A TIME TO SPEAK

BY THE SAME AUTHOR

The Black Unicorn
Thursday's Child

JUNE DRUMMOND

A TIME TO SPEAK

Cleveland and New York
The World Publishing Company

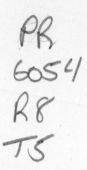

PR
6054
R8
T5

Published by The World Publishing Company
2231 West 110 Street, Cleveland 2, Ohio

Library of Congress Catalog Card Number: 63-14787
FIRST EDITION

HC763

A TIME TO SPEAK

PEACE DRIFT is a dorp; a small South African town, something between a dump and a torpor, on the lower bank of a river that falls cold and brown from the escarpment to the north. The early trekkers found at this point a ford shallow enough to allow their ox wagons to cross, and the first traders, after the casual manner of their kind, named it after Jeremiah Peace, peddler of old clothes, who on a drunken night fell into the drift and was drowned.

At Peace Drift was set up the trading post that formed the nucleus of the present town. The place has grown little in the intervening years, its importance resting solely on the agricultural produce of its hinterland. Although the main road is tarred, and lit by modern street lamps, the motorists who use it seldom stay long. A few stop at the Garage to refuel; have a meal, perhaps, at the Hotel opposite; but most people dash straight through, heading for the trunk road that leads to the cities of the north and south. The side streets are a treacherous amalgam of stone and sand, flanked by trees; jacaranda, syringa, the kindly kaffirboom that provides shade in the heat of summer, and in winter a consolation of scarlet flowers.

At the southernmost end of the town lie the railway sheds, bedeviled by the scream of the sawmill and the pervasive stench of the tannery. Once, sometimes twice, each day, a string of trucks, loaded with hides, skins, or neatly stacked timber, clanks slowly up Railway Hill, and heads east along the Ridge toward Hopetoun, some thirty miles distant.

North of the station is a row of small shops. The largest belongs to Archie Oakes, who sells everything in the world—canned foods, seedlings, popcorn, dustbins, liniment, pince-nez, and native blankets imported from Birmingham. Archie has substituted a plate-glass window for the original wooden shutters, but he has preserved the old-fashioned stoep, with its three steep steps down to the street. African customers like a stoep, which provides them with a place to meet, talk business, gossip, suckle a baby, or rearrange a load that must be carried home along several miles of twisting hill path.

Behind the shops are the poorer living areas. These small, square houses, with their square sandy gardens, seem awash in the shadow of Railway Hill. Above them the track climbs laboriously, zigzagging to the top of the Ridge, and the prevailing wind blows a fine black grit over all.

Next door to the shops is the Garage. Motor services form the least part of its trade, for it helps to maintain the heavy agricultural machines of the backcountry. The land around Peace Drift is not naturally rich, but it is doctored into wealth by tractors and plows, automatic milkers, powersaws, and bulldozers.

Beyond the Garage the houses, still square and squat, are larger, roofed with tiles instead of corrugated iron. Dr. Strasser's, near the Garage and nearly opposite the Hotel, sports a white porcelain stork on its chimney; hardly a suitable emblem, as Tim Sullivan once pointed out, for a bachelor establishment, but Strasser is notably lacking in humor.

Beyond that again, on the river bank, the Anglican and Dutch Reformed Churches face each other across the road. They mark the oldest part of the town. Behind the Dutch Reformed Church the first Victorian houses survive, their fretted porches upheld by ornate metal pillars. Karl Ebenezer owns one of these, the one next to the schoolhouse.

On the right of the main road, between the sawmill and

the Dutch Reformed Church, are the Bank; a land agency; a
few business offices; the Town Hall with its fine gilded clock;
the Hotel; the Police Station; and the Clinic, which is no more
than a cottage hospital for white people. The Elizabeth Hospital for nonwhites stands above the town, among the plantations of wattle and seligna pine that clothe most of the Ridge.

This Ridge half-moons from Railway Hill, right around to
a point well east of the Hospital. The railway line runs along
it, being joined, at the center of the curve, by the road running
up from the town.

From the lip of the Ridge, at times when the plantations have
been extensively thinned, one can see the slow swell of farm-
land rolling to the escarpment: the broad valley farmed by
Julius Kruger, pierced by the narrow course of the Peace River;
further east, the steepening fields of Tim Sullivan, that run to
the foot of a great krantz, rose-red, splotched with clumps and
runnels of natural bush; and east again, the Mission land, where
church and school sit pigeon-squab among fat rows of bean,
cabbage, and sweet potato.

Behind the Mission the terrain falls sharply toward the Native Reserve. This land is barred to white owners—a beautiful
but backward area, scarred by erosion, denuded by generations
of peasant farming, a place where hawks find the living hard,
and each man's prayer is a prayer for rain.

All the Peace Drift territory is hill country. Farming country. Not rich, but able to make a living. Its center a dorp where
doors and windows are screened against insects, where the ice
cart still delivers its foot-square cubes, where water-borne sew-
erage is a recent innovation. Where there is a good market for
fertilizers, cotton cloth, and Bibles.

And the people? Sturdy, inquisitive, opinionated, black,
white, and brown, much like the people of other dorps and yet
convinced of their unique character.

Look in the face of Peace Drift and you may imagine its eyes
are closed in sleep. But be advised, you who are a stranger. It
watches you cannily, under its lids.

2

AT THE MISSION HALT, the train slowed, sighed, and stopped altogether. William Nevis, who had slept untroubled through the lurching descent from the foothills, woke up and glanced at his watch. The air in the carriage was permeated by the hot reek of coal, but there was something else, a resinous brightness, remembered over the years. Nevis swung his feet to the ground.

The right-hand windows revealed a wall of cut earth. He moved across the carriage, jerked the shutter free, and slammed it down. He could see them now, a row of gum trees, their peeled silver trunks obscuring the more distant plantations of wattle. A little to the left, beyond a narrow concrete platform, the main road was joined by two skinny farm tracks.

There seemed no reason for this delay. A uniformed policeman ducked under the crossing barrier and fell into conversation with the ticket collector. A group of African passengers climbed down from the nonwhite carriages and began to make their way back toward the road. Their voices, raised in altercation, faded quickly in the motionless air.

Nevis leaned his elbows on the window frame. The sun drenched him to the bone, a sense of remoteness overtook him. He wondered if the train would ever move again, and decided the question was not of any consequence.

Presently a spiral of dust appeared above the larger of the farm tracks. He caught the drumming of a heavy engine, a lorry, perhaps?

"That'll be Sullivan," said a voice. Nevis turned his head.

A man stood at the next window, one brown forearm braced against the frame, the hand clasping a briar pipe. A felt hat, pulled far down, hid his eyes. His nose was pendulous, his mouth long and flat, his jowls showed a faint gray stubble.

The formidable thickness of his shoulders and diaphragm appeared to be muscular rather than fatty.

The cloud of dust along the road grew higher, and they heard a klaxon blare. The big man said dispassionately, "He's maybe heard Mafeking was relieved." He spoke with a heavy Afrikaans accent.

Nevis smiled. "Sullivan? Where's he farm?"

The other stabbed the stem of his pipe toward the north. "Up there."

"That'd be . . . Redcliff?"

"That's right." The man pushed his hat further back on his head and studied Nevis. "You been here before?"

"I was born here. My name's William Nevis. My father practiced in the town when I was a kid."

"Doc Nevis? You his son? Well, well, eh?" A gleam appeared in the man's small blue eyes. "You won't remember me."

"I think I do. Kruger. Mr. Julius Kruger."

"Ja, that's right too." Kruger seemed pleased. "So what are you doing here? Is your Pa still alive?"

"He's practicing in Joburg."

"They used to call him Ben. Ben Nevis." Kruger laughed, fingering his jaw.

"They call us all Ben."

Kruger nodded. "And now, tell me"—he settled himself more comfortably against the window frame—"are you also a doctor?"

"Yes."

"Where did you train?"

"First Wits, then Edinburgh."

"And you're staying here a while?"

"About a month. With Dr. Strasser."

"Working?"

Amused at the curiosity in the old man's face, Ben said, "Unofficially, yes. As a matter of fact, it's a case of mutual aid. I'll help Strasser during the polio campaign, and he'll give me board and lodging."

Kruger appraised him. "Wanted to see the place again?"

Ben said unwillingly, "Something like that."

Kruger seemed disposed to press his questions, but at that moment an open lorry lurched down the track to the Halt, bumped on to the grass verge, and reached a precarious rest. The Africans who had alighted from the train clambered onto the back of the lorry, handing up bundles and baskets. The driver, a thin, sandy man, leaned out of the cab and burst into vociferous speech, shouting a greeting to the policeman at the crossing, haranguing the Africans in rapid, inaccurate Zulu that drew from them a burst of delighted laughter.

Ben turned to Kruger. "I don't remember him."

"He's been here six, seven years."

"You don't like him?"

"Doctor, I like all children. But not to run farms. That one's not a farmer. You want to see his land. He lets his kaffirs go jaunting off to the towns. . . ." Kruger had lapsed without thinking into Afrikaans. It gave Ben a warm pleasure to hear again, after long absence, the particular burr of this valley. There sprang to his mind, like a schoolroom chant, the place names of the farms, and he said aloud, "Witteboom, Wycombe, Lydensrust, Ikwezi, La Berceau, Alderbarn . . . things haven't changed much, here?"

"You think that?" Kruger spoke with such sharpness that Ben was startled. "Don't make that mistake, young man. Everything is changed." He slipped his pipe into a pocket. An idea seemed to strike him. "You speak Afrikaans. Is your mother still alive?"

His train of thought was clear. Ben's mother had been of Afrikaner stock, his father of English. Kruger evidently gave the mother the credit for having instilled in her son a love of her own first language. Ben said impatiently, "She died when I was seven, the year after we left here. It was my father who made us speak Afrikaans in the home."

Kruger chuckled. "All right, I was only asking. You're touchy, like your Pa, I can see." He continued to chuckle to himself, and to cast sly glances at the younger man.

Ben fell silent, staring at the ground. His resentment, though it might amuse this old man, had some foundation. Nor was it something he could discuss with a stranger. Perhaps not with anyone.

The truth was that Ben was an old-fashioned, stiff-necked patriot. He had left a comfortable job in London and come home because he could no longer stomach the idea of his country's loneliness. Friends in Europe had pointed out, often with justice, the causes of that isolation. While in theory Ben might agree, in practice he wanted to be home, and the longing increased in direct ratio to his sense of approaching crisis.

What caused his resentment was the fact that, once home, he met with a state of mind as unsatisfactory as the uninformed criticisms of Europe. Many of his old friends, bewildered by the speed of events, or embittered by the sanctimonies of hostile dictatorships, were taking refuge in insularity. If Ben voiced an opinion, they eyed him with suspicion. He found himself a foreigner in every camp, and there were many, society having broken into a mass of small cliques, each at war with the next. He was, in Johannesburg, more alone and at sea than ever he had been in London or Paris.

He had decided to revisit Peace Drift much as a dog seeks to roll in familiar earth. Perhaps, here, he would recover his natural color, and become acceptable to his own kind. Yet even before he left the train, this old man Kruger was trying to confine him to this or that sectionalism. Even here, it seemed, there might be no South Africans.

A few moments later, the carriages, with a squeak of couplings, began to edge forward. Ben thought, two miles to the bridge, ten minutes down the Railway Hill bends.

He drew back from the window and began to assemble his possessions.

3

THE STATION OF PEACE DRIFT was not elaborate. On the street side, a parking lot accommodated the few ramshackle buses that served the outlying districts. The railway offices opened directly on to this yard. An archway in the center of the building led through to the main platform. Beyond the tracks was another platform, and the goods sheds.

Three men waited for the train to arrive. The tallest, a compact, square-faced man, scrupulously neat, stood a little apart, fists on hips, and watched the engine negotiate the hairpin bends of the Hill. He paid small attention to the other two men, who appeared to be involved in some discussion.

"It stands to reason," the smaller one said, "you and I both know it, you can't mix politics with business. I say that the way I vote is my affair, and the same goes for you or me or anyone. That's what I say. And tell the truth, I'm not interested in politics. I can see good in everyone. I know my job, and I stick to it, and so do you, doctor, and it's a pity that more people can't say the same. It'll all be the same in a hundred years, so why should we worry?" He was a dapper little figure, and despite the heat wore his black alpaca coat tightly buttoned. The lardy bulge above his collar was dewed with sweat. He held a folded dog leash in one hand.

The man he addressed gave an irritated twitch of the shoulders. "The train is late again. There is no system."

Oakes rolled his eyes. "Hanging about at Mission Halt, you'll see. I don't know why they have to do that."

The other man made no reply, but looked at his watch with raised brows. His face, high and narrow in the forehead, small-chinned and pale, was indefinably foreign. He wore a khaki bush shirt over light drill trousers; fawn socks, and suede shoes. There was a nervousness in his stance, a sort of cold

16

immobility, as if he were possessed by a well-contained but
perennial impatience. His eyes were pure, clear gray. The
townsfolk had never seen Dr. Strasser lose his temper. They
would have liked him better if they had.

Archie Oakes wondered for the hundredth time what made
the doctor tick. Archie liked to get to the bottom of a man's
foibles. Know a man's weakness, you could sell him anything.
Good for business. But Strasser never talked about himself.
Not natural, that, in a place like Peace Drift. As always with
Strasser, Archie felt himself snubbed. He said in a loud voice,
"I agree, the trains are shocking, these days. Something ought
to be done."

Strasser addressed himself to the third man. "Sergeant Reimer, you didn't move that van of mine, did you?"

The policeman said, without turning his head, "I'm not a
traffic cop, doctor, thank God."

Strasser muttered, "I have to get the vaccine into deep freeze,
at once."

The train edged into the station and stopped. A carriage
door swung open and a young man sprang down, looking about
him. He was of medium height, and his thick, unruly hair,
cropped rather short, suggested a Van Gogh cornfield. Strasser
watched him. There was something . . . not exactly pugilistic
. . . no boxer, that, the jaw too light and the eyes not deep
enough in the sockets. Not enough weight for a wrestler. Then
why this suggestion of the fighting ring? Strasser's brow
cleared. A fencer? Astonishing, in this land of the bourgeois,
but possible. There was strength in the wrist and thigh, and
lightness in the carriage.

Strasser moved past the policeman and walked toward the
young man.

"You are Dr. Nevis?"

"That's me."

"Strasser."

They shook hands, the young man smiling. Strasser studied
his face with care. A smile was a sure guide to character. One

saw here intelligence, humor, lack of guile. It was a type that people, in Strasser's experience, found attractive. He said abruptly, "Where is the vaccine?"

"In cold storage. I had the devil of a time convincing the guard it couldn't get at him through the door of the fridge."

Strasser was already striding toward the rear of the train. Ben set down his suitcase and followed. At the van, a small fat man was in conversation with the guard. He turned eagerly at their approach, and said, "My little dog's in there. Hear him? Knows I'm waiting. He's a champ, really, I mean it. A champ. I just sent him off to a prize bitch in Hopetoun. Couldn't take him myself, can't leave the shop, you know." He leaned his head through the open door of the van and shouted, "O.K., boy, I'm here. Just wait, now."

"Stan' clear, please, sir." The guard hauled at the fat man's shoulder. Milk cans, a few crates, and a bag of mail were unloaded. The guard climbed up into the gloom and released the catch of a wire kennel. With a scrabble of nails on metal, an Aberdeen terrier hurled himself across the van and leaped straight out into the fat man's arms. Set down, he streaked away in a wide circle, barking hysterically.

Strasser said peevishly, "And now, perhaps, we may unload my humble little consignment?"

"Soon as we get to it, doctor."

"I have work to do. I can't wait all day."

"We all got work to do," said the guard, under his breath.

The Aberdeen made a dummy pass at Ben's ankles, and threw himself on his back at the fat man's feet. Ben extended his fingers to the dog, who gave them a cursory sniff and wagged his tail halfheartedly.

The fat man bent and clipped a leash to the dog's collar. "They're one-man types," he said.

"He's a fine little chap."

"Sure, like I said, a champ. Cost me a lot of money, but he's worth it."

Ben glanced at the other's face. There was something repellent about it. The eyes, perhaps, unevenly spaced, or of slightly unequal size? They were hard, inquisitive, jealous eyes, curiously unsuited to such a soft pale frame of flesh. Now the man was holding out his hand. "Pardon, my name's Oakes. Archie Oakes."

"I'm William Nevis."

"The new chap for the Bank, perhaps?"

Ben shook his head. "Only visiting. I'm staying with Dr. Strasser for a month."

"Is that so? Helping with the polio campaign, I heard? That's nice. I'm really very keen on that sort of thing, you know. A personal interest in everything medical, you could say. I put out the best line in patent medicines in this town. Oh yes. 'Course, I'm a general storekeeper, but I do quite a nice line in medical appliances. I expect you'll see me again, if you're going to be here for a bit."

Strasser's voice cut him short. "Dr. Nevis, may I have your attention for a moment?"

"Yes, sure. Sorry." Ben moved away, and Oakes waved a plump hand. "Well, I must push along. So long, Dr. Nevis."

"Goodbye, Mr. Oakes."

Strasser and Ben transferred the containers of concentrated poliomyelitis vaccine, packed in tins of dry ice, to the station wagon parked in the yard. On the way, Strasser said, "Take a word of advice. Don't confide in Oakes. He's a fearful climber, he'll bore you to death."

Ben said nothing. The warning annoyed him. Oakes had been welcoming, Strasser had not. But as they drove off, a glimpse of the shopkeeper in avid conversation with a woman on the street corner did something to temper his annoyance.

4

WHEN THE POLICEMAN CAME out of the office, where he had been talking to the booking clerk, the platform was nearly deserted. Only old Kruger loitered in the shadow of the archway. He waited for the policeman to come up to him.

"Well, Mannie," he said.

The policeman dropped an arm around the old man's shoulders. "Well, Uncle?"

The greeting was affectionate, rather than a claim to kinship, but the bond between the two men was almost that of father and son. Julius had married late in life, and had lost his wife on the birth of their only child. He could not bring himself to marry again, but when Mannie Reimer was orphaned at the age of ten, Julius took the boy into his home, to be a companion to his own Andries. The two grew up together, as close as brothers, though very different in temperament.

Mannie was stolid, shrewd, conventional. He had no wish to live anywhere but in Peace Drift, and no ambition to be anything but a policeman. Andries, on the other hand, could not wait to leave home. As soon as he was through high school, he went to Pretoria, to study law. There, in the cultural heart of strict Afrikanerdom, he turned rebel. He deserted the Calvinism of his family and professed agnosticism. He broke with old associates, adopted an air of contempt for the customs of the platteland, spent his holidays with people known to be heathens and freethinkers. He also learned to fly, and when Jan Smuts took his country into a foreigners' war, Andries Kruger was among the first to volunteer for service with the Air Force.

Only Mannie knew how deeply all these defections hurt Julius, who in duty bound forbade his son the house, and bore in silence the unspoken reproach of his circle. And only Mannie knew that when Andries' war medals came home without him

20

to Peace Drift, they were given honorable resting place in the drawer that held the family Bible.

Andries was never mentioned by name, but his memory was alive, in the shape of Mannie Reimer. The boys had been lovely and pleasant to Julius in their lives, and in the death of Andries they were not divided.

As the two men walked through the archway, Mannie said, "How did sales go?"

"Quite well. Prices are lower than last year. What are you doing here?"

Mannie said blandly, "Captain Larkill's away, so I'm taking the day off."

Kruger tried again. "Looking for someone?"

"Why should I look for people, Oom? I got enough already."

Kruger grunted. Like Mannie, like most of his race, he was intensely insular. He looked on the valley as his preserve, and disliked any form of interference from beyond its borders. He had lived in Peace Drift for seventy-three years. A loyal supporter of the Government, he nevertheless considered that politicians, through being forced to spend their time in Pretoria and Cape Town, suffered a serious handicap. Politicians might know the country and the world, but he, Julius Kruger, knew Peace Drift.

He had not failed to notice the policeman up at Mission Halt. And now, here was Mannie, hanging about the station. If there was anything on, no matter how trivial, Kruger wanted to know about it. He tucked his thumbs in the waist of his trousers and said, with a sideways glance at his companion, "Naturally, a skelm will buy a ticket and come to town in the best style. No doubt this afternoon he will call on you in person, at the Police Station."

But Mannie had his own idea of what concerned the public —even as represented by Uncle Julius—and what did not. He shrugged, smiled, and turned the subject.

After a while the two parted, and Kruger made his way up the street to the Garage, where he had left his car during his two-day absence. Several people greeted him as he passed. He acknowledged their smiles abstractedly. His mind was on Mannie's reticence.

Serious crime was rare in the valley. Petty thieving, Saturday-night drunkenness, token fighting between the rival Vuli and Pembe factions, that was about the extent of local misdoing. But in Hopetoun, Kruger had heard rumors. There had been a bus strike, purely a question of economics; but faintly, hardly breathed upon the air, came the word, "agitator." One knew all about agitators. The plague of big cities, scavengers who fed on small grievances, bullies who made life unbearable for ordinary, law-abiding folk, black or white. One knew that Africa was a good field for the professional agitators. One expected them to flourish in the stink and clamor of the industrial towns. But Hopetoun was not much more than a stock market. And it was only thirty miles from Peace Drift.

The old man disliked being left in the dark. Head bent, eyes fixed on the ground, he turned the problem over, like a mason seeking the flaw in a flint.

The tall double doors of the Garage stood open. Kruger walked through and stood blinking in the gloom. An African was working in one of the service pits, and Kruger beckoned him peremptorily. The man came forward, wiping his hands on a piece of cotton waste.

"Is my car ready?"

"Yes, Baas Kruger."

Kruger tossed over the keys of the car. The African caught them deftly and limped away up the ramp that led to the parking gallery. In a short while he returned, driving Kruger's Buick. He brought it to the door with an expert twist, climbed out, and held the door while Kruger wedged his bulk under the steering wheel.

"Was she de-carbonized?"

"Yes, Baas, I saw to it myself."

Kruger eyed him. Many people, he knew, disliked Abel, because he was an educated man. There was no doubt he was a skilled mechanic. His long thin hands touched machinery as if it were alive. If the firm had a good name, it was partly due to Abel's work. Abel must know that. Was he perhaps too big for his boots? Kruger thought not. Meeting the eyes of the African, he saw there patience, the old sadness left by physical disability, but nothing of insolence. Kruger nodded. The man stepped back, and the Buick edged into the street, turning north toward the Ridge.

Kruger farmed Witteboom, on the upper reaches of the Peace River. When his grandfather first came to the place, there was nothing, no farmstead, not one stone laid upon another, nothing but hills of pale grass and a few scattered native kraals. Now Julius could stand on his stoep and approve the work that God had given his family to perform; the fields fenced, tilled, and planted, the cattlesheds and barns stocked and stacked. There was a dam big enough to see him through a two-year drought, and, along the rocky highlands that cheated the plow, showed orderly rows of trees.

After any absence, no matter how short, it gave Julius deep satisfaction to reach the crest of the Ridge and see before him this plateau of achievement. The only fly in the jam, at such times, lay in the view also afforded of Tim Sullivan's property. Sullivan was Kruger's eastern neighbor. He owned less land than Kruger, and of poorer quality, but he was undoubtedly a rich man. That such capital should be squandered struck Kruger as a form of insanity. Sullivan was a horrible, an execrable, farmer. His passion for gadgets was equaled only by his inability to make them work. Kruger found it hard to spend five minutes in his company without losing his temper, but, like most people, he admitted one had to like the fool. Sullivan was good with a horse, a gun (and, it was said, a woman), and he had a sense of humor—of a sort.

Now, with a sinking heart, Kruger saw from far off the flash of a vehicle drawn up on the bank of his river. Certainly it was

Sullivan's bright blue lorry. He had enough to do, God knew, without worrying over Sullivan's problems. There was undoubtedly a problem, or the thickhead wouldn't be down there, waiting. Kruger drove on in a sour frame of mind. At the bridge he drew up and waited for Sullivan to amble over to the Buick.

"Afternoon, Mr. Kruger. You back all right?" Sullivan's long thin body always gave the impression of being beyond his control. He had a stumbling gait, his hands and feet flew out at odd angles. Only his eyes seemed perfectly co-ordinated. They were large, bright, and remarkably observant.

Acidly, Kruger said, "You saw me on the train this afternoon."

"Did I?" Sullivan seemed confused.

"I was merely stating . . ." Kruger controlled himself. "What do you want?"

"As a matter of fact, I came down to look at your dam. I want to build one myself. I thought I'd tap your brains."

"Where?"

"Eh?"

"Where do you want to build this dam?"

"Oh. Oh well, somewhere near my house."

Kruger shook his head. "The land there is too porous. Also rocky. It would cost too much, even for you." He gave Sullivan a slightly malicious smile.

"Expect you're right. I thought you'd know the best place."

Kruger glanced away to the east, to the krantz above Sullivan's farm, the red cliff from which it took its name. He knew it, all right. As a child, he'd learned the face of this valley like a child learns its letters. René van Zyl had owned Redcliff then. René would not have had to ask where to build a dam. Out of temper, Kruger leaned forward and flicked the ignition key. He said brusquely, "I'll come over some time and show you a good place." Before Sullivan could thank him, he drew away.

The farmstead of Witteboom stood on a small rise, fairly close to the river, in the center of a square of trees. Coarse

turf surrounded it, except where, on the left, four oak trees
rose from a stretch of moss-spangled earth.

Kruger parked his car under the oaks, climbed out, shouted.
As he advanced toward the house a garden boy ran to take
his case and hat, and a second servant appeared in the open
front door.

"Coffee," the old man told him, and sat down on a cane chair,
bending to unlace the town shoes that hurt his feet. In a short
while the servant reappeared, in one hand a small tray of coffee
and oatmeal biscuits, in the other a pair of coarse leather slippers. He set them down, straightened and clasped his hands
politely before his chest.

"Well, Solomon?"

"Baas, old Gwevu is here."

"Where is he?"

"In the cowshed." Solomon's hand lifted to cover a smile.

"Ask him to come, in a little while." A faint amusement
touched the corners of Kruger's mouth. How old Gwevu loved
cattle! To him, the fine sleek beasts were a subject for gloating,
just as a miser gloats over gold. Kruger poured himself coffee
and drank it red-hot, wrinkling his face. One of his earliest
memories was of Gwevu, then his boon companion, directing
a stream of warm milk straight from the cow's udder into his
upturned mouth. Kruger had emulated the custom. To this day,
milk from a glass tasted cold and joyless.

He sighed and sagged lower in his chair, unable to throw
off the irritation of the day.

He was not a man with much breadth of imagination. He
read little except the newspapers, his Bible, and the farming
manuals. Although he was comfortably off, his house was bare
of luxury. That was how his people had always lived, stern,
narrow, steadfast. That was how he would like to live. There
was God, whom one served with all one's strength; and the
Afrikaner people, whom one also served, under God. For God
and the Volk had been made the sacrifices of the past. The
history of his race was the story of a struggle for self-preserva-

tion. Exodus, trek, the fight for religious, economic, and cultural survival. For the sake of this national identity the Boers had subdued a wilderness, conquered the regiments of the Bantu, fought a war against Britain. They had fought and won the long, cold war of Union, working to establish their own language, gaining a foothold in industry and commerce, driving on toward the longed-for Republic. In all this, by lineage or actual presence, Julius Kruger had played a part. He had paid his price—yes, even to the cutting off of his right hand, his only son—and he had taken his reward. The fact of Republic was his personal triumph. In his flesh he had helped to build it. He could look at what had been accomplished, and say, "I also was there."

But in the success lay the dilemma. His grandfather had lived isolated, he had his family, his house, his land, stock, dogs, gun, but no neighbors closer than Hopetoun. Now a farmer found himself part of a system. Associations, boards, conferences. The building of the new State had ended the protective isolation of the old, and allowed the world to rush in unchecked. Nowadays, a man couldn't be a good farmer alone. He must be also a businessman. Now, how was old Julius, whose life spanned three-quarters of a century, to arrange things? The truth was, he had given up the agricultural patterns of his youth, and willingly—that was the point—willingly. He was a house divided against itself, part cleaving to the old ways, part moving to meet the challenge of the machine age. He saw that challenge in every phase of life, in the home, in the Church, in the inmost being of his people. Such a strange, ironic thing . . . that the battle to preserve a tradition must bring about its dissolution. Change begot change, and the greatest changes of all were still to come.

He was an old man, in a shifting world. Not that the weight of the world alarmed him. The man, the nation, the continent did not exist that could deter Julius Kruger from the tenets of his faith. One of those tenets was that God, in making him

white, had laid upon him certain advantages, and certain responsibilities.

He had, several years back, pledged himself to support the
policy of separate development. White and black must have
their own areas, where each could retain a separate identity.
(For were not many of the blacks as anxious to preserve their
traditions as the Afrikaner was to preserve his Volk?) The
policy seemed to him just and workable. It remained only to
bring it into effect. The first steps were already taken, Bantu
authorities were being established, new territorial delimita-
tions set. Land was being allocated for Bantu ownership. It
was necessary, now, to eliminate those black spots which
marked settlements of Bantu in the white man's areas.

The matter moved, thus, into his own sphere, in fact into his
own life. It lived and breathed in the person of old Gwevu,
whose family owned land in the valley of the Peace River.

Kruger, who had never spared himself in the making of personal sacrifice, was much disturbed by the decisions that lay
before him in connection with old Gwevu.

Unlike his friend Karl Ebenezer, Kruger was not concerned
with the mystique of politics. He was, in effect, incapable of
taking the broad, impersonal view. What mattered to him were
the few square miles surrounding Peace Drift.

It so happened that this area was one which would be greatly
affected by the implementation of the Bantustan projects, for
it bordered on land which, in due course, was destined for
African ownership.

Kruger glanced up at the hill behind the farmstead where
Gwevu's kraal lay. Its neat round huts, cattle fold, and mealie
patch glowed in the burgundy warmth of the sun. It was more
than an element of Kruger's boyhood. It was part of the history
of the valley itself.

Most of the Africans around Peace Drift were members of
the Zongo tribe. Some generations back, a dispute over grazing
rights had resulted in a split within the main tribal group.

The larger Vuli clan, of which old Gwevu was the head, still kept up a bitter rivalry with the Pembe faction. Despite the discipline imposed by the police, any public ceremony, a wedding or a beer drink, was likely to end in a flare-up of the ancient quarrels, in broken heads and stab wounds.

Since the turn of the century, there had been a steady breaking-down of the old patterns of tribal life. Many of the young people left the valley to seek work in the cities. Attempts, in all parts of the country, to dislodge African squatter farmers had increased the flow of the land hungry. Even towns as small as Peace Drift attracted to themselves a proportion of the rural population. Although the older generation remained loyal to their tribes, a young African proletariat was springing up, men and women who had never lived outside a town, whose outlook and way of life were essentially urban. One of the main difficulties of government lay in reconciling the interests of the rural Africans with those of the urban. The choosing of any African who was to assume authority, no matter how small, in the new Bantustan system, was not, in the nature of things, an enviable task.

Kruger and Ebenezer, as two of the most knowledgeable men in the valley, had been asked to give an opinion on the suitability of various candidates. Unfortunately, their views did not tally. Whether higher echelons took much notice of this battle of Dum and Dee was beside the point. It raged, and Peace Drift knew it.

Now, as Gwevu approached, walking slowly around the corner of the house, Kruger watched him with mixed feelings. The old African was still an imposing figure. Upright in stance, he moved with the grace and gravity of a Roman senator. His greeting perfectly combined the giving and expectation of respect with the ease of long friendship.

There was a similarity between the two men, Kruger in his creaking chair, and Gwevu sinking down on the stone edge of the stoep. Brought up on the same land, enduring the same drought and flood, taking each other's measure in time of emergency, they shared now the same doubts and frustrations, aware of the end of their proper epoch.

For some time they talked of small matters, while lights sank low in the valley and a welcome cool touched face and neck. Finally Kruger came to the point.

"You know, of course," he said, "that there is a plan to move some of the people from land around the town to their own place, toward the Reserve?"

Gwevu nodded. "I have heard of it, yes."

"The new farms are better land. No doubt it will be to their advantage to move."

"They don't want to move." Gwevu raised one hand, palm upward. "They want to stay here. Our fathers worked this land. They are buried here. The spirits of our ancestors are close."

Kruger sighed. He had heard the argument before, many times. It was merely the opening gambit in a familiar game. He said, "Nevertheless, you would do well to think of the advantages of owning your land in the new area."

"The Vuli and Pembe factions will quarrel when the land is allocated. When I go, who will control my clansmen? Even now, it's hard for me. Young people are not what they were, they have less respect."

"If you were chosen as one of the leaders in the new place, that would increase their respect."

"With some, not with others." Gwevu's eye took on a shrewd, not unhumorous gleam. "I may end up with an assegai in my chest. Consider. If I am chosen, my own people of the Vuli will be angry because they blame me for helping to move them from these old lands. Then, the Pembe will be angry because a Pembe has not been chosen. Oh, the trouble! You'll see! Fighting, fines, men in prison. And in the very center of it, who do we see? Why, Gwevu, possibly dead. No. I say it's best to leave things as they are."

"But," said Kruger patiently, "the Government has decided that things cannot be left as they are."

"Then why does not the Great One tell the Government?"

inquired Gwevu with an air of sweet reasonableness. "He is a father to us. He is an important person. He should tell the Government not to do a foolish thing."

"It is just possible that the Government may not listen to me."

"The Government will listen." Gwevu dismissed this childish plea with a flick of the hand.

"Still," said Kruger, pulling out his tobacco pouch and pipe, "some of your people are anxious to make the move."

"Some is not enough to keep the peace between us."

Kruger tried another tack. "It would be an honor if you were chosen.

"What do I need more than I have? When I was young I wanted more. Now I know how much meat my stomach can hold. Why must we make these changes?"

Kruger shifted in his chair. "It may seem strange to you and me, because we are used to our way of life. But in other parts of the country, especially in the towns, things are different. There are too many people, lusting after too little land, too few jobs. Those people desire a voice in the ruling of their own territories. If they are given no place of their own, there will be conflict between black and white."

"I see no fighting. Peace Drift is a big place, with room for everyone. I see no fighting here."

"Don't you? I see it, here in Peace Drift. What about your grandson, what about Sizwa? Is he content? Does he think as you do?"

Gwevu's eyes grew bright. "He is young, and young men chatter."

"It wasn't chatter that sent him to prison."

"Wise as you are, you know that that was a small affair, a fight over a woman when he was too young to realize no woman is worth the effort. Moreover"—Gwevu emphasized his point by tapping the stoep with one hand—"in this matter of moving to new land, Sizwa agrees with me."

"No." Kruger shook his head. "No. He disagrees with the

plan, but his reasons are not yours. You want to avoid trouble. Sizwa wants to make trouble. He blows on embers to start a flame. One day he will go to prison again."

Old Gwevu's lips trembled. He said, with some sharpness, "He is only feeling his strength. There have been other young men who wanted to feel their strength."

Kruger's eyes fell. He said, more gently, "That may be true. It is also true that Sizwa does not recognize your authority, or mine. Yet there has to be authority. We can't allow things to fall into the hands of those who will use young men like Sizwa as their tools."

Gwevu looked away, across the turf to where a section of the river gleamed between trees. "When I was a boy," he said at last, "my great-uncle killed three men—in self-defense— down there. He stood there, in the gully, you see it? And took them one by one. The next night others came, fired his huts, disemboweled his cattle. Oh yes, wherever that man went, there was trouble. Yet there was no one like him. In the end, he went to Johannesburg, to work in the mines. The rock fell on him, he was crushed like a beetle. What a way to die, in a hole in the ground, like an insect! He had his faults, but I remember him clearly. A real man, one to reckon with. Sizwa is very like him."

Kruger said carefully, "No doubt there will always be those to whom trouble sticks like a blackjack to a fleece. One must try to keep such men away from trouble, now isn't that so?"

Gwevu looked at him. He understood quite well the import of the discussion. He said at last, "I will speak to Sizwa again. But times have changed. I fear he will not listen to me."

Kruger spread out his hand and stared at the palm, thinking of his conversation, that afternoon, with Mannie Reimer. He said suddenly, "Who are Sizwa's friends?"

Gwevu shook his head. "He knows everyone."

"Anyone from other parts?"

"I don't think so." Gwevu's expression became guarded. It

was clear he was not prepared to discuss his grandson further. Soon he rose to his feet and took his leave, walking between the oaks to the path that wound up to his kraal.

Kruger sat on, frowning. Gwevu was not a great cog. But then, Peace Drift was not a great wheel. To keep the little wheel turning, the little cog was needed.

When he next looked up, the stretch of river shone blood-red in the last light. The sight affected him like an omen. He heaved himself to his feet and went quickly into the house.

5

DR. STRASSER had decided that the vaccine for the polio campaign should be stored at the Clinic. He drove there with Ben from the station, and they transferred the tiny bottles of concentrated fluid to a deep-freeze unit, where it could be maintained at the requisite temperature of minus twenty degrees Centigrade.

Standing beside Strasser as he arranged the bottles in neat rows, Ben studied this man with whom he would work during the coming weeks. He guessed that few people would claim to know Strasser well, even after long acquaintance. The pale cameo of his face betrayed nothing of his feelings. The word "alien," unusual in polyglot South Africa, rose to Ben's mind. On impulse, he said, "You weren't born here?"

Strasser paused in his task, then said, "In Vienna."

So much, thought Ben, for Viennese gaiety. "Where did you train?"

"Munich, Leipzig, Berlin." Strasser rose from his knees, brushing his hands together. His fingers were short and strong, with small square nails. "Shall we go back to my house? I expect you will like a bath and a drink?"

He said nothing on the short drive back, nor did he indicate points of interest, as might have seemed natural. He ran the station wagon up a narrow drive beside the house and parked it under a pergola of Golden Shower.

Strasser's home was undistinguished. Built of brash yellow brick, it stood square in the middle of a flat, orderly garden. A brick path bisected the narrow lawn that lay between house and road. Ben noticed that this path led to the kitchen door. The front door was hidden in a side wall. Like its owner, the house turned a shoulder to the world.

Strasser led the way in. Most of the interior seemed to be given over to one large living room. On the left lay the kitchen quarters, on the right a wide verandah overlooking a more spacious lawn and the rise of the Ridge. Strasser crossed the living room and went through an archway to a short bedroom wing. He opened a door. "Here is your room. You have your own shower. The bathroom is at the end of the passage. I'm afraid baths are restricted to four inches, due to the drought. You need not hurry. When you are ready, we will have tea or a drink on the verandah."

The bedroom was large and airy. There was a high iron bedstead, covered with a white cotton quilt. The mattress was inner-sprung. Blue linen curtains hung at the windows, an electric fan stood in one corner, there was a cupboard, a chest of drawers, a curtained recess with tiled shower and washstand. A shelf below the window was loaded with paperback Westerns. The floor smelled of carbolic. Above the bed dangled an old-fashioned push-bell. Ben resisted an impulse to ring for the nurse.

He stripped and took a shower. The water was slightly brown, with a metallic smell. Reservoir must be very low. Changed into shirt and shorts, he walked through the living-room to the verandah.

Strasser was seated in a deck chair, a tray beside him. As Ben appeared he said, "Would you rather have tea?"

"No, a lager, thanks."

Strasser picked up a glass and held it to the light, handed

it to Ben with an opener and a bottle. "For lager one must have a long glass. Also for champagne, did you know?"

Ben smiled. "I don't have much practice with champagne, sir." He settled himself in a chair and took a swallow of beer. "That's a nice little Clinic you have there."

"It is terrible. Most cases go into Hopetoun. The Hospital for nonwhites is better. That I planned myself. It is not large, but excellent. Tomorrow I'll show you. Now, about the polio campaign. It is not the first, as you know. There have been three, all of which concentrated on covering Europeans, Coloreds, and Indians up to the age of thirty, and African children up to the age of nine. The response was good, but not good enough. What I plan to do now is go over the ground again and catch those who missed the chance before. For the town, it's easy. We have a regular inoculation day, once a month. But the outlying areas are the test. I'm laying the emphasis on getting the vaccine to the people, not the other way about. I have publicized the campaign as widely as possible. I have arranged three mobile units, to tour the outer districts. I'll explain details later. I have arranged for interpreters and African clerks to accompany each unit. Also loud-speakers. What I want now is some form of entertainment, to draw people in."

"Bread and circuses?"

"A circus, unfortunately, is beyond our scope, although that is the principle of the thing, of course."

Ben blinked. There was no trace of humor in Strasser's eye. He was simply considering a method of approach. With a touch of despondency he said, "I have records of native music, and I hope to arrange for some dancers . . ." He sipped his drink. "Do you speak any native language?"

"I used to speak Zulu, as a child, but it's pretty rusty."

"You must polish it. You must speak at least one Bantu language. South Africans are very slack about this. I have been here only ten years, but I speak two with reasonable fluency, enough for medical purposes. The Indians, of course, speak English better than I do, so there we have no problem. You will have to remember that, in medicine, confidence is all. One must be able to speak to people in order to obtain their confidence."

Crushed, Ben relapsed into silence. In the garden next door, a child was swinging on a gate. The squeak of the hinges carried clearly. Strasser's house was almost the last on this side of the town. Directly above it, the lion's back of the Ridge broke into a dark mane of pine trees. To the left of them, a woman walked, balancing on her head a long bundle of rushes. The sky behind her was saffron, turning to gray.

Ben turned his head and found Strasser addressing him. He pulled himself upright. "I'm sorry, what did you say?"

"Nothing important. You were far away."

"On the contrary, right here, for the first time in years. I hadn't realized how much I missed the hills."

"They are very healthy, certainly, but for me it's a matter of indifference where I live, provided I find the work I wish to do."

Ben reflected on Strasser's reputation for brilliance. It was strange to find a man of his capabilities here in Peace Drift. He said, "You don't miss Europe?"

He received a look that startled him, one of sharp repudiation. "I do not miss Europe." Strasser rose to his feet. "Do you like wine?"

"Very much."

"Good, then I will order it for dinner. If you will excuse me, I have some visits to make, now. I will be back at six-thirty. We will eat at seven, if that suits you?"

Left alone, Ben wandered into the living room. He found there the same aseptic atmosphere that characterized his bedroom. There were no pictures, no mirror, even. The only evidence of self-indulgence was the splendid stock of medical writings in the bookcase. All the best and newest authorities. No expense spared.

Not a likable man, Dr. Strasser, but, it seemed, a dedicated one.

6

AT SIX-THIRTY, Mannie Reimer left the Police Station and set out to walk home. The blade of the day was blunted, only the church spire held a shaving of light, and he took his time, choosing the long way round, past the Hotel and the Town Hall. He knew that Marie would keep supper for him. She was used to his odd hours, and he wanted time to himself, to think.

Habit made him cast an eye over the closed face of the Bank, the burglar guards on the Hotel windows. A billboard outside the Hotel announced that on Wednesday night there would be a film starring Brigitte Bardot. Mannie grinned. Mr. Ebenezer would have something to say to that. Sex kittens weren't somehow in Mr. E's line.

He squinted up at the street lights. Too pale. They should maybe have some of those orange lamps, for misty weather. Across the road, the mechanic Abel was sitting on the wall outside the Garage. He still wore his overalls. Looked as if he was waiting for someone. Turning past the Town Hall, Mannie reflected that Abel was a bit of a puzzle. He gave no trouble, but he was something that Mannie mistrusted, a man without friends. You couldn't fix him anywhere. The men at the tannery spoke of him as clever, but they didn't treat him like a pal. Perhaps they were envious? Abel was a smart boy. They said he had his Matric certificate. More than I have, thought Mannie, more than Archie Oakes, more than plenty of people hereabouts. It didn't put him level in earnings, though. So no one was happy. It was dangerous, that, to educate the blacks, and then, when there wasn't enough jobs, to make laws to keep the jobs away from the people you educated. Using the brake and the accelerator at the same time. . . .

Abel kept his nose clean. Abrahams at the tannery said he'd been helpful, explaining things to the labor. The decimal

36

system, for instance, and the new working conditions. Still, you had to watch out.

A cat on a gatepost flexed its neck at Mannie, who stopped and tickled its ear. He could call by name most of the pets in the town, and all of their owners. He often said to recruits like Venter, remember the man's name, his face, his gesture . . . you had to be friendly . . . but not too friendly. And strict, but never the Judge. It was hard not to slip one way or the other. You could end up with so many pals you couldn't do the job any more. Or with no friends, only an outsize hate. . . .

He gave the cat a slap on the rump and walked on, taking a narrow footpath across a stretch of open ground. A tin half full of water lay in his way, and he kicked it over and stamped it flat, a reflex action from his days on the Coast, when malaria was something to scare the pants off you.

. . . Some people didn't think much of the police. A mug's job, they said, not much pay, not much brains to it. The truth was, you could be good or bad at it, same as anything else.

Sometimes it could be the helluva lonely job.

Then, sometimes, the friends was the hardest part.

He should have been quicker off the mark with Oom Julius. He loved that old uncle, but he was certainly into everything, worse than a fly around dead meat.

Stories always got out, in the end. But this one, this rumor, was different. Say it was true, then here was a man, picked for nerve and cleverness, taught all the tricks, given cash and special equipment, just to help him beat the law. You couldn't trace him through his associates or friends. He had none. No beginning to him, and no end.

The alert had suggested the man might be heading south, toward this area. No doubt the big brass was on the job, already.

On the other hand, some people thought you just lift up a stone and underneath there's an agitator. Some people had agitators on the brain. Larkill was one of them.

Approaching his own house, he heard the leather grunt of a

football, and smiled. The kids would go on kicking it about until you couldn't see your hand in front of your face.

He stopped at the gate. His eyes lifted to the hill behind his roof, the high country, fold after fold, over the Elizabeth Hospital, the Mission, away over to the Reserve. How many places, up there, a man could hide? Jesus, how many?

Mannie was afraid. He'd known real criminals, one or two of them dangerous, and didn't think much of them. Vain, stupid characters, who kept on making the same mistakes, over and over . . . but this could be different. This could be like the Bible said: Satan walking up and down in the world.

He was afraid, and that angered him. This was his territory. His people, to look after.

He pushed through the gate and walked around the house to the kitchen, where Marie would be seeing to his supper.

7

ARCHIE OAKES lived alone, in a flat behind his shop. He looked after himself. Although he employed two Indians to help him in his business, one as driver of the van, the other in the stock-room, he refused to keep a domestic servant. He said he didn't like anyone to touch his belongings.

In that dockside slum where Archie was reared, poverty had jumbled together black and white, Colored and Asiatic. His childhood had been spent between walls blotched with damp, giving off an eternal reek of garlic, sweat, and fish. His father had been a ganger on the Railways, until chronic arthritis lost him his job. In the Depression, when large companies crashed, and small men threw themselves from high buildings, Archie's family lived on charity. There was a Colored family next door, clever people. They made money, and moved to a better area.

Once, when he was a little chap, he struck up a friendship with one of these boys, but it was short-lived. The boy's mother, wary of insults, had put an end to it.

Archie's people were white. That was their talisman, through all the hardships they had to endure. That alone gave them ascendance over the skilled Colored craftsmen, over the rich Indians of the Coast, who drove big cars and sent their sons to University. That alone gave Archie the power and the will to drag himself from sucking despond, to claw toward the light of education, to scrimp and save a capital sum, to escape to Peace Drift and build up a real nice little business for himself.

Color, for Archie, meant the color of his youth, the color of degradation. His white skin was his union ticket. But the price of its possession was an ineradicable sense of guilt and fear.

Fear made him guard the privilege of whiteness. It gave him his pathological dislike of the nonwhite, that expressed itself in a passion for order and cleanliness. He could not bring himself to eat food handled by an African or an Indian, because, he said, you couldn't teach them to be clean. If one of his nonwhite customers brushed against him, he felt contaminated. These emotions brought their own sense of shame.

Fear and shame acted and reacted in Archie Oakes. Expediency made him treat his nonwhite customers with a show of friendliness, but he knew they were not deceived. They saw through to the antipathy he tried to hide. The knowledge in their eyes increased his fear of them.

He would not discuss politics with anyone, because politics had become almost exclusively a question of race relations. Not for him the certainty of Karl Ebenezer, the lighthearted indifference of Tim Sullivan. Better for Archie Oakes to take refuge in silence.

In business matters he was thorough and conscientious. He allowed no credit, his experience being that those who did went under pretty quickly. He was generous, though, and had more than once given financial help to people hit by drought or illness. He subscribed regularly to charity, took an interest in the affairs of the town, was a staunch churchgoer, prided himself on being a member of the Sports Club.

He truly loved only one thing, his dog. Since he entered his teens, he had never been without a dog, and through the years had become so knowledgeable that the townsfolk often brought sick pets to him rather than to the veterinary surgeon.

Tonight, welcoming his terrier back after its brief absence, Archie was as happy as a parent reunited with a child. He bustled about his kitchen, preparing the evening meal, and directing a flow of talk at Jamie.

"You a smart one, eh? That's a fabulous haircut you've got, know that?" He reached down to stroke the dog's back, close-cropped against the approaching heat of February. "Ah, you smiler! Know what's for supper? Liver, your favorite. Then we'll go over to the Hotel. The boys'll be glad to see you. Been asking for you. True's God, they have."

He set down a dish for the dog, beside his own chair. When the meal was over, he washed up with meticulous care, using plenty of hot water and rinsing each plate twice before putting it in the rack to dry.

He made a tour of the house, checking all the locks, particularly the ones on the stockroom leading off the back of the store.

Satisfied, he returned to the kitchen and reached for Jamie's leash. The little dog began an ecstatic caracoling.

"Sit!" said Archie. "Lemme get at your collar, man. How can we get going when you're dancing about?"

He snapped on the leash, guided Jamie through the back door, closed it carefully after them, and set out toward the lighted verandah of the Hotel.

8

IN HIS HOUSE on the bank of the river, Karl Ebenezer sat over his accounts. He had drawn the red plush curtains of his study, and the room was close, but he felt no discomfort. He sat on the edge of a hard chair, his papers before him. His beard jutted, his eyebrows rose and fell, he murmured to himself as he worked, completely absorbed and completely happy. To him, it was a pleasure to compile figures, to observe the beautiful simplicity with which they obeyed fundamental rules.

Ebenezer was an exact man. Before his retirement, he had been a statistician. Now a town councilor, he prided himself that the affairs of the Council were in apple-pie order. Like Pope, he looked on Order as Heaven's first law.

He was small, thin, and sallow, with dark eyes and white hair. Summer and winter he wore the same old-fashioned cut of suit, a white shirt with a stiff collar, and a narrow black tie. He was a heavy smoker. The fingers of his right hand were roughened by frequent scrubbing with the pumice stone.

He was a graduate of Stellenbosch University, and of Oxford. It did not disturb him that he should end his career in a backwater like Peace Drift. In fact, it suited him. In a small, provincial place, it was possible to be effective. Big towns were messy, one could not arrange them according to one's wish. He had, after all, been born in Peace Drift, so there was no reason why he should not die there.

Perhaps his love of the exact was the result of his upbringing. His father had been a rover, who, when Karl was ten, dragged his family away from the Peace Valley, and moved it across and across the subcontinent of Africa, never staying in one place for more than a year. Karl's childhood and adolescence were a landscape in motion, now the fringe of shining seas, now the pallid inferno of fever country, now a rented

bungalow in the shadow of rusty derricks. No need to tell Karl
that the earth revolved. The ramshackle days had seemed to
him not opportunity, but the loss of it. The problem had been
to snatch a little time at school. In maturity, he disliked the
haphazard. Seldom afraid, he was unusually wary, ready to
attack any threat immediately, at source. That was the way
to defeat fear. Attack, regularize, appreciate danger and legislate against it. One must enforce order and clarity where there
had been laxity and confusion.

He was an idealist and a perfectionist. Passionately devoted
to his country and his people, he was often, like Julius Kruger
and Dominee Bond, described as a typical Afrikaner. In fact he
was not typical, but exceptional, a man printed in italics. The
Calvinism that in Julius was ruggedly practical, in Bond humble and self-denying, reaching in Karl the white heat of bigotry.
Ideas were more real to him than human beings.

He had certain unreasonable prejudices, he was capable of
maturing a small antipathy into a major hate, but these too
occurred in the realm of ideas rather than of personalities. He
spun for himself great, shining generalizations, in which he
placed great faith. Thus he hated the Crown, while admiring
the character of the Queen of England. He mistrusted the press,
but lost no chance to cultivate the friendship of pressmen.
Though he was an easy man to criticize, it must be said that
his critics were often unjust to him.

His chief love was Afrikanerdom. Afrikaans he frankly regarded as the most beautiful language in the world. He was
convinced that the English-speaking South African could never
be absorbed into the national life until he had shed the out-
ward marks and symbols that distinguished him from the Afrikaner. He was not, he maintained, an isolationist. All white
South Africa should combine in the beautiful harmony of the
new Republic.

Abrahams, the tannery owner, said that the trouble with
Karl was not that he was mad, but that he was not quite mad
enough. Abrahams professed himself terrified by a man who

applied a yardstick to every aspect of life, who formed a theory
and followed it through to the end. But Abrahams was notably
illogical in his own dealings with life.

Karl lived parsimoniously. If God had guided his people to
power, it was not that they might know ease. Not for them the
land of milk and honey. Rather must the way be hard and the
reward slight, so that the spirit should not soften and be turned
from its purpose.

He was a selfless man. A lifetime of work had left him rela-
tively poor. His health was failing, yet he drove himself to the
limit of his strength. In his self-denial and devotion to duty
he was almost saintly. The townsfolk respected him deeply.
(Except Abrahams, who called him The Inquisitor.)

. . . The clock ticked softly toward the hour. Ebenezer laid
his pen in the tray, tucked away the folded bills, closed his
desk, and walked on to the porch.

In the shadows at the far end, a rocking chair squeaked
rhythmically. Ebenezer said, "Nella?"

"Yes, Pa?"

"Have you nothing to do but sit in that chair?"

"It's cool out here." The rocking ceased. A young woman rose
to her feet and walked toward the doorway. As she drew level
with the man, he said, "Look at me."

She raised her eyes, dark and smoky, vague, as if she had
been recalled from some dream life out there in the dark.

He touched her face with an anxious finger. "You're over-
tired, again."

"No, I do too little." Her voice was flat. "Don't you see, Pa,
that nothing is so tiring as being idle? There isn't enough to
occupy me at the Clinic."

"No doubt you are thinking of Dr. Strasser?"

"Perhaps."

"Strasser cares nothing for women."

"And I care nothing for Strasser, as a man. However, as a
doctor, he belongs in the top rank. It's a miracle we have him
here. He has plans which he can't put into force because he

hasn't the personnel. And I play about at the Clinic, when I could do really vital work, with him. He can't afford to cross you, Pa. If I asked him to take me on, he'd refuse. I'm bored. Why do you have this feeling about Strasser?"

"He is not a good man."

"You say that because he is an atheist?"

"Of course. And because he's unscrupulous in small matters."

"Yet he's done wonderful work here."

Ebenezer sighed. "That doesn't make him a good man, my dear. However, we can't discuss this now. Our friends will be arriving. Will you see the coffee is ready, and brandy, please?"

The girl went into the house. It was Ebenezer's custom, on Thursday evenings, to invite Julius Kruger and the predikant to his house. Now he heard the crunch of boots on the road. He went and stood at the top of the verandah steps.

The rotund figure of Dominee Bond loomed out of the darkness. He moved up the garden path in a fluttering, irregular course, hovering over the flower beds like a giant moth. At the foot of the steps he bent and pulled a leaf of rose geranium, rubbing it between his fingers with an exclamation of pleasure. "Good evening, Karl. How lucky you are to live by the water. My poor garden is dead, only dry sticks." He began to mount the steps, one hand braced on his knee. "Ah, how short of breath! Is Julius here?"

"Just behind you," said Ebenezer.

"Good Heavens, yes. Julius, you creep up on a man like a cat."

Julius, whose two hundred pounds were anything but feline, laughed as he followed the predikant up the steps. "You make so much noise, you wouldn't hear a rhinoceros. Man, but it's hot, still. Will we sit out here, Karl, in the dark?"

Ebenezer led the way to the end of the verandah, and pulled forward three chairs. He said, "Well, what is your news?"

His voice was a little strained. The three men had been friends for a very long time, but of late a rift had opened between Karl and Julius. It was noticeable that Julius now hesitated before answering, and to breach the gap the pastor said, in his gentle voice, "Were the sales good in Hopetoun?"

Julius shrugged. "So-so." He lifted one heel to the verandah rail. "Karl, I had another talk with old Gwevu tonight."

"And?"

"He still needs time to adjust. . . ."

"There is no time."

"Oh come, now, Karl. One can't rush these things."

"We have to make haste. You know it's essential that we get on with the implementation of separate development. The world is not going to accept mere talk. We have to prove our sincerity, we have to make action our key word. Things can't stand still because one obstinate old man . . ."

. . . "It isn't a case of an obstinate old man. We need the support of men like Gwevu. And for him, this is not an academic decision. He already has plenty on his hands, persuading his people to support the soil conservation plans. He knows some of his young men don't favor Bantu authorities. He pointed out today, a decision may involve him in some personal danger."

"He's an obstinate old man, and moreover, as slim as a jackal. He uses you, to hinder me. I therefore feel that our success will lie with the Pembe faction, not the Vuli."

Julius took out his pipe and began to fill it with slow, careful movements. He said, "The Pembe faction is worthless."

"You keep saying that, like a parrot, the Pembe faction is worthless. . . ."

"Wait." Julius raised one hand. "Listen, now. Old Gwevu hinted, this evening, at what I have always thought . . . that the Pembe are a group who will say 'yes' to anything, if it seems to carry an immediate profit. Do you want it said that we want a band of yes-men? Because that will be said, if we work through the Pembe. Cast your mind back over the years, Karl. In the Zongo tribe, every man with any guts or brain has been of the Vuli faction. They may be difficult to handle . . ."

. . . "Difficult? Impossible!"

. . . "But they have character, sand, bottom, whatever you

like to call it. They are the ones that will produce your leaders. Not the Pembe. That is why it is important to give Gwevu time, to use tact."

Karl's hand began to tap rapidly on the arm of his chair. "I disagree. I disagree."

The predikant said, out of the blue, "When I was a boy at school, I was troublesome, until they made me a monitor. My teacher said, only a rogue can catch a rogue." He chuckled. "Authority often makes stability. You have to think of it from the black point of view. The personality of the leader is very important. He must have . . . what can I call it . . . the winning streak? I agree with Julius, the Pembe are glib, but unreliable from our point of view. And from the other point of view, colorless."

Karl looked straight ahead of him. "There is no time to stall and talk and debate fine points. I am beginning to doubt whether I can count on the loyalty even of my friends."

"Don't say things you will regret, Karl." The predikant spoke with unusual sharpness. "We are three old friends. We can say what we think, without question of loyalty."

"Very well. Then let me simply say, in a time of crisis, one cannot call for more and more time."

Bond folded his hands on his chest. "And haven't you forgotten that this whole matter is not one which will be decided by three old fogies on a stoep? It is only our opinion that is sought, not our blood. We must keep a sense of proportion."

"Opinion counts for something in a place like Peace Drift."

The predikant gave no answer except a shake of the head. Ebenezer leaned forward.

"This year," he said, "we are in the valley of decision. And this year, the answer must be given. You, as well as I, will be required to face the fact."

Kruger, who had been silently puffing at his pipe, suddenly leaned back his head and shouted, "Nella!"

The girl appeared in the lighted doorway. Julius said, "Don't I get any coffee?"

"It's coming, Uncle."

"Bring it yourself, and come and talk to us. We're boring ourselves to death, here."

When she brought the tray out, she said to him, "Uncle, there must be pure coffee in your veins."

He laughed. "You tease me, but I'm nice to you. Listen, I met a young man on the train today. A doctor. Handsome."

She shot him a look.

Kruger ladled brown sugar into his cup. "He's staying with Dr. Strasser. I wonder now, is he married? I don't think so. Fair hair, blue eyes. What do you say to that?"

"Has he got all his teeth?"

"I never counted."

She shook her head. "You should have looked at his teeth. One can't be too careful."

She stayed talking to them. Julius seemed to cheer up and her father spoke occasionally, but the predikant fell silent, his chin on his chest, as if he were trying to hear his own heartbeat.

9

BEN'S FIRST DINNER in Strasser's house offered further proof that his host was an unusual man. The meal was admirably cooked, and served by a young African in white ducks and a scarlet cummerbund. Surprised to find such a servant in a country town, Ben studied him with some interest. He was tall, over six foot, with the broad shoulders, long torso, and long limbs typical of the region. It was a physique that made the classical Greek seem effeminate, and the modern muscleman grotesque. The face was bluntly, almost brutally strong, the nose short and broad, the cheeks rounded and the jaw very full. The wide, thick lips were compressed in concentration. Under scrutiny, the man raised his eyes briefly, and Ben was startled to see in them a look of derision that mocked this dinner, the whole stylized performance of an ineffectual rite.

When they had been served with coffee and were alone, Ben said to Strasser, "Where did you find a chap like that?"

"Sizwa? I've had him for several years. He came to me as an umfaan, about thirteen years old. He cooks and does the housework. I have a garden boy, Simeon, and a wash girl, Lena."

"Who taught Sizwa to cook?"

Strasser helped himself to sugar. "I did," he said, "in the finer points. I really could not endure the efforts of the usual sort of farmhand, and I didn't want an Indian. They never mix well with Africans." He sipped his coffee. "I have taken a great deal of trouble with my servants. I cannot bear ineptitude. It's expensive, of course, but I have few luxuries. I believe good service in my home increases my efficiency elsewhere. Don't you agree?"

Thinking of the expression in Sizwa's eye, Ben hesitated, and Strasser smiled faintly. "Of course," he said, "he despises me. You noticed it?"

"Well . . . I'd have said he found all this . . ."

. . . "trivial? Possibly." Strasser seemed to give the matter only cursory attention. "He is, you see, descended from a warrior caste. Naturally he feels contempt for such soft creatures as we. In fact he expresses contempt openly. He's a . . . what do you call it, a balladeer? He makes up rude songs about everyone. Once he was sent to prison, for assault, quite a short sentence. I wouldn't call him an estimable character, but interesting. They tell me he's a natural orator. Some of his people have that gift, which in our race has been debased to teaching schoolgirls to recite little poems."

"If you dislike him," said Ben quietly, "why do you keep him on?"

Strasser seemed surprised. "He's a good cook. I'm not at all interested in what he, or anyone else, thinks about me. He won't leave me because he wants the money. It seems a perfectly satisfactory arrangement."

He turned the conversation, then, to medicine. He was, Ben found, extremely well informed on the malnutritional diseases. "Malnutrition," he said, "is the great problem of the world, particularly of Africa. If you want to treat tuberculosis, kwashiorkor, industrial accidents, you come face to face with malnutrition." But when Ben questioned him on the educative side of the problem, asking how far he co-operated with the land and farming authorities, Strasser showed signs of annoyance. "I'm a doctor. I don't concern myself with things outside my field."

Soon after, Strasser rose from the table and said, "If you like we can go over to the Hotel? We've no club here, but we meet at the Hotel most nights. I usually get a game of bridge, or billiards."

They set out together. As they walked down the path, Ben caught sight of Sizwa at the kitchen window, drying dishes. He was singing to himself with considerable gusto. Ben had the uncomfortable feeling that the song was newly composed, and unflattering to someone, possibly himself. He decided to take Strasser's advice and polish his knowledge of the local dialect.

10

THE LOUNGE of the Hotel was large, high, and overfurnished. Easy chairs covered in orange cretonne lined the walls. In the center of the room was a clear space, surrounded by glass-topped tables and white wicker chairs. Over the empty fireplace at one end of the room hung a picture of a sailing ship, a Coca-Cola advertisement, and the stuffed head of a wart hog. A felt hat dangled from the wart hog's right tusk.

The room was fairly full of people, sitting at the tables and standing near an inner door marked "Bar." Among the latter Ben saw Archie Oakes, his dog at his heels.

Strasser said, "I'll introduce you to Sullivan," and led the way to where the thin man sprawled on a sofa, one arm around the shoulders of a plump blonde. Sullivan grinned, reached up an arm, and pressed the bell over his head.

"Sit down. This is Maisie." He pulled the girl closer to him, and Ben took the empty end of the sofa. The waiter appeared, and while they were still ordering drinks, the swing doors from the verandah opened, and a small man with a heavy round head pushed through and stood surveying them. Maisie gave a welcoming shriek, and the new arrival began to thread his way through the tables to them. Strasser muttered something about billiards and disappeared toward the Bar. The small man fetched up opposite the sofa, turned one of the wicker chairs to face it, and sat down.

Sullivan said, "This is Teddy Abrahams. He owns the tannery. Teddy, this is Ben Nevis. No cracks, he's heard them."

The little man smiled and nodded. He was an odd figure. His little feet, in highly polished shoes, hardly reached the ground, and the fingers which he now clasped around a brandy glass looked like cocktail sausages. His forehead was deep, and he wore thick spectacles. Ben thought, pituitary? And then was embarrassed to find that the eyes behind the distorting lenses were studying him shrewdly. Abrahams smiled.

"A little shorter, and I'd have been O.K. for a circus, hmn?" Before Ben could protest, Abrahams began to tell Sullivan a story both complicated and ribald. Ben settled down to listen.

He was enjoying himself. The ugly, crowded room, the sharp surge of talk, was home. Overseas, people had sometimes said to him, "You have no accent, you sound English." It was no doubt meant as a compliment. Hard to explain how one missed the banjo twang of one's own country. The radio in the corner began to thump out rock-and-roll. Sullivan pulled Maisie to her feet and made for the clearing between the tables. Abrahams moved across to sit on the sofa.

"Where's Strasser?" he said.

"Playing billiards, I think."

"He's avoiding me." Abrahams settled comfortably in his corner. "With us, it's like those little figures on the weather guide. One pops in, the other pops out."

Ben said nothing. Abrahams grinned. "I see you have practice in avoiding gossip."

"I was born here."

"So? And not curious to know why this great feud?"

Ben hooked a chair forward, got his feet up on it. "You hold the ugly secret of his past," he suggested.

"No." Abrahams sipped his brandy.

"He owes you money?"

"Not a cent. Nor I him."

"He's jealous of your success with Maisie."

"No, no. Much more simple. He just hates the sight of me." Ben turned his head sharply. The small, froglike figure beside him was relaxed. "You have to admit," said Abrahams, "that medically speaking, I am not very satisfactory."

"I don't think. . . ."

Suddenly Abrahams became serious. "No, of course that is not the reason. I shouldn't make jokes. Poor Strasser, I remind him of things he wants to forget."

Ben studied him. "Because you're a Jew?"

"No. Because I'm an optimist. Strasser has given up the struggle." Abrahams pulled off his spectacles and polished them slowly. "You should try and understand Strasser. He's a clever man. He lost far more, in his youth, than ever I did. When the brownshirts came to power he was sucked into a system he despised. His skill was wasted in an army medical corps. If he had been without imagination, he would have allowed himself to be carried along, and say afterward, 'I was not responsible, I acted under orders.' But he tried to resist. Not enough, just enough to finish himself with his own family, and not enough to keep his self-respect. You see? For most people, it happens like that. You fight, you win, or you lose. The guilty don't care, it's too late for them. The innocent have their innocence to wear in their hearts. But most people, like you and me, muddle along. We don't mean to be cowards, but we are. We are cruel, you could say, by default. We protest, but only in a murmur. As human beings, we don't quite make the grade. Now, I've seen what sort of man I am. No hero. I'm not proud. I can go on living with myself, I can be happy to be alive. Strasser can't do this. He has lost faith in everyone, most of all himself. And the reason he avoids me is that I understand. I know what he suffers. It must be hard, that, for a proud man."

"Has he no friends?"

"My boy, why would he want a friend? You know what friendship is? To hold a mirror up to yourself. Only a man who likes himself is capable of friendship."

Ben wagged a finger at the waiter, and gave an order for two more brandies. "If you are right, how can anyone stand living with himself. If, as you say, we're all such cowards."

Abrahams began to hum in tune with the radio. He said, almost casually, "You have to have love, it's the only defense." He pointed a pudgy finger at Sullivan, who was dancing with Maisie, both arms around her shoulders.

"That one, that Sullivan. He was in the war. He was in East Africa, North Africa, Italy, a prisoner, escaped. Quite brave, in a war. But now, in a time of attrition . . . pfft. Nothing. If you ask him what will happen here, he'll look away, make a joke. He is like Strasser, settled for second best."

His myopic gaze searched Ben's face. "Africa will be saved from anarchy by a few people with courage. They will draw from the rest whatever they have to give."

He turned the subject, then, talking about his travels. Sullivan returned to them briefly, drank a round with them, and soon disappeared into the night with his blonde. An hour or two later, Ben and Abrahams went out onto the verandah, and Abrahams caught sight of the Town Hall clock.

"Oh my God, look at the time. I came out only to buy soda water. We must meet again, doctor. You come and see my tannery. You'll be interested, if you can stand the smell."

He scurried off to his car. Ben watched him go with a cer-

tain disquiet. He felt that Abrahams guessed why he had come
to Peace Drift. Since he had discussed his reasons with no one,
that made Abrahams an extremely perceptive man.

He crossed the road, passing an African who sat on the low
wall outside the Garage. The man stared at him. Ben was beginning to feel that he had a placard, Stranger, pinned to his
chest.

He walked as far as the river before going home. The willow
fronds barely touched the surface of the water. At this time of
the year they should be half-submerged, the trees thigh-deep
and braced like fishermen against the current.

A damned, inquisitive, drought-ridden town, thought Ben,
and went to bed in a disgruntled frame of mind.

I I

Sizwa, as a domestic servant, was on duty from seven in the
morning until eight at night, with a break of an hour and a half
for breakfast, and two hours for lunch. He could have got
through his work in a shorter time, but haste to him was pointless. He considered white men crazy, who worked against the
clock, red-faced and irritable, and collapsed exhausted at five
in the afternoon. Sometimes he thought he might like the
shorter hours of factory work. Then he looked at Strasser, and
changed his mind.

Two other things had to be weighed. Strasser paid him very
well, and old Gwevu wanted him to stay with Strasser. Gwevu
was always lecturing him on the importance of working hard
and showing respect to his employer. Domestic workers, Gwevu
said, were safe, they didn't starve in a drought, and they didn't
get paid off in a slump. Also, Sizwa should remember that although he'd worked in Peace Drift for some years, he hadn't
been born there. He had no right to think of himself as a towns-

man, he could have his work permit canceled and be sent back
to the bosom of his family . . . a prospect that both Gwevu and
Sizwa found extremely unattractive.

So Sizwa remained in Strasser's household. He didn't feel
good there. Strasser was not one who made this nice feeling
around him. He was stingy, counted the groceries, and locked
the cupboards like an old grandmother. He never smiled, or
chatted, there were no women in his life, he was altogether
an unsympathetic person.

Yet in one respect, Sizwa was content. Strasser, he felt, was
a man of his word. There was a certain understanding between
them that could be counted on. Sizwa kept his share of it,
which was to cook well and look after the house. He expected
the bargain to hold, until he'd saved up enough money for his
taxi.

Nobody knew what an effort it was to him to save. There
were so many things to buy in the shops, and women who were
never satisfied. And relations, that was another thing. Gwevu
was always after a cut, prosing about the need to send money
to this or that dependent of the family. Gwevu was adamant on
the subject of family duty. It was a nuisance. Sizwa had no time
for these old-fashioned ideas. Let old people cling to old things.
In the new times coming, there was need for young men with
new ideas.

He'd found that out, listening and watching. Men came home
from the cities to talk about a new Africa. Some of them said
quite openly, "We will do this, we will do that." These men
knew something. Were something. Sizwa watched and listened.
He spent his spare time hanging about the tannery, the sawmill, even the Hotel, anywhere that men worked in combination rather than for an individual household. He had the strong
community sense of his people, but the community to which he
was drawn was not the traditional one of home and family,
but the new, shapeless society of the town. Moreover, he could
read a little, he knew how to turn on a radio. He thought it odd

that white people, discussing Africa, writing about it in their papers, should think their views were a secret to Africans.

Not that Sizwa analyzed the catchwords . . . nationalism, freedom, Pan-Africanism . . . that throbbed in the talk of educated men. He was not educated. He had only his natural resources: the force of character that had made his forebears leaders; great physical courage; an egotism so large it allowed of no self-pity; a humor pungent and resilient; and the emotional sensitivity that gave him access to the lightest of another's thoughts.

Those of his country's laws that irked the minds of his learned friends affected Sizwa only through his emotions. He felt the Pass regulations, the restrictions on residence, travel and ownership of land, the difficulties of job reservation, not in any social sense but as a direct, personal threat. He also understood that they provided a means of influencing his new community.

Sizwa was, in some sense, the rough Africa, from which time must shape the cutting point of rebellion, or some safer, flatter facet. Such a stone was not safe in the care of a man like Strasser.

Strasser, for his part, could not remain blind to Sizwa's potential. The irony was that the doctor, being white, refused to acknowledge the effect of Sizwa on his own life. He would have been disgusted by any suggestion that he envied his native cook. Yet this was the truth. Strasser envied Sizwa his vitality, his sexual prowess, his capacity for enjoyment; and envy, in time, had bitten down to the level of malice. It was this wholly unconscious reaction that had made an impression on Ben, almost as soon as he entered Strasser's household.

Sizwa had one close friend, in Abel. It was a surprising friendship, but it endured, and it was to Abel that Sizwa carried first impressions of this newly arrived young doctor.

Abel lived at this time in the outhouse quarters of his employer, Turnbull. Abel's mother had been nurse to Turnbull's children, and was now the family washerwoman. It was Turnbull who had paid for Abel's education, and, as owner of the Garage, secured him a job as garage hand.

The room he had was not much. It overlooked a stony yard littered with the skeletons of dead machines. There was no water laid on, except in the nearby washhouse, and no electric light.

Sizwa approached the quarters by the lane running past the side of the Garage. He banged on a back window, walked around, and pushed open Abel's door.

The room was square, lit by a paraffin lamp attached to a hook in the ceiling. Against one wall was an iron bedstead, with a thin mattress, and two brown blankets folded across the foot. Beside the bed on a wooden box stood a stub of candle in a saucer, and a box of matches. There was a chest of drawers in one corner, a looking glass nailed above it. A red coir mat covered the center of the cement floor, and in the middle of the mat, placed directly under the light from the lamp, was a brown wooden table and chair. Everything was minutely clean, and in good repair.

At the table sat Abel, papers and a book before him. When the door opened, he looked up with a sigh, and a corner of his mouth lifted slightly.

Sizwa slid down to a seat on the doorstep, braced his bare toes against the opposite post, and reaching into his pocket, brought out a small cotton tobacco bag which he tossed over to Abel.

Abel caught it in one hand. "What's this?"

"Snuff. From the old one."

Abel, who disliked snuff, was touched. "That's very kind of him."

He laid the bag carefully beside his papers, and turned sideways in the chair to face his visitor. "When did you see him?" He had a great respect for old Gwevu, and knew he worried about his grandson.

Sizwa shrugged. "Last Sunday, it was." He looked at Abel with suspicion. "Are you reading again?"

Abel smiled. He picked up the book at his elbow and held it to the light. His hand caressed its new, sharp edges. He opened it near the end, for the pleasure of hearing it click as the pages separated for the first time.

Sizwa said kindly, "It's a very fine book," and Abel smiled more widely. He had an attractive smile that showed the whiteness of his teeth and the kindness of his eyes. He said, "Has the new doctor come?"

"Yes, on today's train."

"What's he like?"

"Quite small, not fat, but strong. One tooth is broken, at the side, here. Hair that stands up like a dandelion, but short. His eyes see everything." Sizwa considered. "He speaks very little, and smiles often." He was not quite sure how to put a value on the new man, and after a moment changed the subject. "Tusi from the factory told me this afternoon there was a policeman up at the Mission, asking about someone."

"Gavine brewers," suggested Abel.

Sizwa squinted at the palm of his hand. "They're afraid of agitators." He glanced up slyly.

Abel grunted. "So am I. I've seen them at work."

"Where?"

"In the locations, in the cities. Believe me, they're something to be afraid of. Pulling people off the buses when they come home from work, beating them up, burning the school and the beer hall. They get hold of idlers and teach them to terrify respectable people."

Abel contemplated Sizwa's profile. He understood him so well. Abel knew himself what it meant to live through these times. It meant fear and confusion. The old protectors were failing, the tribal chiefs and the white men with their paternalism. Both had been ready to carry ordinary men on their backs. Now both seemed corrupted by fear and ready to abdicate. People felt betrayed. Now both belonged nowhere. So they looked for new leaders, with courage, leaders who could bind them together again, make them secure, interested, hopeful. They looked, thought Abel, for someone like Sizwa. Sizwa was very young, but when he spoke to a crowd, one forgot his age. Abel's eyes shifted to the book before him. He said, "You shouldn't talk about agitators, Sizwa. You know nothing about them."

At once Sizwa was angry. He leaned forward, jeering. "You are afraid of the sound of words. You're afraid to move. You sit here and read your books. And what does it do for you? You work in the Garage, get yourself covered in grease, and what are you paid for your trouble?"

"Enough to save. . . ." began Abel, and increased Sizwa's annoyance.

"Save? What for? Can you buy a house in a nice area? Of course not, it's impossible. You can buy more books, so they'll call you a cheeky Kaffir, for knowing too much. Why must I be quiet, and wait, wait, wait? Will that make me rich, put food in my mouth? I tell you, a man with a vote doesn't starve. Is that in your books? It should be! Do your books say that a man should be proud in his own country? They should say that! Are these lies I'm giving you?"

Abel opened his mouth but Sizwa interrupted him. "All true, all. Those who want good things must ask, and fight. White people won't give anything to a silent man. Their judgment peeps out of one eye. We must ask, take, be ready!"

Abel stabbed a finger at him. "And there is no way of taking unless the price is paid. Stop shouting and listen. I'm not saying that you can't beat the price down. You can. But there is always a just price to pay. Another thing. There are people, white people, who are prepared to deal fairly. You know that."

Sizwa threw out his hands. "How many? Ten? Twenty?"

Abel looked steadily at him and said nothing. Sizwa's hands waved more violently. "Those have no power to change anything. Their own people won't listen to them. If you joined one of their Parties, do you know what would happen to you? The police would come at two in the morning, to arrest you. The Whites care nothing for us. They are throwing us away, every day. We are rubbish to be thrown away." He cupped his hands as if they held something delicate that might escape. "When they talk of giving us our own place, it will be a place for Gwevu, perhaps. For a person like that. But where will there be a place for me, and for Tusi, and for you? There will be no factories in that place, no machines. How will we live? And if we stay here, what power will we have in that other place, and what power here? I tell you, we are nothing!"

His voice had risen to a shout, and Abel said urgently, "Be quiet, Mr. Turnbull will hear you."

"That's all you can say, be quiet, be quiet! For how long have I been quiet, and what have I got to show for it? Where is my house, my garden, my motorcar? What else can I do? Really, I'm not a person at all. You're not a person at all. How many white people, passing us in the street, see us with their eyes? That doctor who came to our place today looked at me. I tell you he saw me, really saw me, and it gave me a surprise. A surprise, because his eyes said to me, 'Who is this we have here, what is his name, what sort of person is he?'"

He flung out his hands, shaking his head. "The first to see me for years. What will I do, living in such a town?"

A faint smile appeared in Abel's eyes. "You're truly wasted among us, Sizwa."

Sizwa nodded. "Yes, I am."

The tension induced in him by the self-hypnosis of the orator suddenly evaporated. He began to sing under his breath, leaning in the doorway, his eyes apparently fixed on the round green star that hung low over Turnbull's roof. "I have saved ninety-eight pounds," he said.

"Really? Soon you'll have your taxi."

"Yes, and it won't be an old crock. This is going to be a taxi smart people will be glad to enter. In a little while, in a few months more." He turned his head. "You can come and see me buy it."

"That will be very pleasant," said Abel dryly. He knew that he should not let the evening slide without warning Sizwa against being reckless. But Abel was a gentle, shy man, and disliked arguments. Now that the awkward subject had lapsed, he could not make himself revert to it. He went on discussing Sizwa's taxi. The opportunity for advising caution was lost.

Later he walked with Sizwa to the end of the lane, and watched him spring away toward Strasser's house. Sizwa seldom walked. He danced, jumped, sang his way about.

Abel sat down on the low wall outside the Garage. It was true, though, what Sizwa said. Few white people had eyes. Either the gaze was averted, or it was blind and hazy. Some saw. Kruger. The old predikant. Oakes, who looked and then looked away quickly, as if the light hurt him.

Abel sat for some time, enjoying the nighttime cool. He was about to go back to his room when the swing doors of the Hotel opened, and Abrahams and another younger man passed through. From Sizwa's description, it was easy to recognize the new doctor. Abel watched him with interest. Would there be something special about these eyes? The young man was coming across the road, toward him. He glanced quickly at Abel, at the thin leg, up into the face. He gave a faint nod and smile as he passed.

The eyes certainly saw. But they were quite ordinary. Blue, a bright blue under the streetlight. Abel watched the young man walk away towards the river, and then, remembering that he had left the lamp burning in his room, slid off the wall and hurried back up the lane.

12

ANOTHER TRAVELER reached Peace Drift during the course of that day. Like Ben, he had retained childhood memories of the shape and form of the valley, memories that were of life-and-death importance to him now.

He had climbed far above the plantation, above the steep acclivity of the Mission lands, and come at last to a small platform of rock that overlooked the whole of the Peace River bed. Thick natural bush surrounded his eyrie, continuing down the banks of a stream that fell in a series of pools and cascades to the foot of the krantz.

The man lay resting on his back, screened by the overhang of the rocks above, and the vegetation below. He seemed half-asleep, his arms outspread, his fingers limp. He was in fact very tired. The problem of survival occupied his whole remaining strength.

This man, who lay so relaxed, felt neither hope nor despair, neither passion nor interest, in the people of the valley. He belonged nowhere. A doctor had once described him as being unable to identify himself with the emotions of others. He had not been told of this opinion, but if he had, it would have caused him no concern.

His eyes, of a singularly dark brown, watched the heavens with the unblinking stare of a child. Policemen and welfare workers took warning from his eyes, round and cold as the eye of a pistol.

He rolled over at last and pulled his rucksack under his chest. Through a break in the bush he could study the town far below; he scanned the rooftops, picked out the warning lights on church spire and town hall, the flat black pool of the station roof, the double necklace of lights on the central highway.

Easy, he thought. But he would have to wait for rain, even a little rain.

When at last he dropped his head, the after image of Peace Drift danced briefly on his vision.

A little, soft, open town. An oyster ready to be gouged from its shell.

13

MANNIE REIMER'S OFFICE at the Police Station was a high, square room overlooking the courtyard and the main road. In a summer such as this, it was stifling, and Mannie, who had to catch up on a good deal of paper work after the Christmas and New Year holidays, had taken off his coat and hung it on his chair. Even so, the back and armpits of his shirt were darkened by sweat, and the papers under his wrist stuck to his flesh.

Just after ten, he heard a car drive into the yard and stop with a familiar squeak of brakes. Almost immediately, young Venter, who lived in perpetual hopes of drama, put his head around the door and said, "He's back!"

Mannie smiled, got to his feet, shrugged into his jacket, and buttoned it. When Carptain Larkill came into the office he was standing waiting, his hands clasped behind his back.

Larkill's eyes swept around the room as he greeted Mannie. His voice was hard and awkward, his body hard and deft, for he was a man who preferred action to words. He made little secret of his contempt for Peace Drift, and looked on his term of duty there as an interlude designed to improve his knowledge of native languages.

He had served as a commissioned officer in Egypt and Italy, during the war, and the experience had left him with a taste for authority. Although not a particularly intelligent man, he was efficient and ambitious, the sort of officer who wins the grudging respect of his subordinates, the trust of his superiors, and the liking of no one. Little escaped his attention, and less penetrated as far as his understanding. He was a disciplinarian, and often expressed the opinion that Reimer was too soft with lawbreakers.

The lack of sympathy between the two men was not lost on their associates.

As soon as the door closed behind Venter, Larkill sat down opposite Mannie and said, "While I was away, I took the chance to call in at Division. I spoke to Wolmarans. He told me quite a bit about the man Black." He drummed the fingers of his right hand on the desk. "It seems he's coming this way."

"What makes 'em say so?"

"I'll tell you. He is an agitator known to have been operating in the Transvaal for two years, but up to four months ago nothing was known of his identity, although his methods tallied with those of an operator who was active on the Portuguese border, several years ago. Then, four months back, this drug addict called Mendal was convicted of forgery in Joburg. While Mendal was inside, he couldn't get his dagga, and he started to throw ing-bings. In hospital he admitted to having forged some documents, passes, and permits, and so on. He said he'd supplied them, in exchange for supplies of dagga, to a gang working in the Sunvalley Location. Our chaps ran down two of this gang. One of them said he'd obtained certain forged papers from Mendal, for Black, and he also said Black was the one who organized the disturbance in the Location in April of this year. Now, if Black was ready to work in with a lot of dagga junkies, that makes us think he's pretty hard-pressed. Once we had a line on him, we got the feeling that he's out on a limb, funds caput. The guess is that he's no longer what you could call an accredited agent. About three weeks ago the boys thought they'd cornered him, but he shot his way out, stole a car, left Joburg. Five days after that, information was he'd been seen over toward the border of Portuguese East. Then they lost him. But last week, a trading store on the border was raided by a man answering Black's description . . . which isn't much, I grant you. But that store's less than fifty miles from here as the crow flies."

"Who says he's a crow?" muttered Mannie, and then added, "What happened at the store?"

"The owners are—were—an elderly couple. The man was down with flu, and the woman was alone in the front precincts.

A man walked in in the middle of the afternoon. Must have asked to see blankets, there were some out on the counter. Probably offered her a high-denomination note, and when she opened the till, he clubbed her and cleared the contents. She got a fractured skull, and they don't think she'll regain consciousness. May be dead already. Anyway, the old man at the back heard the scuffle. Came as quick as he could. He saw the man from a distance, and gave a description. It tallies with Black's."

"And the car?"

"He couldn't see one, but there are trees around the store."

"Did they find the stolen car?"

"Yes, up near the border."

"Then there's nothing to connect Black with the robbery at the store. The description isn't much. About five-ten, brown eyes, wearing jeans and a dark jersey, that sort of thing could be anyone. Could be you, sir."

"The man who robbed the store was driving a stolen car. It was found abandoned, about ten miles from the store. And that car was stolen last week from Nelspruit, which is quite close to where the Joburg car was abandoned. They reckon the chap left one, stole a second. They checked the mileage on the Nelspruit car. It wasn't driven to the trading store direct. Likely, Black stole it, headed for the border, found it too hot there, doubled south."

"Why south, though?"

"Making for Swaziland, perhaps."

"Or the coast. Maybe has Russians waiting to take him off by submarine." Mannie chuckled.

"This is a serious matter."

Mannie rubbed his neck. "You don't think we are getting a bit too keen, sir? After all, there's nothing to say the same chap stole both cars, is there? Black mucks about on the border. Someone else nips a car and does the store job. My experience is, a professional doesn't gash old ladies. That's for tramps and ducktails. Not a political agent."

"Black is no longer a political agent. He's a man on the run, looking after Number One. If he's wanting to clear the country, there's at least a chance he'll come this way. Perhaps a thin one, but we have to take anything these bastards give us and follow it up."

"Ja, that's so." Mannie picked at the edge of the blotter on his desk. "Why are they keeping the Press out of it? Seems to me the thing would be to circulate a description and get everyone looking for this boy."

"I've told you, he's not a bloody amateur. If we have the whole district out playing cops and robbers, we won't get a sniff of him."

"That might be a good idea." Mannie looked at his superior thoughtfully. He wondered if he'd heard the full story. Larkill was a monkey. Liked to keep one little piece in his cheek, just for himself. He said bluntly, "Even if Black did the store, why do you think he'll try and pull something here?"

Larkill's eyes shifted toward the window. "It's a question of being prepared. This isn't the only town he could use, but it's the most likely. Plenty of cover, not too big, on the route to the coast or Swaziland. He may try to contact someone here. We'll have to keep an eye on every suspicious type in the area, but we must do it quietly. We don't want the thing to blow up into a panic. So far as the Press knows, the store robbery was a straight smash-and-grab. I don't want the public squealing like pigs. Most likely the whole thing'll fizzle, but in the meantime we don't want publicity. That's the instructions and that's how it'll be. I want to handle this myself."

Mannie thought, I'll bet you do. Out-special the Specials, show us how it's done.

His resentment increased as he listened while Larkill gave detailed instructions. Larkill hoped Black would come their way. To him Peace Drift was a springboard to something more worthwhile. A goat tied to a tree, so Larkill could get his tiger.

Mannie didn't believe the store had been done by any agitator. He didn't want to believe it, either.

After Larkill had left the office, Mannie crossed the room and stood at the open window. If it was a big thing, they'd have sent more men down. If it wasn't big . . .

He ran a finger around his collar. If it wasn't big, then it wasn't any use getting in a muck sweat about it.

If it would rain, that'd ease the heat, and the tempers.

With a sigh, he turned back to his desk and settled down to work through the papers in his tray.

14

ON SATURDAY MORNING, Strasser took Ben to see the Elizabeth Hospital. As they drove up the Ridge, past the Mission Halt, and on around the curve of the plantations, Ben said, "Bit off the beaten track, isn't it?"

"Not when you consider the area it serves. The Bantu are used to traveling far greater distances to hospital. Up here, we're within easy reach of the town, the back country, and the Reserve. We are, in fact, a true border area."

Ben though that over. It was the policy of the Government to develop industries and public amenities in the territories adjoining Reserve areas. Strasser went on:

"I saw the need for a hospital here, years ago, soon after I arrived. I have worked on the idea ever since. A good deal of money is sunk in it, one way or another. In a few years, we will have a model hospital, one of the finest in the country. We'll be able to treat everything ourselves. One day, we'll serve as dispersal point for health teams to visit the remoter districts." His voice held an entirely new note. He gave Ben a shy, oddly endearing smile.

"There it is," he said, and halted the car at a pair of white gates in a wire fence.

The Hospital stood in a large clear acreage. Behind it, rough

veld ran to the surrounding forests. There were several buildings, newly white-washed. Strasser took the car down a sloping
approach to a concrete apron in front of the central block. He
stretched out a hand. "This is Medical. Surgical on the left,
with the theater in the tower. The theater is air-conditioned—
the file on that makes very good reading, I assure you. Emergency is there, X-ray and path labs here. Behind is the Day
Clinic and Maternity. One day, someone will endow a proper
research laboratory, and I will make this the main center for
the treatment of the malnutritional diseases. It will be a revolution, don't you agree?"

"Not entirely."

Strasser's eyebrows rose in amusement. He climbed out of
the car, and as Ben followed, said, "Qualify that statement,
please."

"Well, sir, as I see it, the main centers for the treatment of
malnutrition are anywhere but in hospital. They're out in a
thousands farms too small to be called by the name. People
have this idea that mammoth projects are the answer for Africa.
A sort of Kariba complex. But we'll have to cure malnutrition
out in the backward areas, and down there, in those corrugated iron shanties."

"And what about the poor patients?"

"I'm thinking of them. If you will pull them in to hospitals,
and patch them up, and send them packing to the same conditions of wrong feeding, what purpose has been served? Their
families have learned nothing. The patient has been ill for
nothing. It's not enough to cure a disease in hospital. You have
to use the disease, get something out of it in the way of human
learning.

"When I was touring in Italy and Spain, I saw what was
being done to reclaim the peasant farms there. It was a small
but profound revolution. They told me that production went
up only by inches, over years, but the inches carried the people
above the breadline. It was the difference between starvation
and viability. If you were to tie your research in with land-

reform teams, now . . . they're already in existence . . . and bring in legislation to enforce their decisions, and give them better finances, then you'd have something really big."

"You don't call that a mammoth project?"

"In a sense, yes, but not a whale. Rather, a very big shoal of sardines."

They began to walk toward the Hospital. Strasser said drily, "Well, perhaps you had better plan this El Dorado. I've enough on my hands."

"I didn't mean to belittle what you've done."

"I know." Strasser sighed. "Rhodes," he said, "was not an edifying character, but at least he appreciated the size of Africa."

At the entrance of the hospital, they passed an African in a white coat, who glanced up and smiled at them. Strasser said, "That was Mdunge, my senior resident." He led the way around the buildings. The Hospital was small in relation to the number of patients it must serve, but it was designed for expansion, and the equipment, though incomplete, was of excellent standard. Ben's respect for his colleague increased steadily. When at last they returned to the main door, he said, "How did you get so much?"

Strasser scratched his chin. "Bullying, persuading, writing thousands of words. Getting up on platforms. Pulling every string there was." He smiled. "I had help."

"Whose?"

"Never mind! If I wanted to reach a man, I reached him. You see, I'm a Vicar of Bray. I have no moral standards. I play left against right, politically and economically. I don't care about anything except getting my own way."

"Then," remarked Ben placidly, taking out a pack of cigarettes and proffering them, "I'm sorry to have to tell you, sir, that you've had your day."

Strasser waved a hand. "No thank you. Why do you say this?"

"October fifteenth, 1961. The Day of Declaration."

Strasser's pale eyes studied him briefly. "Are you one of these very boring Progressives?"

"Well, yes, but that's not the point. The October Election was the end of Bray. People will have to declare, now, for separation or integration. You too."

Strasser said waspishly, "My dear boy, you misunderstand me. I'm not one of those who disguise their political sympathies for business reasons. I don't trim my politics, I'm simply not interested in them. I have none, they are quite unimportant to me. My only loyalty is medicine, and my only ethics are medical ethics. You may be humanistic, or patriotic, or anything you care to be, but not I. I have no emotions at all. I don't even love my successes. I like my patients, a little, so long as they are ill. When they recover, I forget them. I have been able to do what I have done because I have no personal stake in it. I try my utmost to make people see this, but being for the most part grossly sentimental, they persist in crediting me with altruism. I repeat now, don't look for the idealist in me. It is not there. You see?"

He went away to complete some business in the almoner's office, and Ben waited for him in the car. As the sun climbed, the trees round about shone as if with sweat. Their aromatic freshness was dulled by the smell of water-starved soil.

When Strasser reappeared, his temporary loquaciousness was over. They drove back to the town in silence. As they ran down the hill, Ben heard a droning in the western sky, and saw a red spotter-plane move slowly across the valley. He said to Strasser, "What's that for?"

"Probably a met. plane. Or a fire-spotter, if the fire hazard figure has reached danger point." He pursed his mouth. "There is not enough organization. They should have more planes, and more water-storage points within the forestry area. Wardens should have radio-telephones. Volunteer firemen should be trained. This town is slipshod." He slowed down to negotiate the Drift. "It is an appalling town, really."

They drew up at the Clinic, an unimpressive building with a long verandah on three sides. As they walked in, Strasser reiterated his dislike of it. "Nobody stays here long. It's either Hopetoun or the cemetery for them."

Two rooms had been set aside for the polio campaign. Trestle tables already bore neat stacks of forms for completion by the applicant. Strasser said, "At the first inoculations, we asked for too much detail. Now we have concentrated on name, age, and race. We have clerks for the nonwhites, as so many are illiterate." He was explaining the process of diluting the triple vaccine in saline when a young nurse came in, carrying a large, old-fashioned screen. Ben went over and took it from her.

"Where do you want it?"

"Here, please sir, in the corner."

Ben set it up. Strasser said, "Nevis, this is Sister Ebenezer. She will be helping us with the campaign."

The young woman murmured some reply. She was small and light-boned; her nose was narrow and aquiline, her skin smooth, with color on the slanting cheekbones; and her eyes dark gray, the iris ringed with black. It was a sharp, bright, uncompromising face. Ben found it oddly familiar. It reminded him of a picture he had had in his nursery, of a boy on horseback, the head arrogantly poised, the hand doubled on the hip. Yet when she smiled, her face sparkled, and Ben found himself wishing she would laugh.

As he left the building with Strasser, Ben said, "I think Sister Ebenezer should be on my team, sir."

Strasser said absently, "She's an excellent nurse. I could use her to better purpose, but her father doesn't like me."

"She's over twenty-one, isn't she?"

"It's easy to see," said Strasser, "that you know nothing of this town. Her father is one who believes himself to be of the Chosen People, which is not, of course, the Jews. There are three magic circles around that little princess. A strange man, Ebenezer." After a moment, he said, "Do you know the Afri-

kaner song and poetry? There you find the hiemwee, the longing for an identity, for a quiet place on the earth."

"I know them, because I'm half Afrikaner."

Strasser seemed amused. "Ah, but also half English. Take
my advice, Nevis, leave that girl out of your calculations. She
isn't for you."

Ben grinned. "Too fast, give me time." They reached the
road. "Is her mother dead?"

"She left Ebenezer, years ago, they tell me. I never met her.
Apparently she was rather beautiful, and rather clever. She
wrote a book of poems, quite good. Her family was famous
for hospitality, argument, and sexual indiscretion. The marriage
must have been fated from the start. There were three children.
One boy is, I think, an engineer, the other went back to the
Cape and entered commerce. Neither has been home since I
came here. Nella is like an only child. She should leave, but
she has great loyalty to her father. In my view, it's only a matter of time. Some crisis will arrive, and she will go."

"What's he like?"

Strasser shrugged. "He's the unofficial Government in these
parts. He's an honest man. I don't advise you to cross him, but
if you must, speak loud and hold your ground, or you won't
last a moment."

Walking home, they passed the Police Station. A dapper,
muscular man ran down the front steps, and seeing Strasser,
gave a curt nod. Strasser muttered under his breath.

"And who's that?" asked Ben.

"Captain Larkill. A great, stupid, local busybody."

Ben reflected that if Strasser disliked Larkill, his dislike was
evidently keenly reciprocated.

15

WATERY SUNLIGHT, shining on the brass knobs of the bedstead, woke Ben early. He lay still for a few minutes, then got up, bathed, shaved, and dressed. The house was quite silent. Perhaps if he spoke aloud his mother's voice would come in swift reproof, "Hush up, now, it's Sunday."

He went out into the garden, into the street. The Sabbath deepened. Thick dew clothed the hedges, and on the sidewalk the body of a caterpillar glittered with a hundred diamonds. Must have rained a little in the night. The cloud ceiling was low, threatening showers.

Ben strolled up to the Drift, turned right along a red sand road bordered with trees, continued on until the houses gave way to open veld. Further up, the road dwindled to a track, then a path, skirted a patch of native shanties, and faded into a blue wall of pine trees.

He was about to turn back when he saw an old man in black hurrying down the track. When he was quite close to Ben, he suddenly turned aside, sat down beside the road, and put his head on his knees.

Ben crossed quickly to his side. The man did not look up. Ben put his hand under a cold, damp forehead, took the wrist, and felt for the pulse. He said, "Lean back against the bank."

The old man obeyed. Ben saw that he wore a predikant's collar. Presently his eyes fluttered open and he said, "I lose my breath." His hand faltered toward his coat pocket. Ben slid his hand into the pocket, found a small ampoule, looked at the label, wrapped it in a clean handkerchief, and broke the glass in his fingers. He held the handkerchief under the man's nostrils. The man tried to move and Ben said, "Sit still, sir. Don't worry."

They sat in silence for some time. At last Ben saw the strug-

gle for breath diminish. The old man said, "Sorry." He essayed
a smile. "I chose my victim well. Dr. Nevis, isn't it?"

"That's right." Ben studied the heavy, gray face, lined like
a bloodhound's. "You shouldn't walk so fast, you know. Skelt-
ing down the hill like that."

"It's the pine trees, in dry weather. Set me off." The man sat
up straight. "My name is Bond." His limpid eyes gazed at Ben
with friendly curiosity. "Tell me, are you an Anglican, like
your father?"

"I suppose so. Not a very good one."

"I remember your father. Let me see, now. My sister's child
had diphtheria. In those days, many cases died, but he saved
her. He had an old Ford car, I remember. How it used to boil
and bang! My sister would say, 'Who would think an angel
of God could travel with so much noise and smoke?' He shook
his head. "I can go home now, I think."

"To rest," suggested Ben, and the old man chuckled.

"Oh, you are not yet my doctor. Sunday is my busy day."

"Where do you live?"

"Just up there, behind the Church."

They went slowly along the road. The predikant's house was
small, the garden full of roses withering in the heat. "Look at
them," the old man said. "With water so precious, these poor
things must die."

"It looks like rain now."

"We will get a few showers, not nearly enough. Day after
day, we wait for the real storm that will break the drought."
He thanked Ben profusely, and then insinuated himself through
the narrow garden gate. "Have a good breakfast." He waddled
away up the path, much too rapidly.

Back at the house, Ben found Strasser, up, dressed, and in
a bad temper. He said sharply, "Wherever have you been?"
and before Ben could answer, continued with a gesture of his
square hand, "There is no method in this place. The law is an
ass."

They took their places at the breakfast table. Ben said, "Why the law, particularly?"

"Captain Larkill." Strasser shook brown sugar over his porridge with delicate precision. "Weeks ago, he promised me four native policemen to help in my campaign, which means from tomorrow. Now, this morning, at short notice, he has withdrawn his promise."

"Perhaps the men are needed elsewhere." Ben watched Strasser with curiosity. His anger was no less evident for being perfectly controlled.

"I am not interested in reasons. My plans are upset. The polio campaign is far more important to the community than any sordid police activity." Strasser ate for some moments in silence, and then said, "Larkill is incapable of seeing a thing from any viewpoint but his own. A careerist throughout."

"Did you protest?"

"Naturally, but not to the point of animosity. In a place this size, one can't afford high words. We shall have to get on as best we can without their help."

He left the house after breakfast, and Ben, whose work did not begin until the next day, took a chair into the back garden. He read for about half an hour, but was driven indoors by a sharp shower.

At ten o'clock, the bell of the Anglican Church began to peal, and presently the deeper note of the Dutch Reformed bell joined in. Behind and above them, *vox caelestis*, sounded the Mission bell.

Ben walked to the garden gate. There were cars coming down from the Ridge, and many were already parked on both sides of the street. People passed in pairs, in families. Some of the women wore long-sleeved, high-necked black dresses, black stockings and hats. A Colored family turned in through the Anglican gate, but the people in the yard of the Dutch Reformed Church were all white. The nonwhites of that community, Ben knew, attended the Mission Church on the hill.

Two figures appeared on the main road near the river, a

girl in a dark dress and an old man. They walked briskly. The girl's face was concealed by the brim of a hideous hat, but her movements seemed familiar. Ben watched them turn into the Dutch Church. Then he raced back to his room, changed hurriedly into his one dark suit. He had no hat, but snatched one of Strasser's from a hook in the hall.

The courtyard of the Church was nearly deserted. He caught up with a couple entering the building, slipped inside, and took a place among the men. Glancing around he saw Nella Ebenezer sitting across the aisle. Her hands were folded in her lap, and her eyes downcast. She looked not demure, but like a small, thoughtful cat. Ben smiled.

When he looked to his front, though, he found himself close to old Julius Kruger. There was a glint in his small bright eyes. Ben was not sure whether it betokened amusement or warning.

16

AT THE FIRST SOUND of the church bells, Archie Oakes went to his desk in the living room and lifted out a prayer book and a hymn book, placing them beside his hat on the center table. His terrier cocked its ears and shifted its feet uneasily. Oakes crossed to his bedroom, checked that the windows were locked, took a clean handkerchief from the bureau drawer and folded it carefully into his breast pocket. He went back and picked up hat and books, bent and stroked the dog's ears. "Back soon, boy. Look after things nicely until I get home."

The Indian who helped in the stockroom did not live on the premises, and was never there on Sundays. Archie let the dog into the back garden, locked the back door, and closed the garden gate behind him.

He walked along the side of the house. As he reached the main road, his attention was caught by an African on the stoep of his shop. The man stood close up to the display window, his hands pressed flat against the glass. Oakes halted, his pale cheeks suffused with color. He said loudly, "Get away from that window!"

The man's head turned toward him. Oakes recognized Strasser's cook. He clambered up on to the stoep. "You hear me? Get your hands off my glass."

The man stepped back. He said nothing. His mouth drooped a little and his eyes narrowed. Oakes peered at the glass. He said, "Look at that. Your greasy marks on everything. I've told you before." He pulled out a handkerchief and scrubbed at the hand-prints, breathed on them, scrubbed again. When he straightened, the man was watching him expressionlessly. Oakes swung his arm, pointing. "Get off my stoep, I said, go on, right off."

The man dropped to the street. Oakes said, "Next time, I'll tell the police." He stepped back to the pavement and walked up the road to the door of the Anglican Church. There he turned and peered back at his shop. The bells were still loud in the air.

Sizwa sat on the edge of the stoep until they stopped pealing. He saw the new doctor run from Strasser's gate, and cross the road. The street was deserted, now, all the people at breakfast or in church. He heard the music of the hymns swell out. He returned in leisurely manner to the window, placed his hands deliberately on the glass, leaned his forehead between them.

The guitar lay in the center of the display of goods. Its yellow body was picked out in black and red, its round, black mouth seemed already singing. Sizwa bent his arms up, strummed his fingers across his chest. He sang to himself. Then he laughed, and flung out his arms, dismissing the guitar. He sauntered to the edge of the stoep, jumped down to the gutter, and shuffled along it.

As he reached the corner of the store, he saw a man standing beside the high paling fence that surrounded Oakes's garden.

The man wore faded blue jeans and a black jersey. He glanced up at Sizwa, turned his back on him, and leaned a shoulder against the palings.

Sizwa moved on, his bare feet scuffling the dust. He was composing a speech. Oakes figured in it, but Sizwa felt little more than a contemptuous amusement for the shopkeeper. Everyone knew he was rotten with fear, like an old tree full of white ants. A flurry of raindrops fell, and Sizwa began to hurry. It was time to eat.

The man by the Oakes's fence watched him go.

17

BEN WAS AMONG the first to leave the Church. Some of the congregation moved off homewards, but the greater number lingered in the courtyard. Many of them would be from the outlying farms, and glad of a chance to talk to their friends. Here in the shadow of the spire they were stiffly circumspect. Ben smiled, thinking of the conflicting aspects of their nature that made them by turns dour and ribald, frank and devious, passionately vocal or close as a clam.

Julius Kruger appeared in the doorway with the predikant. They began to walk slowly toward the gate, stopped when they saw Ben, and greeted him with affability. The pastor's eyes twinkled. "So you've changed your allegiance, Dr. Nevis?"

Kruger chuckled, looking back at the door where Nella Ebenezer stood with her father. Ben watched them approach. The old man looked small and frail, even negligible, but the people round about, even the two stalwarts beside him, stiffened in deference. Ben found himself folding his hands behind his back like a schoolboy.

Nella herself seemed different in her father's presence, or

perhaps it was her heavy, dark dress and ugly hat that subdued her vivacity. The small man greeted his contemporaries and then fixed a cold stare on Ben.

Nella said, "Pa, this is Dr. William Nevis."

"Good morning." The beard nodded once, the eyes continued to study him. Ben looked at his feet, and the predikant said, "The doctor was very kind to me this morning, when I felt unwell."

Ebenezer's head turned stiffly. "You were hurrying again?" He glanced back at Ben. "Was he?"

"Hurrying slowly," said Bond.

"Hurrying rather fast," said Ben, and felt a traitor.

"You are too old to act foolishly." Ebenezer crooked his arm. "Nella, my dear." She slipped her hand through his elbow, and said in a soft, rather anxious voice, "You'll come to midday meal, Uncle?"

Kruger nodded. "I'll follow you."

The old man and his daughter moved through the gate. The other two men looked at each other uneasily. Ben saw that each had taken Ebenezer's coldness to his own account. The pastor seemed perplexed and unhappy. Kruger's thick brows were drawn down in an uncompromising scowl.

Ben said, "Did I offend him?"

Bond shook his head. "He's a sick man." He left them a moment later to talk to other parishioners. Kruger said, "What is it they say in English? Not a good address? You have not a good address."

"I certainly didn't win him."

"No, no. I mean you live at the wrong address, with Strasser." Kruger shrugged. "You can keep trying."

He went off up the road, toward the river, and soon Ben, knowing no one else among the people gathered, left too. The Anglican service was over. A few people remained on the strip of lawn near the river. Others were dispersing through the surrounding streets.

Ben was halfway across the road when the outcry began, a

man's voice, pitched to a womanish scream, rising, rising in an
outrageous clamor of grief.

A woman on the pavement exclaimed, turning about to seek
the origin of the appalling sound.

Down the road appeared the figure of Oakes. He lurched
grotesquely toward them, half doubled over. Ben leaped forward and got his arms around the shopkeeper, lifted him bodily
through Strasser's gate and up to the back door.

Oakes sank down on the steps. Tears poured down his face,
there was blood on his cheek and on the front of his Sunday
suit.

Tightly clasped in his arms was the body of his black terrier.

18

BEN OPENED the back door and half-lifted the shopkeeper
through it. With some difficulty, he freed the dog from Oakes's
grip and laid it on the kitchen table. Oakes kept reaching out
toward it, and Ben had to thrust his hands away in order to
examine the terrier. It was quite dead, the head battered in.
The limbs were limp and warm.

Ben took Oakes by the arm and drew him into the living
room, pressed him into a chair. He found an old ironing cloth
in the kitchen and threw it over the dog, then went to the cupboard in Strasser's bathroom, rummaged through a pile of
pharmaceutical samples, found a bottle of sedative pills, and
made Oakes swallow two.

He said, "How did it happen?"

Oakes leaned back in the chair, his head rolling from side
to side. "I feel . . . it's all . . ."

"Take it easy."

"I'd been to church. And, and . . . I found him, in the garden.
I'd been to church, and when I got back. There. Kind of laying

there, in the hydrangeas by the back door. And I thought . . .
sometimes, he'd hide, see, then jump out at me? It was his
little game. So I patted my knee for him to come. I said, 'Come
on, I can see you. You can't fool me.' But he never moved. So
then I went, and I saw him like that . . . I ran . . . I don't know,
I ran. . . ."

Ben put his hands on Oakes's shoulders. "Stop it, now."

Oakes nodded. "Sorry." He pulled out a handkerchief and
rubbed it over his face. A step sounded on the back porch and
Strasser came in, stopping short just inside the door.

Ben said, "Some bastard's killed his dog."

Strasser looked puzzled. "A car?"

"I don't think so. We'd better get down there."

Between them they got Oakes on his feet. He was trembling
in a violent reaction. They walked back to the store, Strasser
carrying the body of the dog still wrapped in the cloth. A few
people watched them from a distance.

They stepped through the gate in the paling fence. The
small, square garden could not be overlooked from the road.
Strasser laid the dog down, next to the fence.

Oakes pointed to a thick clump of hydrangea shrubs by the
back steps. "There," he said.

Ben went over to the place. The gravel path, still damp from
the showers of rain, was much trampled. One of the half bricks
edging the flower bed was missing. Reaching into the wet un-
dergrowth, he felt for and found the brick. It was stained with
blood and short black hairs. He glanced up at Strasser. "Someone bashed the poor little devil."

But Strasser was already trying the door. "This is a Yale,"
he said, and over his shoulder called to Oakes. "Did you leave
this unlocked?"

Oakes came up slowly. "Pardon?" Strasser repeated the question and Oakes nodded dully. "I always lock up carefully because of the stock."

Strasser said, "You can open a Yale with a piece of mica.
You should have mortise fittings." He led the way into the

house. The dark little living room seemed undisturbed, but the doors leading to the store and to the stockroom had been forced. There were a few small, precise scratches on both lockboards. Oakes went into the stockroom, glanced around, looked in a cupboard, and came out again. "My gun's gone, and some cartridges."

He stood rubbing one soft, pale hand over the opposite wrist like a puzzled child. Shock and the sedative were having their effect.

While Strasser went over to the telephone and dialed the police number, Ben persuaded Oakes to enter the shop and try to make a rough guess at what had been stolen. Oakes glanced at the shelves, and coming back, slumped down on the stool near the till. He ran his fingers along the brass measure set in the counter. Ben prompted him, "What's missing, Mr. Oakes?"

Oakes looked up, his eyes hazy. He said, with sudden vicious force, "My dog."

"But anything from the store?"

Oakes mumbled, "Some canned stuff, a pair of trousers, cigarettes, matches, a pair of shoes, I think."

Strasser appeared in the doorway. "The police will be here soon."

Oakes made no answer. Strasser and Ben moved a little apart. Through the display window they could see the street, people waiting in watery sunlight. A child pressed its face against the glass and a woman pulled it away.

Ben said, "He's very upset."

"His affection was abnormal."

"So are the dog's injuries."

"I agree, the violence was exceptional. Unpleasantly so."

After a moment, Ben said, "Have they got tracker dogs here?"

"I don't think so. They'll send them up from Hopetoun, I suppose, but they won't help if the rain continues."

They waited without further speech until a knock sounded

on the back door and two men walked through into the shop. The older of the two Ben recognized as the man whom Strasser disliked. He went straight over to Oakes and began to question him. The other man greeted Strasser and was introduced to Ben as Reimer. He gave Ben a brief nod, and went out of the shop and into the back premises. They heard him go into the bedroom, the kitchen, and the stockroom. Strasser said, "I looked there, too, but nothing seemed to be disturbed. He was selective, apparently."

Presently Reimer reappeared. Ben said to him, "Is there anything we can do?"

Reimer's light, calm eyes studied him. "In a minute, sir." He went across and said something to Larkill, came back and said "Well, the little bee put up a good fight, out there. Reckon he got someone by the trouser leg. Wonder no one heard the row."

Strasser shook his head. "I was out."

"You, sir?"

"I was in church," said Ben. "I should say most people were."

"Not the blacks. And not the chap who did the job."

"As to noise, a real fighter doesn't bark much. He goes straight in, biting."

"That's true."

Larkill now came across and questioned them briefly. Then he said, "We've got a lot to do, in here. Perhaps you can wait a while in the garden?" As they turned to go, he said, "Please don't discuss this with anyone at all. It will hamper us in the execution of our duty if you do."

They stepped into the garden to find the sun had dipped again. The sky hung limp and pale as an unstarched apron. On the Hill nothing moved, leaf and limb subdued alike by the sultry heat.

Ben went over to the fence. Flies were already buzzing on the carcass of the dog. He picked it up, carried it to the shade of a camel's-foot tree in the corner of the garden, went to the coalshed, and found a spade.

He began to dig a hole in the hard-baked earth. Strasser leaned a shoulder against the trunk of the tree and watched him. "You'd better not put it in, yet. The police may want it for something." Ben finished his digging and laid the dog, still wrapped in the ironing cloth, next to the hole.

Some time later Larkill came out of the house and bent over the bundle, pulled the cloth back, and examined the terrier's head. Straightening, he asked the two men to repeat their statements. His manner was abrupt, shading to rudeness when he addressed Strasser. Before he left them, Ben said, "Do you know who might be responsible?"

Larkill shook his head. He said to Strasser, "Oakes says your cook was hanging around the store this morning. Oakes went at him for dirtying the glass."

Strasser said gently, "Don't be childish."

Larkill reddened, but said no more. As he walked away, Strasser said, "The small intellect, the big conceit. He never misses a chance to annoy me. I'm a little tired of it. He thinks I ought not to employ Sizwa, because he was once jailed for some trivial offense." He yawned and stretched slowly. "I am going home. Coming?"

Ben said, "Don't wait for me." He went over to the two policemen, who were crouched on the path. Reimer gently lifted the overhang of hydrangeas. Ben could see the impression of a toe cap on the edge of the flower bed. He craned for a better view, and Larkill looked up at him pointedly. Ben said, "Can I bury the dog?"

"Sure."

Ben did so, pushed the soil back, and smoothed it. He took the spade back to the coalshed and stood for some time among piles of rusty tools and empty bottles, thinking.

No money taken, but shoes, food, a rifle, and cartridges. That print in the flower bed, of a brogue or walking shoe. Few black men in this town wore shoes. Sizwa certainly did not. Larkill knew that, so why the crack at Strasser? Only done to annoy? Unlikely. Possibly to cut short speculation?

Larkill had gone indoors when Ben returned to the path, but Reimer was still there. Ben said, "O.K. if I go?"

"Yes, thank you, sir."

"Hope you get him."

"Ja, so do I."

"A tramp, do you think?"

"Don't know yet, do we, sir?"

Ben grinned. "You mean, shut up and go home?"

The skin around Reimer's eyes creased more deeply, but he said nothing. Ben sighed. "Some people have all the fun. Will Oakes be all right?"

"Yeah." Reimer shrugged. "It's tough, but he can buy another dog. Lucky it wasn't him instead."

A few people still loitered in the street. One man waylaid Ben, his eyes avid. Ben gave no information, and allowed him to believe that the police suspected some tramp of taking a few cans of food. The man nodded sagaciously.

"They'll get him quick enough."

Thinking of the size of the area, Ben was unable to agree with this opinion.

19

THE MAN who had killed Oakes's dog did not fear arrest. By the time the congregation was filing out of the Anglican Church, he had slipped through the back lanes behind the store and up the hill to the railway cutting. He strolled easily along the tracks, the gun in its gray cotton cover carried at his side.

In the shelter of the plantations, he pulled off his shoes, tucked them inside his shirt, and put on the new pair he had stolen. He waited until a sharp shower broke before leaving the forest for the open country of Mission Halt. The rain was a thickness between him and the world. He ran up the hill paths, singing.

He had come down in rain, and he was going back in rain. Dogs wouldn't find him. They had once, but not again.

By the time the storm passed, he was back in his hiding place, high above the town.

Police dog-handlers arrived that afternoon, with Alsatians. They found no trace of the scent above the railway cutting, but their presence convinced the townsfolk that the police did not look on the burglary at the store as a light matter.

The small, forked tongue of fear began to wag.

20

OAKES'S STORE was open as usual next morning, and Mannie Reimer, out of kindness, dropped in to see how the little man was. The shop was fairly full. Oakes, behind the counter, looked ill. His pale face had a waxen shine and his hands shook. He told his story to each newcomer.

Mannie waited until there was a lull, and then leaned an elbow on the counter. "Well, Mr. Oakes, how is it?"

Oakes said, "Have you got him yet?"

"Not yet. Takes time. There wasn't much to go on. We'll try if we can find any witnesses. Look sir, you sure you're well enough to open shop today? You look dicy to me."

"I'm all right. But I'm not having any more kaffirs in here. One of them killed my dog."

Mannie was startled. "Look, it could be anyone did the job, there's nothing to tell if he's black or white. No good spoiling your business when you're only guessing, now is it?"

"White men don't kill dogs."

"Anyone can kill a dog if it goes for him."

"My dog never went for a white man."

"Never went for anyone, did he?"

"He barked at kaffirs. That's why he got hit, because he barked."

"He went for a burglar entering your house."

Oakes thrust his face forward. "Listen. You do your job, and I'll do mine."

Mannie straightened up. "I'm only saying, it won't help. . . ."

"You mind your business, I'll mind mine."

Mannie shrugged, tipped his cap, and left. Back in Larkill's office he said, "We got a one-man strike."

Larkill looked up, frowning."

"Oakes," said Mannie. "Not going to sell to the natives. Thinks one of them did in his dog."

Larkill leaned back in his chair. "That's all we need now."

Mannie sat down. "He's sick. The way he talks, anyone'd think there's another Zulu Rebellion."

The desk telephone rang sharply, and Larkill spoke into it briefly and slammed the receiver back in the cradle. "Dr. Strasser still wants us to run his bloody campaign for him."

"Why don't you give him one or two men? Next week those polio teams'll be all over the place, even the Reserve. It's one way of asking questions about the burglary. Kill two birds with one stone."

Larkill shot him a glance. "Might do." He added, "Now that my suspicions are confirmed, they're sure to send us extra men, and we can really put on the heat."

"If they agree with your theory about Black," said Mannie, and regretted it at once. Larkill's shoulders bunched up and the corners of his mouth turned down. "What do you mean?" he said.

"Well sir, what I mean is, can we really say Black did the burglary?"

"Those locks weren't forced by a juvenile delinquent. The whole thing was timed when people were in church. . . ."

. . . "in broad daylight. . . ."

. . . "there was rain to cover his traces from the dogs. . . ."

"Maybe."

"You've set your mind against the idea of an agitator."

"That's for sure."

The two men stared at each other. Larkill said, "I'll have things done my way."

Mannie made no reply. Larkill said, "We start with routine questioning. You can begin with the men at the tannery and the sawmill."

Back in his own office Mannie picked up a pencil, weighed it in his hand, wrote "Abrahams" on a memo pad, and threw the pencil into a corner of the room.

21

THE POLIO CAMPAIGN opened the day after the robbery. Strasser, outlining the details to Ben once more, said, "In the earlier campaigns, the dope was given to African children up to the age of nine. While that is still the official target, I plan to give the pill to anyone who comes. I think that that will insure a larger attendance, simply because it gives people one less detail to remember. Once the vaccine is mixed and distributed, there is really no need for a qualified doctor to be present with the team, but I want you and me to be seen about. There is a certain degree of nervousness about the effects of such immunization, particularly in rural areas. We will help at least to equal the prestige of the local medicine man.

"Lastly, I intend to use this campaign for general observation purposes. If we get a good response, it will give us a chance of seeing people who do not normally come to the Hospital. I regard the campaign not only as a medical issue, but as a good-will crusade, and an opportunity to observe the health of the community. You will, of course, examine anyone who seems unfit to take the vaccine for any reason."

At the Clinic, everything was in readiness. There was a queue outside the room set aside for white patients. A tent in the grounds was to accommodate such nonwhites of the town as could not be reached in mass at the school, the tannery, or the sawmill.

Nella Ebenezer was already on duty inside the Clinic. Ben greeted her with some restraint. She smiled at him and said her father would call in later in the day, to give the campaign his support. She spoke quite seriously. Ben made no answer, and after a moment she said, "You musn't worry about his stiff way. He's rather shy, and he doesn't like to talk after chuch, but he was pleased that you were there. He told me to invite you around to supper one night."

Ben picked up a white jacket from the chair behind the screen and shrugged into it. He groped in the pocket, emptied out two torn theater tickets and a burned match. He said, "Tell your father, if you will, that I went to church only because I saw you go in. If that pleases him, I'm happy to know it. I'd be glad to come to supper, provided I'm allowed to say what I think, smoke between courses, and squeeze your knee under the table. As far as the campaign goes, judging by the queues, we seem to be doing all right without him."

She looked at him out of the corner of her eye. After a while she said, "I don't think he'd let you smoke between courses."

Before he could answer, a huge woman sagging under a locust-horde of children surged through the door. For the rest of the morning, attendance was too brisk to allow much conversation.

At noon Strasser, who had been out on routine business, strolled in. He seemed pleased with the pile of completed application forms, and riffled through them, glancing at the names. "If we get as good a response up at the Hospital, we'll have nothing to worry about."

He went off whistling toward the tent in the grounds.

Nella said, "He's always happy when he has a scheme on."

Ben watched her discard used spoons into a bucket behind the screen. He said, "But you know, it's fantastic, all this."

"All what?" She began to set out a new row of spoons on the table.

"This town, this country. Perhaps it seems odd to me because I've only just come back, and because my first three months were spent in Joburg, which isn't typical. But when you think of it . . . here we are in the middle of a huge controversy. Most of the world is actively opposed to us. We've been kicked out of the Commonwealth, censured at UNO. Southwest is a flare point, the Federation may blow up at any time. We may, I suppose, even find ourselves in a shooting war. It would be natural to find everyone in a state of fever. Not at all. Here we are, measuring drops of vaccine on to sweets. Every man his own escapist. Strasser with his schemes, Oakes with his dog, Sullivan chasing blondes, the rest chasing tennis balls or thinking about trips to Europe. It's as if we all had schizophrenia. One body, two personalities. If one life gets too difficult, switch to the other, the one with no memory and no conscience."

She said, "You've very wrong. It never leaves us, the crisis. It's built into our lives, into everything we do and every thought and action. We're small people, here, and we know our world is coming to an end. We pretend it isn't, not now, not today. That's not surprising, it's normal."

"It's frightening."

"Africa is frightening." She hesitated. "Once, when I was a probationer, I was called in to clear casualties from a train smash. Afterward I couldn't recall much, but I did remember two people. There was a man who got the engine driver out, he was scalded by steam yet he went on trying to bend metal with his bare hands. And there was a woman who stole a brooch off a victim's blouse. I think most people just stood about and got in the way, and told each other how terrible it was. But these two—they summed up the whole situation, judged the risks, took their opportunity, one as a hero and the other as a thief."

"You think that always happens?"

"I think, in a crisis, most of us stand by. A few make something out of it." She placed a sweet in each of the spoons. "Have you had your dose yet?"

"No, so I haven't."

She handed him a spoon with its doctored pill, watched him swallow, and said, "No alcohol for luncheon."

"It'll be a struggle. Perhaps you should come and help me fight this thing."

"Switch to the personality with a conscience. I have to stay on duty."

"Ruddy Edith Cavell." He studied her profile. "Tell you what, the two of me will take the two of you to the cinema on Wednesday."

She pursed her mouth. "We'll think about it."

With that he had to be content.

22

WHEN BEN RETURNED to the Clinic at two o'clock, he took Strasser's servants with him. The wash girl Lena, and Simeon the garden boy, accepted the idea of immunization as merely an example of employer's eccentricity, but Sizwa argued against going. He was busy, he said, and had not had his lunch. Moreover, he knew the medicine was only for African children of nine and under. He agreed to come when it was made plain that Strasser ordered it.

They crossed the road in a sort of straggling procession, Ben in front, the two men servants behind, and Lena rolling in their wake. Although he knew it to be a mark of politeness, Ben felt that in Sizwa's case good manners were tempered with resentment. At the far pavement, he turned his head and glanced back. Sizwa's eyes met his with a brief flash of antagonism.

Ben accompanied them to the tent, where three queues were assembled, African, Asian, and Colored. Inside the tent, clerks were taking names and filling in forms. As Sizwa approached the crowd, his manner changed. He shed Ben, as it were, and stepping forward greeted the assembly with casual grace. Some of the men in the queue turned to watch him. He began at once to exchange quips, inducing first unwilling and then uproarious laughter. It was impossible to miss the dynamism of his personality. It was not, thought Ben, only the physical beauty of his frame. He came of a beautiful race, and was in no way exceptional. It was more that Sizwa was a born actor. His voice carried clearly; deep, expressive, effortlessly produced. His movements were spellbinding, the chopping sweep of an arm, the lazy, satiric tilt of his head. He gathered his audience, tied it in a neat bundle, tossed it here and there, and when the time came to go into the tent, abandoned it good-humoredly. Yet beneath the virtuosity was a tension, an oblique antagonism that left Ben interested and faintly disturbed.

Did Sizwa voice the unrest at the heart of every human being? Did he have the quality that makes the crowd cry "Prophesy, prophesy!"

Ben thought that it was so, and that the power of Sizwa's will was already bent, however slightly, toward destruction.

One other incident marked the day. Late in the afternoon, Ben heard voices in altercation on the verandah, and going outside, found a man and a woman arguing fiercely. The woman was scarlet in the face. The man had withdrawn to the head of the steps and hovered there uncertainly. As Ben arrived, the woman turned and said in a voice sharp with disgust, "His queue's over there. Tell him to get with his own kind."

Ben glanced at the man. He was very dark-skinned, his head

covered with tight curls. He turned toward Ben, thrust a shaking hand into his breast pocket, and brought out an identity card. "Look, doctor, look what it says there. White, doesn't it?" He thrust the card under Ben's nose.

Ben took it, feeling sick. He looked at the woman. "He's in the right place, madam."

She leaned down and grabbed the hand of the child standing beside her. "I know what he is. You're a stranger here. Everyone knows what his family is. We're not staying here with kaffirs and kaffir lovers." She dragged the child down the steps. As she passed him, the man suddenly shouted, "You say those things, I'll have the law on you!"

Ben caught his arm. "Come on now, chum, and get your sugar lump." The man still stared after the woman. "Come on, now."

The man relaxed. "O.K. O.K., doctor." He went off into the Clinic. Ben looked at the faces of the people in the garden. They watched him in silence. There was animosity in their eyes, but whether it was directed at the man, or the woman, or himself for intervening, he could not tell.

23

THE FIRST CHANCE Kruger found to visit Sullivan and help him choose a site for his dam was late on Monday afternoon. When he reached Redcliff, he found its owner at ease on the front verandah, a jug of iced lemon squash at his elbow.

Kruger leaned out of the window of his car, and Sullivan unwound his long body and shambled down the steps.

"Like a cold drink?" he invited.

Kruger jerked an elbow. "Come, little man."

"Where to?"

"Get in the car, jong."

Sullivan grinned and folded himself into the passenger seat.
They drove along a narrow farm track, heading north. On their
right the country toward the Mission sank into the sea-quiet
of evening, the hills horny and pink as shrimps under a weed-
green sky.

Kruger pointed at the krantz straight ahead of them. "There's
the water you need," he said. His thick forefinger traced the
line of bush, the flash of cascades. "The springs on top never
dry up."

"Not even in a drought?"

"Man," said Kruger pityingly, "what have we got now?
Floods? This is as dry as it comes. There's still plenty of water."

About a quarter of a mile from the lowest cascade, the stream
broadened in a natural basin. Kruger stopped the car, climbed
out, and led Sullivan to the edge of a little amphitheater.

"That's where you put it. The ground helps you. You have
plenty of room, and with the slope in your favor, you can chan-
nel it off to your house and your fields."

Sullivan was as pleased as a child. He insisted on walking
down into the hollow, and made Kruger go into details about
the size, angle, and possible construction of the dam. Finally
he pulled a Leica from his pocket and took several shots of
the area.

"They won't come out," said Kruger.

"They will." Sullivan spoke with unusual decision.

As they were about to leave, they heard the coughing bark
of baboons, high up the krantz. A troop of the animals broke
from the cover of the bush and swung right, racing for the
high boulders east of the stream. They could see the leader, a
huge old bull, and the sentries posted lower down. Sullivan
squinted across the sun. "Something's scared 'em."

"They're making for their night camp," said Kruger.

But once again Sullivan shook his head with decision. "They
never go east." Kruger half-smiled. Funny fellow, he thought.
Sell him anything, most of the time, and then, over baboons,
he digs in his toes.

On the drive back, Kruger averted his eyes from many signs of mismanagement on the farm. It hurt him to see such ineptitude. He himself was rich because he used the talents God gave him. He paid his labor well, housed them well, fed them well. Now an old man, he could still afford to relax, but he knew he never would. A man didn't farm simply to make a living. He farmed to keep something alive, in the land, and in himself. But this land here was being allowed to die.

Sullivan didn't know the meaning of the word work. Playing childish games, visiting the city, often away for weeks. If he was forced in the coming year to cut down labor, to let some of his blacks move to the new territory, it would mean nothing to him. No sacrifice was required of him.

Why did one tolerate such a fellow? Perhaps, as Ebenezer said, every village must have its idiot, so that charity should not perish from the earth.

Back at the house, Sullivan pressed Kruger to stay for a glass of brandy, and since hospitality lay in acceptance as well as dispensation, Kruger broke his rule and agreed to stay. They settled themselves on the verandah. While drinks were being brought, Kruger asked, out of politeness, whether Sullivan did much photographic work. Sullivan, to his surprise, blushed like a girl, shuffled off into the house, and returned with a bulky album and several large buff packets, which he laid before his guest.

The old man winced. Sullivan said eagerly, "You'll like these best," indicating the topmost envelope. His expression was so trusting that Kruger picked the packet up and pulled out a wedge of photographs.

In a moment, however, he sat upright and began to go through the pictures with close attention. Once or twice he asked a question, and occasionally he shook his head with an expression of incredulity. At last he said, "But, man, this is beautiful work."

The photographs were of southern African flora. They combined botanic clarity with a delicacy of lighting and composition that gave them tremulous life. Kruger selected one from the pile and held it in his stubby fingers with something like reverence. "This one?" he said. "Never did I see this before."

"Star-of-Bethlehem. It's night-flowering."

"Indigenous or exotic?"

Sullivan shrugged. "I just take the pictures. I'm no botanist."

"And animals? You have them too?"

"Some, not so many."

Kruger shook his head. "I don't understand you," he said. "To say nothing, to let people think . . ." He spread his hands. "Why?"

"They mean too much to me."

"Ja, that I can understand." Kruger thought a while, then tapped a finger on the table. "You listen to an old man. This is a matter for serious action. You must make a book, as many books as it takes to record these pictures. You must talk to those with botanical knowledge, classify exactly where and when you found each example. It will be a big work, a big work. If you would let me . . ." he hesitated, his elephantine features creased in a smile. "I confess it, I would love to take a share in such a project. I feel like a man who finds blue clay. You wouldn't deny me a little part in it, would you?" He was evidently puzzled that no one had discovered Sullivan's virtuosity with a camera. "Haven't you shown them to anyone?"

"I've had a few published, but not under my name. Oh, and I showed some of the fauna to Reimer. He wanted a picture of a sable antelope for his kids."

"What did he say?"

Sullivan laughed. "Said I was good enough to be a police photographer."

Kruger gave a snort. "If I could do this, I'd give up farming."

"Can't," said Sullivan. "It's in my contract, so to speak." He sipped his brandy. "See, I'm sort of a remittance man. My father cut me off, and when he died, he left all the cash to his sister. In her will she left it to me, provided I farmed for ten years in what she called the Colonies. Thought it would be the making of me. Odd, isn't it? If my family had approved of me, I'd be in Dublin now, head of a distillery."

Kruger battled with his manners and lost. "Why did your Pa throw you out?"

Sullivan looked at him for a moment and then said simply, "I joined the Air Force during the war."

Kruger sat quietly. It was hard, in the failing light, to see his expression. Finally he said, almost to himself, "My son Andries . . . you never met him."

"There you're wrong. I did."

"Andries? You met him?"

Sullivan knew that the unsayable had been said. The moment stretched between them, a bridge of ice across a chasm. He said, "I never liked to mention it. . . ."

Kruger nodded, turning his glass slowly in his hands. Without looking up, he said, "Where was this?"

"In Italy, during the war. I was doing photographic work, on reconnaissance. Andries was seconded to our unit from the S.A.A.F. He flew me on several missions. He was a very good pilot and a lot of fun. I didn't know him well, of course."

Kruger gave a small sigh. "I haven't spoken of him to a soul for . . . what is it? . . . eighteen years."

"Why?" Sullivan ran the tip of his finger around his glass and won from it a small, soft singing. "It's a question I've often asked myself. What did my father accomplish, what did you accomplish?"

"I thought I would not be a stumbling block to the weak. My right hand offended me, and I cut it off. Or perhaps I cut off my nose to spite my face." Kruger lifted his hands and let them drop. "Now, of course, the skies should fall. But no. The stars are still there. Young man, you may fill my glass again."

He stayed for some while, talking. Truth to tell, he was unwilling to be alone.

It was dark when he returned to his own house. He ate his supper and then went out on to the lawn to smoke a pipe.

I am like a child, he thought, that says what it thinks is a very bad word. But it is nothing. The adults smile and wink at each other, as the stars now smile and wink.

I've grown old, and it is not terrible. I have struck attitudes, been stern, upright, just, and the world has waited kindly, without pointing out that I am a fool.

Under his heel he could feel the grass, brittle with drought. He could hear the crickets singing near him, and high overhead, infinitely high, above the velvet haunches of the hills, the singing of the galaxies that burst like spray against eternity.

Oh Lord, he thought, let me be staunch, but let me not fear, sometimes, to change this thing I call my mind.

24

"CAN I COME IN for a moment?" Through the glass door of Oakes's store, Karl Ebenezer mouthed the words. Behind him on the stoep, several Africans waited for opening time, eight o'clock.

Oakes inched the door ajar, and allowed Ebenezer to slide his spare body through. Still in his shirt sleeves, unshaven, Oakes stared at his visitor like a dreamer. Ebenezer said drily, "May I come in, Mr. Oakes?"

Oakes fell back. As he made no move to invite his guest further, Ebenezer sat down on one of the high stools by the counter. He said, "I came first to express my . . ." he struggled with a sense of the ludicrous . . . "my sympathy in your loss." He paused, and Oakes nodded. Ebenezer said carefully, "I hear that in your . . . very natural shock . . . you have decided not to continue selling to your Bantu customers. Or perhaps I am misinformed?"

Oakes looked up. His lips folded in.

"Am I misinformed, Mr. Oakes?"

"It's my shop."

"Undoubtedly. But since this is the case, surely it will be injudicious to damage your own trade, and antagonize some of your best customers?"

Oakes smiled. "What's your worry? You're a Nationalist, you support apartheid, don't you?"

Ebenezer frowned. "I uphold the law. There is, I think, no legislation that prevents your selling your goods to the Bantu. I don't believe in punishing the innocent for the crimes of the guilty."

"I know who is guilty." Oakes picked up a duster. "Now I have to get my shop tidy, please."

"You have no one to help you? Is your Indian helper sick?"

Oakes shrugged, and began dusting. Ebenezer leaned his elbows on the counter, considering. At length he said, "Mr. Oakes, since Sunday there has been a certain nervous tension in the town. At a time like the present, when people are constantly reading stories of terrorists, murders, threats against the country's economy, etcetera, it's important that all unfortunate events be treated with the greatest tact and self-control. Now, it is bad enough that you were robbed and your little friend killed, without it becoming a source of racial ill-feeling. I'm quite sure that some hooligan from outside our little circle is responsible for this . . . outrage. In a little while, the police will arrest him, and punishment will be applied in the proper manner, by the courts." He paused. "You, sir, must not try to forestall the judge."

There was no reply, and Ebenezer continued, his fingers laced together. "Look at it from this point of view. We are a small community. You supply many of the necessities of these people. They can get much of what they want from other stores, but if you refuse to serve them, you will create ill-feeling that will spread beyond your own shop. There may be a boycott of stores, something like that. You will harm people who have no connection with what happened on Sunday. What you propose may seem a logical action to you, but to others it will seem cruel and unjust. You have to remember that it is just as possible that a white man killed the dog."

"I know who killed him."

"You have no proof. Only suspicions." Ebenezer thought, and malice, great malice.

Oakes turned his back. Over his shoulder he said, "Didn't know you felt so pally toward kaffirs, Mr. Ebenezer."

Ebenezer stood up. He said gently, "I hope, Mr. Oakes, that you will never contemplate placing me in the same category as yourself. The gulf between us is too wide to be spanned by your guesses or my warnings. However, I'll say one thing more. If you want to court trouble, remember that it is not only your affair, but ours. I shall do all I can to discourage you from spreading . . . what is the phrase . . . alarm and despond? Even if it means taking firm action against you."

"Don't make me laugh."

Ebenezer's cold eyes scanned Oakes's face. "Nothing more is to be gained. Good day." He walked to the door, stepped through, putting on his Panama hat. On the stoep, he nearly collided with a tall African, carrying a market basket on one arm. The man sprang back with exaggerated reverence, calling to the others to make way for Ebenezer. Glancing up, Ebenezer caught their mocking smiles.

Sizwa, he thought. Never can his like be brought to a sense of dignity and responsibility. An insolent, rebellious house, the Vuli.

He walked away toward the Police Station. Ridiculous that Oakes should suspect Sizwa, as Mannie Reimer said he did.

Sizwa was an undesirable character, but thought far too highly of his reputation to indulge in burglary. One could not jail a man for impertinence.

Not, thought Ebenezer with a small, sour smile, without incarcerating a large section of the population, some notable clerics, and almost all politicians.

25

Sizwa completed his marketing at the small vegetable shop next door to the Station, and began a leisurely stroll home. He stopped several times to exchange the time of day with friends. Most of them, when they heard of Oakes's latest action, looked on it as ridiculous enough to be ignored, but one or two, who had bought from him for many years, were angered, and some took it as a serious affront.

Idling along the road, the sun warm on his face, Sizwa listened to their jokes, their gossip, and their occasional bitterness. All was grist to Sizwa's mill. The ballad of Archie Oakes was already forming in his mind.

At the Garage he stopped, sat down on the wall, and whistled sharply between his teeth.

Abel emerged from the open doorway. Sizwa beckoned, and Abel came slowly across to him.

"What do you want, man? I'm busy on a job."

"I thought you'd be interested."

"In what?"

"Not important, if you're busy." Sizwa smiled under his eyelashes, enjoying himself. Abel gave an exclamation of impatience and seemed about to go back into the Garage.

"You know that man that broke into the shop?" said Sizwa quickly. Abel checked. Sizwa looked skyward. "I saw him."

"Where?" There was enough sharpness in Abel's voice to recall Sizwa's wandering gaze.

"In the lane, near the shop."

Abel studied his friend. He had known Sizwa too long to underrate his powers of observation, and long enough to appreciate his lack of wisdom. Now he sat like a child that holds a

100

bull's-eye in its cheek and thinks it doesn't show. Abel said grimly, "Did you tell the police?"

"Why should I?"

"If they find out later that you knew, and said nothing, they'll throw you straight in the jail. This isn't a time to play games."

"It's none of my business. I don't owe the police anything."

"Oakes doesn't like you, he might make trouble for you."

"I don't like Oakes."

Abel said, "Then why did you tell me about it?"

"I thought you would be interested," Sizwa smiled. "You can tell the police, if you want to."

Abel stirred uneasily. He guessed that Sizwa was testing him. He sensed danger, and once more it came to him that he ought to be firm with Sizwa, that he ought to go straight to the police. But that seemed to him treachery not only toward a friend, but toward his people. He said quickly, "I don't want anything to do with it." His hand made a gesture of dismissal, and he went off at a rapid walk into the Garage.

Sizwa laughed. Abel really was an amusing person. It was fun to shock him. His eyes so big and round, like a child's. So worried about doing the right thing, always worried about this or that, afraid to listen in case he heard something he didn't like. He was like a chicken in the road, squawk, squawk. As Abel reached the doorway, Sizwa gave voice to an anguished clucking.

He continued up the road in high good humor. He liked things to happen. A joke was best when it held the spice of malice.

His feet danced, he sang to himself. His eyes traced the ridge of hills above the town. He guessed that they concealed the thief. Trouble. And he, Sizwa, knew what that trouble looked like. Oakes could do anything, nothing. He would get no help from Sizwa.

It was a lovely day, full of amusement and secrecy and joyous power. Savoring it, Sizwa sang louder. Across the road, on the steps of the Police Station, Mannie Reimer heard the song, stared, and became thoughtful.

Back in the Garage, Abel worked faster than usual, his head bent, his mouth compressed to a thin line. He looked like a man trying to read in a crowded place, trying to close his mind against distraction.

26

THE AFTERNOON proved to be one of unusual beauty, although what the community longed for was rain. At four o'clock, indeed, huge clouds, round and shining as soap bubbles, broke from the escarpment, but they floated over the valley too high and swift to shed their load.

Coming out of the Clinic, Ben asked Nella whether she had made up her mind to accompany him to the cinema.

She wriggled her shoulders. "It's terribly hot and stuffy in summer. I'd rather go riding. We could today, if you like?"

"You mean horses?" said Ben.

"Uncle Julius lets me borrow his. I'll phone him, and we can go out in my car. Did you bring jodhpurs?"

"They look like Gilpin's Last Ride."

"That doesn't matter. I'll pick you up in a quarter of an hour."

He had no boots with him, and had to make do with brown brogues. His jodhpurs were a legacy from less muscular days, and his only thick socks were bright blue. Surveying himself in the mirror, he hoped the horse wasn't of nervous disposition.

Waiting in the road, he recalled that Nella did not seem to have much clothes sense. Neat enough in uniform, but her church gear was pretty horrible. Or perhaps that was a uniform, too? He was surprised at himself, wanting to take such a female about.

But as he folded his legs into her car, he was glad to see that in riding clothes she looked good, very good. Her breeches and boots were old, but beautifully made. She had on a fine white linen blouse, and a broad belt of soft leather. It was the first time he had seen her bare-headed. Her hair was dark brown, with red and gold and black tones, like sweet sherry. It was secured in a sort of twist at the back of her head.

He said, as they drove off, "My mother used to wear skewers like those."

She put up a hand. "These were my mother's. Real tortoise shell."

"Each time I see you, you look different."

She inclined her head slightly. "How do you mean?" Her voice, with its slight clip, had a vibrancy, as if she were on the point of some private laughter.

"A different personality at each appearance. You don't look like your father."

She changed gear as they splashed through the drift and began to climb the Ridge. "Like my father and my mother."

"Then your mother was pretty."

"They say so. I haven't seen her since I was six. My father put her away."

The Biblical phrase sounded strange, carrying the old sense of disgrace that the word divorce had lost. She said, "But you're like your father."

"Don't tell me. Like a kind horse."

"Kind, perhaps. He was very brutal to me."

"No!"

"He took out my tonsils. They never warned me what was coming. Just slapped me on the kitchen table like a steak, and when I woke up . . . no tonsils. Nowadays that would be enough to make a juvenile delinquent, wouldn't it?"

"You were sterner stuff."

"Next week, your Pa bought me a rag doll. I took it, but afterward, whenever I saw him I'd run like mad."

"Trauma."

"No, just prudence."

He smiled. "Funny I never knew you."

She shook her head. "We were kept to ourselves."

"What made you decide to be a nurse?"

They were crossing the railway lines at the point where, a few days earlier, he had talked to Julius Kruger. Then, and again at the Church, he had been a stranger. Now he felt he had never been away.

They continued up, breasted the rise. She pointed. "That's Oom Julius's farm, over there," and without pause she went on, "I took up nursing to get away from home. I wanted to see a big city, meet new people."

"Did it come up to expectations?"

"Oh yes! I love to travel." They were running through uncultivated grassland. Ahead he saw the river, and far off, the square of trees that marked the farmstead. "Did you go overseas?" he said.

She looked regretful. "To my father, overseas is . . . a sort of treason. He can't understand that one should want anything beyond South Africa. That was part of the trouble with my mother. She wanted to see everything, the world."

"Then, how do you think of yourself? As an Afrikaner housewife, a nurse, a citizen of the world? What? Go on, be truthful."

At that she burst out laughing. He enjoyed the look of her, her bright eyes and small lustrous teeth. "Why should you expect me to be truthful about my private thoughts, when we've barely met?"

"Catching the local curiosity. You haven't answered my question."

"I seldom think about what I am."

"And when you do?"

"How have you lived so long? Well, well then, I rebel against all these definitions. I am myself. I hate tags. People invent them so that they can keep track of their hates. I won't have it. That's why I like working for Dr. Strasser. He's the only man in the valley who won't be put in a pigeonhole."

"It's not only the valley. Everyone, abroad, wears a tag. I'll tell you, at the moment, yours isn't worth much. White South African, colonialist, racialist. Not much catch at all, I'm afraid."

She said fiercely, "That's worst of all, to label what you don't know. I hate these men who sit in Whitehall or New York or Moscow and decide the future of people they don't even know, let alone like or love."

"Even when they're right?"

"How can you know what is right, if you aren't concerned?"

He stared at her. "It's generally accepted that good judgment depends on not being involved."

"Judgment, who wants judgment? Compassion, yes, knowledge, and wisdom. Don't you see, the problems here will never be settled by an International Court, by sanctions, or sabotage. If you think that, you don't know people. Do you think a man like my father, his conviction and dedication, can be outweighed by anything but an even greater conviction and dedication, arising in the country itself? I am a realist. It's not enough to change things on the surface."

He thought of Abrahams, and his casual reference to love as the saving grace. As to Ebenezer, Nella was right. It would need something, to pull that sword from the stone. Aloud, he said, "Why do you stay in Peace Drift?"

"To be with my Pa." Her mouth trembled suddenly. "My Pa is an honest man. I don't care what they say about him."

"Of course not." He fell silent, annoyed with himself.

On the edge of the river, a crane was poised like an old man paddling, his feathers rolled up to his knees. At the car's approach, he rose clumsily and flapped away eastward.

They circled the trees to the farmyard entrance, swept through, and parked the car in the open square between the sheds. As they climbed out, a young boy saluted them and led up a pair of horses, ready saddled.

Nella took the smaller of the two, a bay with a wild eye. Ben found himself facing an enormous bulk, which seemed to be roughly carved out of kitchen soap.

"What is it?" he said.

"Horse," said Nella, swinging herself to the bay's back.

"God, look at those hocks. Where have they hidden his plow? I don't want to be rude, but is it possible to control him?"

"He's Kruger's favorite. You're honored."

The boy beside them suddenly put his hand over his mouth and giggled. Stung, Ben snatched the reins, got a foot in the stirrup, and said, "Let go." He managed to reach the saddle as the beast surged forward. They jolted off toward the road. When speech was possible, Nella said, "Where did you meet Oom Julius?"

"On the train." Ben's mount caught him a playful nip in the leg. Ben gave him a clout that cracked like a pistol shot, and the horse moved his ears in a way that indicated appreciation.

"He likes you," said Nella.

"Not mutual."

"I mean Kruger. He's invited us to go up and see him when we get back. He hardly ever does that."

They cleared the trees and emerged on the road. Nella let her bay into a canter. Ben muttered, "All right, you win," and slackened his rein. As he shot past Nella he called, "Slow-coach!"

They raced as far as the river, and then branched off on a narrow track leading up into the hills. The horses' hoofs were muffled in satin-red dust. The breeze in their faces smelled of pine needles.

They returned from their ride at six o'clock. Kruger watched them walk toward the house from the stableyard. As they drew near, he observed in them a certain self-conscious delight. "Stepping so carefully, talking so eagerly," he murmured. "They will fall in love."

Kruger felt a paternal affection for Nella. She was what a woman should be, strong, warm, practical with the heart. He drew them into the house with such unprecedented politeness that Nella glanced at him in surprise.

"Did you enjoy your ride? Where did you go?"

Taking the proffered chair, Ben said, "Up on the east side of the river, sir. That horse of yours has very good paces."

"Ja, he can go."

Kruger handed each of them a glass of wine and a sweet oat cake. They talked for a time, coming finally to the polio campaign. Kruger listened attentively, nodding.

"You be on time, on Monday," he said. "I've arranged for my labor to be ready in the yard. I won't waste money, keeping them waiting."

He turned to Nella and said, somewhat abruptly, "Does your Pa know you're here today?"

"I don't suppose so, Uncle."

The old man looked at her, and said, "I ask because I'm not in very good favor with him, at the moment."

"Because of Gwevu and company? But you have no quarrel with me."

The old man grunted. "If it would displease your father to have you visit at Witteboom, Nella, then it is certainly not for you to argue the matter, nor for me to encourage you. However, I asked you here this evening to say that if, in the future, it becomes difficult for you to come here, I shall understand. Also, I think it would be wiser if you asked Dr. Strasser to appoint you to a different team from Dr. Nevis, during the campaign. Be a little clever."

Nella put her wine glass down. Her cheeks reddened. "I don't understand. Why should there be any difficulty? Pa would never interfere with any friendship I chose to make."

Kruger settled his shoulders against the chair back. "My child," he said, "you are sweet enough to live in the Garden of Eden. But look now, we men are serpents. I don't say this because I want to spoil. Times are changing. I feel . . . how does the writer say it? . . . by the pricking in my thumbs . . . that we are to be tested. You, Nella, and I, your father, this young man here. It will be a time when each one makes up his mind. So a little tact, eh, a little of being slim?"

He spoke gravely, the words drawn slowly from unwilling

depths. "I do not usually take children into my confidence . . ." they had the feeling that his thoughts were for a moment on the past ". . . but I wanted to tell you myself, if there is a division between me and your father, then I shall expect you to remember your filial duty." He smiled. "And if I see you in the street, I will perhaps wink with my eye, to tell you we know what we are about?"

Nella nodded. The happiness that had lighted her was quenched. Kruger said to Ben, "And you may find it politic to work with another nurse, even though not so pretty?"

Ben met his eye. "That isn't my decision, sir."

"Oh come, now. You can speak to Strasser?"

Ben made no answer. Something like appreciation flickered in Kruger's smile. He said, "Nella will speak, however."

Nella got up and walked out of the house. Ben started to follow her, but Kruger caught his arm. "Young man," he said, "use your head." He settled back in his chair again, nodding dismissal.

At the door, Ben turned. "Thank you for the drink, Mr. Kruger, and for the ride."

"A pleasure, come again."

Kruger listened to Ben hurrying after Nella, toward the yard where they had parked their car. He chuckled. That boy was very like his father. Then he sighed, closing his eyes. Multitudes, multitudes, in the valley of decision. The multitudes of the past and the future. They streamed before his inward sight. He shook his head to obliterate them.

27

IT WAS DURING these days that the idle gossip of the townsfolk hardened into talk of an agitator. Part of the blame for this fell on Larkill. He fought rumor as an impala buck fights a lion, bounding on its heels in an effort to prevent the kill from behind. He called in for questioning the known vagrants and idlers of the area. He pestered his superiors with demands for reinforcements, and when these were not at once forthcoming, he fell to pulling strings. He infected Karl Ebenezer with his theory that the robbery at the store was the work of a terrorist, and Ebenezer got in touch with certain authorities in Hopetoun, creating among them a mood of mingled annoyance and apprehension.

The breach between Reimer and Larkill was steadily widening. Mannie stuck to his view that the burglary was the work of a small-time delinquent, and Larkill, knowing that this opinion was shared by Division, became nervous and truculent toward his own men.

If Mannie had had his way, he would have handled the situation better. His presence, the patient skepticism of his blue eyes, was generally fatal to hallucination. He would have taken Oakes to the Hotel in his off-duty hours, and soothed him; terrified the town's awkward squad into a week or so of immobility; and persuaded the townsfolk to wait and see, a policy to which they were by nature inclined.

But Larkill's vision was narrow and selfish, and Ebenezer's wide and fatalistic. Both treated the robbery as a matter of supreme seriousness, and so, in time, it became.

A telephonist in Peace Drift listened in to part of Ebenezer's appeal to Hopetoun. It became known that Larkill was asking for extra men. Word got around that the police had organized a night raid on an unspecified household, searched the premises, and removed political pamphlets.

By Wednesday, several people had approached Mannie seeking reassurance. The stories they carried were unfounded, but unpleasant. There was a homicidal lunatic about, he was maiming animals. Oakes's store had been forced by means of an explosive charge. More explosive had been found in the Railway yards. A man had been caught in the forestry area, his pockets full of candle ends and matches.

The town buzzed, locked its doors at six in the evening. Old

Mr. Smithers fired a load of buckshot at her daughter's fiancé, who was returning from a trip to the bottom of the garden. Mamie Johansen set her Alsatian on a tramp discovered asleep in the grass outside her front gate.

All this Mannie took in his stride, but when the word agitator became frequent in conversation, he knew the safety limit had been reached. Soon apprehension would spread through the native compounds and shanties. Ordinary folk would panic, and the bad hats would take the excuse to harry officials in the course of their duty. Perhaps someone would throw a stone, light some petrol.

He went to Larkill on Wednesday morning and asked that an official denial of the agitator theory be brought out and given to the press. "Or if not, sir, then for God's sake let them give us more men and we make a really big drive. It has to be one or the other now, or someone'll be hurt. The town's like a tree full of summer bees, all spit and buzz."

Larkill lost his temper, and packed Mannie off to question Abrahams about his employees.

On Wednesday Peace Drift, like a child whose laughter turns to tears, slid casually into disaster.

28

MANNIE HAD MIXED FEELINGS about Abrahams, whose odd humors were a puzzle to most of the townsfolk. He was a foreigner not only by birth but by outlook, sharing few of the prejudices and principles that made up their lives. He laughed when others were grim, and sometimes when others laughed, he wept, literally cried tears of misery or rage.

People watched him as if he were a cracker that might go off in their faces.

He had, on the other hand, made too much money to be

counted insane. He had certain theories he was fond of pro-
pounding. Such as: look after the pennies and the blondes will
look after themselves, women with wide-set eyes are liars, never
employ a man who lives with his mother. What was confusing
was that he seemed to abide by these theories, and still make
money.

When he took over the tannery, it was nearly derelict. Wattle was suffering a depression, plastics were competing with
leather, he should by rights have bought himself a failure. No
such thing. Abrahams had, in the teeth of opposition, come out
on top. He had also forced through his ideas on salary rates
for African labor, pensions, housing, and factory facilities. Although legally Africans were not allowed to join a trade union,
Abrahams established a system of discussion and negotiation
between himself and his employees that side-tracked many of
the difficulties that cropped up in larger urban areas. Moreover, he did it before Big Business and Industry recognized
it as essential. He never suffered any shortage of labor, his
turnover increased each year, and the townspeople learned to
treat him with wary respect.

Now, making his way between reeking bales of hides in the
tannery yard, Mannie wondered how the little man would take
the suggestion that his dream child might be harboring Com-
munist agitation.

He found Abrahams in a small office at the rear of the building. He looked, Mannie thought, like a tadpole just sprouting
arms and legs from an embryonic body. He greeted Mannie
cheerfully, and gave him a cup of stewed tea. Mannie explained that he was making inquiries about the burglary at
the store. Abrahams said promptly, "Well, I didn't do it." He
gave the policeman a shrewd look, and added, "But I'd like
to know who did."

Mannie cleared his throat. "Have you, perhaps, dismissed
any labor recently?"

Abrahams built his fingers into a pyramid. "No. Nor have I
any idlers, vagrants, or agitators on my pay roll."

Mannie eyed him. "Yes, Mr. Abrahams, no doubt you're right there, but we have to make these inquiries. No one's going to come and tell you he's committed a crime, now, is he?"

"They do sometimes." Abrahams grinned. "But I choose my workers very carefully. They wouldn't do a thing like this."

Mannie sucked his teeth and tried again. "That store was cracked by a smart boy, sir. Someone who's tried it before, you follow me?"

"Then it's not likely to be anyone who's lived in Peace Drift all his life. Comes to me that there's not much practice for a professional, here."

"Maybe." Mannie drained his cup and put it on the desk. "I wonder could I have a word with your native foreman?"

"Albert? Sure." Abrahams lifted a telephone and sent an order for Albert to come to the office. While they waited, he said nothing, his eyes fixed vaguely on the window. Presently there was a knock on the door, and an African in overalls came into the room. A white cotton fatigue cap dangled from his hand. His face was beaded with sweat, and he gave off a strong smell of raw hides. He glanced at Abrahams, who moved his head very slightly, and smiled.

Mannie questioned the man about the employees working under him. Albert answered freely and politely, but it was clear he was frightened. He kept repeating that nobody, nobody would ever think of robbing the store. When he had a good job, a new house, who would be silly enough to steal a few cans of food? He was a tall man, heavily built, but his hands trembled as he spoke, and he kept looking at Abrahams for encouragement.

Later he accompanied Mannie to the sheds where the men worked, and stood by while Mannie questioned those who had been in the town the previous Sunday.

It was a wasted morning, and when Mannie left the sheds he knew that all he had done was create feelings of unease where none had been before. He retraced his steps across the yard and found Abrahams standing in the doorway of his office.

"Well?" The frog's mouth was no longer smiling.

"Nothing more for the moment, thanks, sir."

He was about to move away when Abrahams said softly, "Sergeant." Mannie turned back.

"Try not to come frightening us again."

Mannie screwed up his eyes. "No need to be frightened if you haven't done anything, sir."

"What do you call doing something?"

Mannie looked puzzled, and Abrahams said, "Seems to me too many people are afraid of the police. Not only black people."

"Too many people break the law."

"There are too many laws to break. Let me tell you, it's easy to interfere with a man's courage and integrity. You can't legislate it back to life. If you want a town full of rats, go ahead. You will get it. I've seen it happen too often."

"You don't have to be afraid, sir." Mannie spoke as if to a child.

"Oh yes," Abrahams poked the air with a finger. "Oh yes, I have to be afraid. Need be, I can be afraid enough for the whole nation. Now go away, and remember what I told you."

He remained leaning in the doorway while Mannie left the yard. Then he extended his right hand. Sweat ran down the fingers and dripped into the dust. He pulled out his handkerchief and rubbed his hands and forehead.

Mannie strode rapidly back up the main road. Outside the Bank, the manager's retriever, hopeful of a pat, approached him, but thought better of it.

Mannie whistled as he walked, a sign of irritation. Now, he told himself, you don't get mad with Abrahams, nor with Larkill either. Only with the slob who started all this.

His annoyance came into focus. He stopped whistling and walked more slowly.

He'd have to go up and check the shanties again. Might go over into the Reserve.

Opposite Oakes's store, he noticed that the tarmac was

strewn with fine white crystals. Thinking of glass, he crossed
the road and bent to explore the powder, which proved to be
nothing but sugar.

Further up, he found paper bags burst open, rice and flour
and vegetables scattered in the gutter. The street was prac-
tically deserted, but up by the Police Station a crowd was
gathered.

Mannie marched sharply up the road and entered the Station by the side door.

Several people milled in the charge office. Venter sat at the
desk, looking harassed, and in front of him Sizwa gesticulated
and shouted between two native policemen. Mr. Malcolm from
the Hotel hovered uncertainly behind them, with a young
African servant. In a corner, Dr. Nevis bent over a man who
lay with his shoulders propped against the wall. Further up
the corridor, the door to Larkill's office stood open, emitting
sounds of angry argument.

Mannie stepped over to Ben, who straightened up and said,
"It's O.K., Sergeant. Bad nosebleed, that's all."

From the floor, Archie Oakes stared up with dazed eyes, a
blood-spotted towel pressed to his face.

"What happened?" said Mannie.

Oakes heaved himself up on his elbows. He pointed at Sizwa.
"He hit me."

Ben said quickly. "That's a lot of bull!" He met Mannie's
gaze. "I saw the whole thing. It was an accident."

29

MANNIE SIGHED. Now he should separate the sheep from the
goats, take statements, all nice and orderly. But he had the
feeling he'd get no truth that way. He went back to the desk

and nudged Venter aside, sat down, and surveyed the circle
of faces.

He said, "Everyone can please take a seat."

Malcolm, Nevis, and Oakes found chairs on his right, Sizwa
and the young boy settled on a bench across the room. At
Mannie's nod, the policeman closed the doors leading to the
corridor and the outer courtyard. A hot silence settled on the
room.

Mannie said, "All right, Mr. Oakes, you tell me."

Oakes pulled the towel from his nose. A streak of blood
was congealed on his upper lip. He said, "He was making a
row on my stoep . . ."

"Who?"

"The kaffir."

Sizwa's head turned slightly and his eyes fixed on the pale
swell of Oakes's throat.

"You know his name?" said Mannie. Oakes made no answer.
After a moment Mannie said in a tired voice. "Go on."

"I went out," said Oakes, "and I told him to get off my stoep.
I warned him before, on Sunday, I told you."

"Yes?"

"There was this crowd of bucks outside there. I told them,
too, to get off. Some of them did. This one said something, and
they laughed."

"What did he say?"

"I didn't understand." Mannie glanced at Sizwa, whose heavy
features wore a look of complacency. It crossed Mannie's mind
that if more people took the trouble to learn a Bantu language,
there'd be fewer obscene remarks made in public. He turned
back to Oakes. "So then?"

"So I said they could chuck that, and get off, or I'd call the
police. That kaf . . . that one put his hand on my plate-glass
window. Just what I've told him not to do. It was done on purpose, just a piece of bloody cheek. Listen . . ."

"Just tell it, sir."

"I took his hand off. He stood back and said, 'Aiee! Suka!' and I said I'll suka you, you swine. He stepped forward, and I took his arm to push him off the stoep. Then he hit me and knocked me off the edge. I fell on my face. I was knocked out, like, stunned."

"Who picked you up?"

Oakes's eyes flickered. "Mr. Malcolm. And the doctor."

"Mr. Malcolm?"

The Hotel manager, who had been sitting with his hands clasped on his knee, looked up quickly and then back at the floor. He said, "I was back in the crowd. I didn't see, exactly. I saw Mr. Oakes take a dive off the stoep. He came down plunk on his nose. He was a bit dazed."

Ben said sharply, "You were in front of them. You saw."

"Look, doctor," said Mannie, "you'll have your turn. Now I'm talking to Mr. Malcolm."

"Sorry." Ben sat back. He looked at Sizwa, who still lolled on the bench in an attitude of indifference. Ben thought, boy, you don't help yourself at all. Malcolm won't testify for you, not against a good customer. Sit up straight and look as if it mattered. Sizwa caught Ben's stare. His chin sank on his chest, his eyes remained stony.

"How did you get there, Mr. Malcolm?" Mannie said. "Just passing?"

"No, not . . ." Malcolm shuffled his feet. "About twelve, I sent Tickey over to get me some things I needed for the lunches. Half an hour later he wasn't back, and it was getting late. He's new, and I thought he'd got held up somehow, so I went out on the verandah to tell him to put a spurt on. Saw this crowd over by Oakes. I thought maybe Tickey'd got in a fight, so I went over. There was a lot of blacks standing on Oakes's stoep, yelling."

"Yelling, or laughing?"

"Well, both."

"Yes?"

"There was Strasser's cook among them, and I could see his

head above the others, him being so big. There was a bit of to
and fro stuff, then Mr. Oakes took this high dive. Landed right
at my feet. . . ." Malcolm stopped.

Mannie said blandly, "Right at your feet. So you were in
front?"

"Well . . . I was kind of pushed to the front. But I couldn't
see much, there were too many people about, and I was trying
to look for Tickey. I saw him in the crowd, and told him to get
back to the Hotel. He said something about the basket. I
looked, and there were all my groceries in the road. Anyway,
I picked Mr. Oakes up, with Dr. Nevis, and we brought him
back here. He wanted to make a charge against the native."

Mannie spoke to one of the African constables, asking him
whether they had arrested Sizwa. The man replied that he had
joined the crowd just after Oakes fell, that Sizwa had himself
insisted he wanted to come to the Station with Oakes, that he
hadn't pushed anyone and wanted to say so, to the police.

Mannie ran a palm down his face, leaned his elbows on the
desk, and hunched his shoulders. "Now, doctor."

Ben leaned forward. "I left the Clinic at about twelve-fifteen.
I wanted to buy some cigarettes before lunch, so I walked down
to Oakes's store. There were quite a few people sitting along
the edge of the stoep. Also there was a basket full of things,
standing by the top of the steps. I noticed it particularly.

"When I got inside the shop, it was quite full. I waited while
Mr. Oakes served several people; one woman had a lot to order
and it took some time. I waited about ten minutes. There was
a boy there, waiting beside me. He got there before some of
the white customers, but he wasn't served. He was looking a
bit het up. I asked him if he was in a hurry, and he said his baas
wanted some things for lunch at the Hotel. When Mr. Oakes
came along to us, I said, serve the kid first. Mr. Oakes looked
annoyed. He asked the boy what he wanted. The boy said,
chilisauce. Oakes said he didn't have any."

Ben paused, then continued. "The boy pointed to the shelf
behind Mr. Oakes and said that was the bottle he wanted, he

couldn't buy it anywhere else. Mr. Oakes told him to clear out because there were customers waiting. I said I was the only customer left and I didn't mind waiting. But the boy was on his way out already."

"Yes?"

"I asked for my cigarettes, and for a bottle of chilisauce."

Again Ben hesitated. Mannie said, "D'you get it?"

"After a . . . discussion . . . yes. I went out on the stoep. I gave the bottle to the boy and told him to tell his baas he could pay me some time. Then Sizwa spoke to the boy. I understood him to say that the boy musn't take the bottle, that he must return it to Oakes. I told Sizwa to mind his own business. The crowd laughed. The boy put the bottle in his basket by the top of the steps.

"I was turning to go when Oakes came out of the store. I suppose there was quite a bit of noise going on. He told everyone to get off his stoep. Sizwa made a crack, and Oakes raised his arm. Sizwa stepped back and put his hand on the glass. Oakes grabbed his arm and yanked him toward the edge of the stoep, and Sizwa swung his arm to shake Oakes off. Oakes missed his footing, half-turned around, and his feet ran up against the basket. The basket and Oakes went over the edge together. I saw Mr. Malcolm stoop over Oakes, and I dropped down and turned him over. He was bleeding from the nose and partly stunned. The African policeman came from the back of the crowd. There was a lot of shouting going on, and I saw someone reach down as if he might be looking for a stone in the gutter. There's a lot of plate glass around there. I said we should all get over to the Police Station and sort things out in peace and quiet. That's all, I think."

Mannie said, "Thank you, doctor."

He addressed a few questions to Tickey, whose large eyes were round with fright and confusion. Then he turned his attention to Sizwa. His voice, barking fluent Zulu, did not sound amicable. Ben, who understood only part of what Mannie said, gathered that he was giving Sizwa hell. Tickey relapsed into

tears, but Sizwa remained impassive. It seemed to Ben that
there was deliberate provocation in his silence and his indolent
posture. After a while Mannie got to his feet and left the room,
walking along the corridor. He was gone for some time, then
reappeared and beckoned Oakes through the door. They went
back to Larkill's office.

The men waited, not speaking. A cockroach scuttled across
the floor and Venter slammed a foot on it. After about fifteen
minutes, footsteps sounded along the corridor, Oakes appeared,
and behind him, Karl Ebenezer. They walked to the outer door,
looking at no one. Mannie came back to the desk. He stood
beside it and said, "You gents can go now, thank you."

Malcolm and Ben stepped into the sunlight. Malcolm walked
a little way off to the shade of a stunted mimosa. Ben felt in
his pocket for the new pack of cigarettes, began to peel off
the cellophane wrap. He wondered whether Malcolm would
remember to pay him for the chilisauce. He lit a cigarette and
leaned against the wall, listening to Reimer's voice rise and
fall in the charge office.

In a few moments, Sizwa and Tickey came down the steps.
Tickey went off with Malcolm, Sizwa lounged across the courtyard. He shot Ben a glance as he passed. Ben was about to
move off himself when Mannie came out of the building, with
Dr. Strasser behind him. Strasser nodded briefly at Ben and
marched through the gate and over the road.

Reimer folded his arms and looked at Ben. Ben said, "No
charge?"

"No charge."

"Big guns," suggested Ben, "they twist Oakes's tail?"

Mannie nodded. "Thanks for moving the party over here,
doc."

"Don't thank me. I suppose I started it."

"In small towns, you have to move gently."

Ben shrugged. "Oakes gets my goat. What did Ebenezer say
to him?"

"A nice piece about everyone has to be polite, black and

white, and we have grave responsibilities and no privileges. You couldn't teach that to Oakes in a million years. Nor to Sizwa. That's just two who want trouble. Don't worry, you didn't start it."

But when Ben was out of hearing, Mannie added to himself, "And you won't end it, either. Not you or the whole bloody Army."

30

As BEN WALKED into the hall, Strasser offered him no greeting. Ben went through to his room and washed his hands. When he returned to the luncheon table, Strasser said, "I'm afraid we'll have to serve ourselves."

"Hmn?"

"Until I can replace Sizwa."

"You mean you've fired him?"

"May I have the salad, please?" Ben passed him the bowl and Strasser ladled lettuce on to his plate. "Yes, that is what I mean."

"But you can't do that. He hasn't committed a crime."

Strasser began to eat, without speaking. Ben said, "Sir I was there, you know."

"I know."

"Then surely . . . the man's been with you for years. You owe him something?"

Strasser sighed. "Dr. Nevis. I spent time at the Police Station this morning. A very unpleasant situation has been avoided by what I, and Mr. Ebenezer, said there. We heard all the evidence. This is not a time when one can be naive."

"I'm not being naive."

"Oh yes, very." Strasser's thin mouth curved in a smile. "You see yourself as a Galahad, I suppose. But I have to consider the health of this town. That is all. To do my job, I have to avoid trouble, and keep in with the authorities. Sizwa has always been a potential troublemaker. His behavior today was incitative. Now he must go. I gave him one chance, but I won't give him another."

"There was provocation."

"For the boy, perhaps. Not for Sizwa. You have to realize that Sizwa is born to trouble as the sparks fly upward."

"You employed him."

"And now I have dismissed him. He has the proper wage compensation. It is perfectly fair."

"Fair to sack a man because he's an embarrassment?"

Strasser said coolly, "Yes, I think so. He would not have hesitated to leave me, you know, when it suited him."

"Perhaps. But a man in your position has certain responsibilities toward the African."

"My dear chap. Antique paternalism is not for me. Nor, I understand, for Sizwa. Lately he has been declaiming to the hills that Africa must throw off the white hand. That means you and me. Why do you imagine he instructed the boy to hand back the . . . what was it, chilisauce? . . . an apt commodity. He did it because he has the troublemaker's nose for an incident. There is tension in the town, and Sizwa, out of malice, is making the most of it. Therefore I would be foolish to give him further harbor."

Ben began to eat his salad. At last he said, "You don't think that if you fire him now, he'll make capital of it? Unjust dismissal?"

"Perhaps. Now or later, what does it matter?"

"He may try to get even with you."

"I can look after myself."

"Yes, but . . ."

"Dr. Nevis, I am not terribly interested in your views."

They finished the meal in silence. The garden boy, wearing Sizwa's much-too-large jacket, cleared away the plates.

Ben went out into the garden to smoke a cigarette. He could

not dispel the unease induced by the morning's events. Perhaps if he'd kept his mouth shut, at the store, and not supported the boy? Let Oakes impose his petty spite? But why the hell should Oakes get away with it, after all?"

Leaving the house to return to the Clinic, he saw Sullivan and Abrahams talking on the pavement outside the Hotel. He went over and told them about the quarrel at the store and Sizwa's dismissal.

Sullivan shrugged the whole thing off. His face tightened in a deprecating smile. Like a sea anemone, he closed at the slightest stirring of the shallows around him. Soon he excused himself and ambled away.

Abrahams watched him go, and then studied Ben, his large head drooping to one side. He said, "Strasser is right about one thing. The man would have had to be dismissed sooner or later. Sizwa has the combative sense overdeveloped. In England, he would be a shop steward. There is a type of man who must always oppose, and when one obstacle is overcome, another must be found. There is nothing positive in such a man, although he makes slogans to win support from the masses. That is the real danger of African nationalism, that it will promote leaders who have nothing to offer except more opposition to more and more ideas. Who thrive on turmoil. Who are not fitted by their nature to do anything else but whip up the emotions of a mob. They are produced by an evil situation, they perpetuate it, and finally it destroys them."

"And we can do nothing about it?"

"Certainly we can do something. We have to alter the situation, recognize rights, and above all, conquer fear. We must not be afraid of being submerged, nor must we pander to those who would submerge us. We have to recover our courage and our moral sense."

"Recover?"

"Oh yes. South Africans are very soft, you know. This is the only remaining country in the world, I think, where one can live like a mollusk, and the time for that is very short. The pin is already digging, isn't it?"

They walked up the road together. Abrahams said, "What I fear most is bullying, lethargy, and the fragmentation that comes when negotiation fails. The country might well become another Algeria, unless we can keep open the channels of discussion and compromise." He stopped as they drew level with the Clinic. "But as for Sizwa, I don't see that you can do anything about him. It's too late for that."

3^I

ABEL DID NOT HEAR of Sizwa's dismissal until late in the afternoon, having been sent to an outlying farm to work on a combine harvester.

When he was told of the scene at the store, he walked to Strasser's house and asked the garden boy to call Sizwa. The boy told him that Sizwa had been sacked, had taken his possessions and left at once.

"But did he go down to the employment office?"

"I don't know."

"Did he say where he was going?"

"No." The boy ran a finger delicately down his neck. "He was too angry for talk. Perhaps he's gone home."

Abel thought this likely. He returned to his room, much concerned. What would become of Sizwa, without work, angry? What could anyone do to help him? Nothing.

He carried a bucket from his room to the wash house, filled it with hot water, and went to the concrete alcove in the yard that served as his bathing place. He washed himself, went and put on a clean shirt and trousers. His thin face was wrinkled as at some sourness in the mouth. Sizwa was a grown man. There was nothing anyone could do.

He lit the paraffin lamp and hung it on its hook, then went and stood in the doorway. Sizwa should have told the police about the man he had seen at Oakes's store. Then this thing would have been avoided. He himself should have persuaded Sizwa to go to the police.

Even now, if the story was told, it would calm Mr. Oakes. Abel thought of the questions of the police, the disturbance, the notoriety. It was Sizwa's business. No one else could do anything.

Abel didn't want anything to do with it. He had a job, he'd worked hard, he didn't have to put his head in a hornet's nest.

He went back to his chest of drawers and got out his books, spread them on the table, sat down. There was nothing to be done about Sizwa, nothing.

32

"Do you know where he is?" said Kruger. Old Gwevu, standing beside him under the oak trees, shook his head slowly.

He had made the long walk from his kraal to speak to Kruger, and the heat had tired him. "The Master knows that this morning my grandson was sacked," he said. Kruger waited for the old man to marshal his thoughts in his own way.

"The quarrel at the store was provoked," said Gwevu. "Mr. Oakes accused my grandson, to the police, of killing his dog. We have heard that, but it is not true. Now Mr. Oakes has said that my grandson tried to hit him. That is a lie. The new doctor, what is his name? With hair the color of butter?"

"Dr. Nevis."

"Him. He spoke for my grandson. He was there. He saw it."

"Yes?"

"Nevertheless, Sizwa has lost his job. That is not right, Inkosi." The old man spoke with care, and with great hurt in his
voice. "Sizwa came to me, very angry, and took food and went
away."

"You should have kept him at home until he cooled down."

"How can one keep a full-grown man at home against his
will?"

"It is possible, though difficult. You don't know where he is?"

"Where would he go? He has no permit to go to another
town. There will be trouble. People are angry."

Kruger did not question it. Already, he knew, the story would
be spreading, borne with the milk cans and the bread delivery,
called from hill to hill by herd boys, gossiped over from one
end of the valley to the other. Kruger named certain people
names for their ineptness. Sizwa should have been charged,
and sacked; or not charged and not sacked. The way things
were, he'd been handed a grievance, ready-made.

He stood frowning, trying to estimate the effect of the affair,
trivial in itself, on larger matters. He sighed, considering the
old man beside him. Why were there not more like Gwevu?
Gwevu was not only responsible, he was knowledgeable. Kruger, that essentially practical man, understood that Gwevu possessed certain gifts not open to himself. For Gwevu the dust
still spoke with tongues, the sky was eloquent. He gathered
scraps of information as readily as a lamp gathers flying ants.

Kruger said, "What is the matter with the people of this
valley?"

Gwevu took his time in answering. Then, lifting his hand,
he pointed to the northeastern hills that rose to the escarpment. "The medicine man up there says that one has come over
the mountains. It is said he is from far away, even from beyond
this land altogether. He is evil, and his presence makes the
police afraid. Therefore the people are nervous and afraid."

"Afraid of one man?"

"I'm telling you what is being said, not what I can explain."

"And the burglary at the store?"

Gwevu chose to misunderstand him. "The people are angry because Oakes has refused their custom. Many of them have bought from him for a long time. They have been faithful to him. Now they are told not to go there."

"But was it this man from the hills who robbed the store?"

Gwevu shrugged. "I don't think a man would come such a long way to rob a store."

Kruger pressed the point, trying to discover whether any information had been given that might identify the thief, but Gwevu plainly knew nothing more that he could, or would, disclose. At last, Kruger said, "Why do they suggest he is a man from another country?"

"They say it," was all the answer he got. He wondered if the rumors had spread from Hopetoun. He told Gwevu that he would speak on Sizwa's behalf at the labor bureau, and also undertook to find Sizwa employment on his own farm if he reappeared.

Thanking him, Gwevu asked, "Why did not Dr. Strasser speak up for my grandson? You would speak for your workmen. The new young doctor spoke. Why did the old one throw him off? It was not a good thing to do. Not right."

Kruger hesitated. "I do not know all the facts. Perhaps the old doctor had his reasons. I will ask him when I see him. He works hard for your people at the Hospital, you know."

Gwevu seemed to hold this of small account, set against Strasser's personal failure toward Sizwa.

After Gwevu had left, leaning heavily on the shoulder of the young boy who accompanied him, Kruger called to mind the lands that lay in the hills to which Gwevu pointed. Redcliff, and Loubacher's land, possibly; Bill Maxwell's plantations at La Mercy; the Mission territory and the Reserve.

With a sour shake of the head he went indoors to telephone Mannie Reimer.

33

EBENEZER reached home that evening with a severe duodenal pain. The day had been tiresomely hot, he was worried about the rumors in the town, about the babblings of the fool Oakes, the scene at the store, the report of Sizwa's disappearance. Sizwa had been seen marching up through the shanty area, shouting and swearing.

Ebenezer went straight to his study, closed the door, and sank down wearily in his wing chair.

It was the only place he could find peace and order. It was a nice room, a beautiful room. On the dresser stood the blue and white china that his mother had taken on their travels across Africa; besides the cups, the long-barreled pistol that had belonged to his great-grandfather, and the stabbing-assagai that that redoubtable man's servant had thrust between the ribs of a lion, piercing the heart. Above these material trophies were Karl's own diplomas, framed in black wood. His wife had once said that the room depressed her, but to Karl it was beautiful.

He leaned over and jerked open a small drawer in the table at his elbow, extracted a packet of faded sepia photographs and selected one. It showed his wife, in an ankle-length black dress, standing between two of her brothers. All three had the same look, sharp cheekbones, long noses, and an arrogant poise of the head. A wild lot, given to fierce rages and bursts of up-roarious laughter. His wife had been capricious and unstable. Dark and bittersweet as wild honey. In their final quarrel—which had arisen, as God was his witness, because he gave her an umbrella for her birthday—he had cried at her, "You're drunk, woman, drunk with your own foolishness and imbecile laughter." And she had said with one of her piercing looks, "It's a pity, Karl, that you can't get a little merry on the same spirit."

She had stayed too long. Her presence had done damage. She had stayed until his sons opposed his will, corrupted by her fancies. Now they were strangers to him. One thought only of money and the other never thought at all. Nella remained, but he knew it was from a sense of duty more maternal than filial. She treats me sometimes, thought Ebenezer, as if I were a cripple or a half-wit.

He put the photograph away and closed the drawer gently.

A knock came on the door. He leaned over the arm of his chair and called, "Come in!" Julius Kruger appeared in the doorway.

Karl sat back. "Come in, Julius."

Kruger approached, and drew up a chair. Neither man smiled. Kruger's face drooped in ponderous folds. He said, "We have to talk."

Ebenezer nodded. His face was impassive, but he felt a pulse beat in his throat.

Kruger said heavily, "I have been speaking to Gwevu again, this afternoon. He is upset about the dismissal of Sizwa. I have promised that I will try and find Sizwa employment."

Ebenezer's eyelids flickered, but he said nothing. Kruger went on, "Karl, I want to ask you not to allow this storm in a teacup to influence your decisions."

"About what?"

"About the Vuli faction generally."

Ebenezer shook his head. "I thought we agreed that I have no authority in the choice of a nominee."

"But you carry weight, and so do I. Just a little weight in a little town, but enough to count as a responsibility. That is the situation that we must face. We both have friends at court. I don't want to become embroiled in a quarrel with you."

"That is hardly likely. What happened at the store today does not alter my opinion, it merely confirms it, that the Vuli are troublemakers, and will not co-operate in a responsible manner." He tapped his fingers together. "That is it, in a nutshell."

"Not quite." Again Kruger hesitated. "Karl, I decided to come to you tonight and speak my mind. We aren't really talking about this or that incident in the day's work, are we? I'm not thinking only of this or that faction, or indeed of any one problem. I am thinking of you and me. Particularly, perhaps, of me. We've been friends for a long time . . ."

"And?"

". . . so long that I have fallen into the habit of playing Follow-the-Leader. I've allowed myself to agree with you always, because you are a good friend but a bad enemy. Oh yes, I know you. I know that now, as we talk, you're making plans." Kruger smiled. "Working out who will support you against me, if it comes to that point. What I want you to see is that I am supporting you, in friendship, even though I may disagree with you on a special question.

"For a long time, you've been losing faith in my friendship. Sometimes I feel that you have ceased to trust me. So I wanted to give you fair warning. I intend to oppose you if I feel it is right to do so. That is why I'm telling you that although I agree with you that Sizwa is a troublemaker, I am offering him a job. I believe that that is a safe move in an explosive situation. I say, don't put ammunition in his hands, or make a martyr of him. A little diplomacy will serve us well, here."

"You call it diplomacy. I prefer to call it weakness." Ebenezer pulled a cheroot from his pocket, nipped the end, and lit it. "All my life," he said, "I have never shirked a difficult task. I didn't expect to find you among the shirkers, Julius."

They were now talking at two levels. They were setting the mood for the future, and each saw in the other's face the shadow of things to come.

Kruger said, "Times have changed. One cannot apply the methods that worked ten, five, two years ago."

"Times have changed, and you with them, I see. What you are saying, under the surface, is a criticism of present policy."

"You consider that a weakness? To say what is on one's mind, on one's conscience?"

Ebenezer said coolly, "I say it is desertion in the face of the enemy."

Kruger reddened. He screwed up his eyes and said very gently, "Karl. You speak as if you were the Party, and I something outside it. Let me remind you that we have taken an equal share in its creation, that we exercise the same rights and carry the same responsibilities. I have no enemies, as yet, in this valley, although I have some opponents."

"You will have enemies."

"You among them?"

"If you prove renegade."

They stared at each other in silence, each shocked at his own thoughts and yet unable to call a halt. Karl said, "Good, then. It's come to a head. Good that we say what has been unsaid for too long.

"Your loyalties are divided, Julius. You allow personal comfort and expediency to blind you to the urgency of the times. You want the bread, the butter, and the jam as well, to support a policy up to the time when it hits you personally, and then withdraw. Now, you say, 'I've had enough.'" Ebenezer looked at the cheroot in his hand. It had gone out, and he ground it into the ash tray at his elbow. "All you want is the dream. But the reality is hard. There is no room for doubters among the men who govern a country."

Kruger thought, Karl always does this to me. He's quicker than I am, and more ruthless. But this time, I must find an answer.

He leaned forward and pointed a finger. "Karl, you've gone through life knowing you were in the right. Not thinking, but knowing. Now for me, it's not like that. You see things larger than I do, but you don't see the fine points. You don't see the people in your plans. Now I have to tell you that you have sometimes been wrong, since all men are fallible.

"Look, now. Two days ago, something happened that made me realize my own fallibility. In short, I found my son again. The prodigal father returned, and the son forgave him. It seems to me that God requires only what He says, that we shall love one another. I'm a clumsy man, not good at saying things, but I'm your closest friend. I can speak to you as I've never spoken to another living soul. As your friend, I warn you. You are losing touch with people. Soon you will lose your friends, and perhaps, one day, your daughter."

He stopped. Ebenezer looked at him levelly. "I'm not blind. I know what I stand to lose, but I see what you do not. There is no such thing as a slight deviation. It continues and increases, until one reaches quite a different destination. You must go your way and I'll go mine."

Kruger got to his feet and stood looking down at the thin man's face. He shrugged and said, "I'm not equal to you, Karl. Whatever I say isn't enough, I can see that. One day, however, you'll meet an opponent worthy of your sword. When that time comes, try and see him for what he is. Respect him. That is your last hope."

Long after Kruger had gone, Ebenezer sat on in the darkened study. He was very tired, to the point of illness. He fell at last into a half-sleep. Shadows moved. He seemed to hear his wife laughing, saying, "Karl, such a long journey, and you've forgotten to pack your warm friends."

34

IT WAS GROWING DARK when Kruger left Ebenezer's house. The pale green sky seemed thick as a jelly, the town solidified at the bottom of the bowl.

Mannie Reimer, passing as Kruger made his way to his car, saw that the old uncle was in a somber mood, and would have avoided an encounter, but Julius spotted him and bore down on him.

"Why in Heaven's name," said Kruger, still ten yards away,

"cannot the people in this town behave like adults, instead of like moronic children? Why didn't someone at the store make a joke, tell everyone to go home, anything rather than make a big scene of it? Where were you?"

"At the tannery."

"Much use you were!" Kruger pushed his hat far back on his head and wiped his forehead. "I saw Gwevu this afternoon. He says there's an agitator up in the hills. I passed the message to Larkill. Do you think it's true?"

"No."

"Then who does think so? Someone does. This town has more rumors than a cotton boll has weevils."

Mannie smiled at him. "You're in a very nasty temper."

They began to walk together toward Kruger's car, parked in the main road. Kruger said, "When are you going to catch him, whoever he is?"

"We're trying."

"Well, try the northeast territories."

"Only those?"

"Don't be sarcastic." At the car door Kruger said, "I called on Mr. Ebenezer tonight. We quarreled."

"Ah well, everyone quarrels with him sometime."

"He thinks I'm a deviationist."

Mannie chuckled, and Kruger dealt him a sharp blow in the ribs. "I'm old, but there's fight in me yet." He climbed into the car, started the engine, and leaned out of the window.

"Gwevu says Sizwa has disappeared."

"Where to?"

"Don't know. Think he's got ideas about this agitator?"

"Uncle, I left my crystal ball at home."

Kruger withdrew his head, then stuck it out again. "Well, if you see him, tell him I'll give him a job."

Mannie lifted a hand in acquiescence. The car drew away from the curb.

On the way back to Witteboom, Kruger turned on the radio set. At the tailend of the news, the impersonal voice of the announcer told him that the drought was unbroken throughout the province, and in the forestry areas the fire hazard now stood at the danger point of ninety per cent.

35

ON THURSDAY NIGHT Ben, shirking the awkwardness engendered by Strasser's dismissal of Sizwa, left the house and went across to the Hotel in search of company. On the steps he found Abrahams and Sullivan, the former agitated, the latter undeniably drunk. They presented a curious spectacle. Sullivan trailed across the shoulders of the factory owner like a creeper on a sagging porch.

Somewhat breathlessly, Abrahams said, "Take the other side." Ben looped Sullivan's free arm around his neck, captured a wrist and grasped it firmly. The trio maneuvered in short bursts toward Sullivan's car. Abrahams opened the back door and Ben attempted to guide Sullivan through it. Sullivan's limbs, springy as coils of wire, rebounded from the polished body work. Forced at last through the curbside door, he emerged smoothly from the far one. When his captors converged on him, he showed signs of tearfulness. "Two to one isn't fair." He sat down suddenly in the road. "Only a little chicken wire." He put his hand on his heart. "Tha's not much to ask, just a li'l bit of chicken wire?"

"God knows why he wants it," said Abrahams, wearily loosening his tie.

"I need it," said Sullivan. "Tha's all you know on earth, and all you need to know." He got a grip on the door handle, pulled himself upright, and leaned back. "I need it. There are fairies at the bo'om my garden. Steal my ducks."

Ben said to Abrahams. "I'll drive him home, if you'll follow and bring me back."

"First catch your duck," said Abrahams. They circled cautiously, but Sullivan darted between them and careened toward the center of the road, causing a motorist to swerve violently and shout a pithy phrase. It was evident that Sullivan would be induced to go home only after some attempt had been made to procure chicken wire. Looped together once more, the three made their way toward Oakes's store.

They negotiated the gate and reached the back door. Abrahams knocked, saying under his breath, "We'll just apologize and get him away home."

But though they knocked several times, there was no response. The darkened store seemed utterly silent. Ben's eye roved to the window of the living room, and froze. The curtain was slightly lifted. In the crack was the pale puffy outline of a face, and below it, pointed straight at them, the bluish gleam of a shot-gun barrel.

Ben said gently, "Let's get out of here," and Abrahams, after one swift glance at the window, wheeled with him and marched Sullivan swiftly back the way they'd come. Sullivan, luckily, was now half-asleep. They got him into the back seat of the car, where he wrapped both arms around his head and sang to himself.

Abrahams said, "Maybe we'd better buy Oakes another dog. Some time he's going to shoot someone."

"His nerves are in a mess."

"Mine too, doc."

They took Sullivan home, Ben driving his car, Abrahams following in his own. A toothache moon was well up in the sky. As they approached Redcliff, a kaffir-dog ran out from a sleeping kraal and barked hysterically. The ripple of barking spread to the other kraals and homesteads, a ripple of unrest. In the back seat of the car, Sullivan snored.

They carried him to a settee on the verandah, and pulled off his shoes and tie. Ben released the cord of the sun blind, which rattled down without breaking Sullivan's slumber.

On the way back past the poultry yard, they stopped and

Ben got out of the car and walked around the wire fence. There was a breach at one place, clumsily mended with palings and cord.

As he got into the passenger seat he said, "I suppose he's told the police."

"Probably not, I think. He's very lazy, you know. He'd think it too much trouble, for a duck or so."

They bumped along the track, climbing with the Mission fields above them on their left. The squat belfry gaped like an open mouth, the bell hanging limp. Moon and heat bleached the earth, imposed a languor even on the crickets, yet there seemed to fall from the sky a tingling note like the tremor of silver wires.

Ben shook his head, and Abrahams, with a faint smile, said, "They are singing, eh?"

"Hmn?"

"The stars. You hear them sing? Why deny it? The smallest child knows that in Africa the stars sing. You try to explain it away, of course, because you come of rational stock. To me, it's the wonder of Africa that it is like a Rosetta Stone, on which we see ourselves written, infinitely old, and subtly different from what we think ourselves to be. We have here a chance to study ourselves. Think of the implications, for example, of witchcraft, its connections with suggestion and with psychotherapy. Or again, think what a chance political philosophers have to study the type of revolution that has not taken place in the Western world for three hundred years. Fascinating, umh? It is as if, in our sight, an operation of history has laid bare the brain of Man. No wonder the world watches. Such a continent this is, so old and remote, the cradle of mankind, perhaps. And yet so new, the rising phoenix of the world. That is what makes us afraid, the sight of our own origins and destinies. It is something to provoke wonder, and fear."

He lapsed into silence. Ben lit a cigarette and leaned back in his seat. There came to him a sense of the vastness, the physical vastness of the continent to which he belonged, the vastness of the problems that beset her. He thought, Abrahams is right, the brain is exposed, and the scalpel in our hands. The idea filled him not with fear but with exhilaration.

About to flick his cigarette stub through the window, he remembered the risk of fire, and stubbed it out carefully in the ash container.

36

PEOPLE WHO WATCH from a safe distance the onset of disaster are usually puzzled by the manner in which its victims seem to invite rather than resist it. This may be because the human disaster, unlike the calamitous act of God, is a cumulative affair. Its elements, occurring again and again though not perhaps in fatal combination, produce a corrosion of the spirit. Discussion crumbles into barren acrimony, energy becomes apathy, the way is yielded to the weak, the brutal, and the complacent. Finally the threat of danger produces no healthy reaction. The final holocaust is accepted, almost looked forward to, as natural and inevitable. A nation succumbs to morbid euphoria.

Against this, what defense exists? Only that of desperation. The solitary watcher at the bridge, the martyr, the prophet alight in the wilderness.

Nor does calamity always bestride a high black horse. Often he limps ludicrous into town, a raggle-taggle mumbler scuffing the dust.

On Friday night Ebenezer and Kruger, at a meeting called to discuss the Republican celebrations, fell into public and undignified argument over the purchase of bunting. At about the same time Archie Oakes called Mick Loubscher a nigger-lover and was thrust forthwith into the gold-fish pool near the

Town Hall. On Saturday, Strasser's garden boy, frightened by a light in the vicinity of Sizwa's old room, declared that Sizwa had employed the services of a witch doctor to help him work off his grudge against his employer. Strasser himself, scornful of superstition, ignored the boy's hysteria, but was unable to treat so lightly the discovery that, while he was attending an operation in the Elizabeth Hospital, someone had let the air out of all four of his tires.

Larkill, his temper much exacerbated by recent events, asked Mannie Reimer why nothing had been done to prevent a particularly large brew of gavine being sold in the shanty area, and Mannie took the chance to point out that lawbreakers were bound to thrive if the routine work of the police was neglected in favor of wild-goose chases.

There was, in short, plenty of evidence of that fragmentation of good will which Abrahams had foreseen.

Meanwhile the heat increased hour by hour, unbroken by the electric storms that rolled to the north and south. The water in the river fell so low that mud was exposed on either bank, dark, cracked, and odiferous as alligator hide.

Only two men in the valley were entirely satisfied with life. One was the man in the hills, who took his ease, his stomach soothed by Sullivan's prize ducks, tastily stewed with potatoes, onions, and tomatoes from the Mission fields.

The other, oddly enough, was Sizwa. He was his own master. He basked in the sun of popular sympathy. He possessed a real and workable grievance. Even the weather, by imposing a strain on other people's nerves, served his ambition. He felt himself a king.

Calamity observed Sizwa, spoke soft words to him, nudged and giggled and traced a plan in the dust.

37

As THE TOWN HALL clock struck two, Karl Ebenezer closed the file before him on his desk, reached out a hand, and pressed the old-fashioned button-bell that summoned his secretary. The stained grease-proof wrapping that had held his luncheon sandwich caught his eye, and he screwed it up and threw it into the wastepaper basket.

He spent most of his mornings in this building, now that he had retired from his profession. There was plenty of work in the town for a man who was ready to serve the public without expecting remuneration. Usually he devoted himself to those dull matters that interested him least, but on Saturdays he allowed himself a little relaxation, turning to the things close to his heart, the cultural pursuits of the town, his scheme to create a proper lending library, the work to be done on improving local roads. He had a finger in every pie. His worst enemies—and he was a man who made enemies easily—admitted him to be a good organizer and an excellent Committee Member.

The door opened and Miss Labuschagne came in. He indicated the papers on his desk with a wave of his hand. She picked them up without speaking and carried them out to her own office. Ebenezer stood up, stretched, walked over to the wide, dusty window that looked down on the main street. He could see Oakes putting up the shutters of his shop, and Strasser walking briskly toward his house. Ebenezer nibbled a fingernail, thinking of the second phase of the polio campaign, due to open on Monday. Strasser was efficient. It was a pity that politically and morally he was a twister.

Ebenezer jerked the cord of the green sun blind and lowered it, walked over to the next window, which looked south over the roofs of the tannery and sawmill. A small frown pinched his brows together. Abrahams now. A Liberal, or merely liberally-minded? Was it in him that the challenge lay? Was it at that little man with the big head and the large generosity (for Ebenezer always gave credit to generosity), that the needle of intuition pointed? Ebenezer shook his head.

He lowered the second blind, and crossed the office in a green gloom. He took his hat, the cream Panama that declared his generation to the world, and walked through the outer office. Miss Labuschagne had already left. He locked the outer door, moved down the stairs, avoiding the tread where the linoleum was cracked, turned right past the treasurer's office, and left the building.

Outside in the yellow afternoon light, he hesitated a moment. His thin face, with its jutting beard, absorbed the brilliance of the sun, took on the stony glow of a gargoyle. He was in fact going through the small, secret act of steeling himself to the public gaze. He must conceal the approach of old age, the pain in his duodenum, the way his hands trembled after a few hours' work. Endeavor was the watchword. Confidence. Calm. He had this month canceled a much-needed holiday at the seaside, so sure was he that, this year, his country and his people would claim the utmost of every loyal supporter.

Lifting his chin, he set off briskly along the road. The year of the Republic . . . young people did not appreciate what it meant . . . the years of struggle, of utter devotion, the hard-won achievements. The victor's laurels on the brow of the Volk. His step slowed as he visualized the celebrations they would hold. Oh, a happy time. A great service, a holiday for the school children, a parade, with dancing—decorous, traditional dancing—and in the evening a solemn dedication on the steps of the Town Hall. There must be special celebrations for the non-white population. He frowned, thinking of the squabbles of the Pembe and Vuli. Certainly this was not a time to sharpen their differences. Calm, unity, that was the country's greatest need, a mood in which there was no weakening, no pandering to those who were ready to let the work of fifty years slide into ruin.

His steps faltered and stopped. He stood teetering on the edge of the pavement, neat and exact, hands grasping the lapels of his coat. Then, abruptly, he turned back and made his way to the clearing behind the Church. It marked the spot where the old Church Hall had stood, where the new one would go up, when funds were available. Thick wild grass clothed the site, a track led across it to the small Pastorie where Dominee Bond lived. Ebenezer picked his way quickly across to the garden gate.

He saw that he had caught the predikant at his only self-indulgence . . . the few moments of idleness in his garden that he allowed himself each afternoon. Ebenezer watched the old man with affection. He stood now with his hands clasped behind his back, gazing at a rose bush. Presently he put out a stubby finger and touched a leaf. There was tenderness in the action. How good the old friend was! Everything he did had simplicity, humility of the heart. Just to watch him turn the pages of the Book was to feel comfort and security. He seldom spoke of justice or love, but these things flowed in him as naturally as the blood in his veins. Principles that other men used as weapons were in his hands as harmless as his flowers; like water lilies opening in the sun.

The gate creaked under Ebenezer's hand, and the old man in the garden looked up, smiled, and crossed the patch of sun-baked lawn between them.

"This is nice, Karl. Have you come for a chat? Shall we take coffee together?" He drew Ebenezer toward the stoep, calling for his servant to bring coffee and rusks. When they were settled, he took off his old-fashioned metal-rimmed spectacles and polished them vigorously on a colored handkerchief.

"Well, now, what is the matter? You look tired. I can see the little black devil on your shoulder, there."

Ebenezer made no answer. Why were thoughts so easy, and words so difficult? The predikant said gently, "I heard you quarreled with Julius."

"Who told you?" said Ebenezer, more sharply than he intended.

"Someone who was at the meeting last night."

"Oh . . . that."

"It wasn't the first quarrel?"

Ebenezer ran a finger over the hat on his knee. The Panama felt sticky in the heat. He laid it aside. "Julius has changed, toward me."

"That I don't believe. There's no one more staunch. Perhaps it's simply that his opinions differ from yours, Karl."

"We have differed before." Ebenezer leaned his head back, looking at the sky. "This is more serious." He moved restlessly. "You know what this year means to us? The year in which we will be tested to the limit of our strength? There's no room for dissension. Julius, you, me, we've lived in this town for so many years, we've differed sometimes on the surface, but in spirit we have always been united. Each of us, in his sphere, a facet of the whole, but part of the same gem. How can I persuade Julius that he is wrong, that is my problem."

A faint smile touched the predikant's mouth. "In what way?"

Ebenezer hesitated, and then said painfully, "He is, I believe, confused by the speed of world events. He raises a flood of small points, suggests this little diversion, or that. I can't make him see, what I recognize so clearly, that our policy is all of a piece. There is no illogicality in it. Since integration is national suicide, we must, in justice to the nonwhite peoples, press forward with separate development. The Bantu in particular must have ultimate independence in his own territory. We have reached the moment of truth. The thing is ready to be taken to its critical stage. We must go forward. It is that, or failure. Yet Julius talks of modifications, of concessions. Of excepting the Colored peoples, and so on. I cannot make him see that these little divergences, as he calls them, lead straight to integration. To the merging of the races, the supremacy of black nationalism, the downfall here of Western civilization. And, logically, to the misery of everyone in the country. You see that?"

"I understand the argument."

"Not so Julius. He talks as if this were a matter of degree and not of principle. That, at a time when Africa is in turmoil. People who walk in the middle of the road, I have told him, are run down and killed, and it serves them right."

He leaned back in his chair, his face pale. Mr. Bond said, "Drink your coffee, Karl, it's growing cold." He noticed the way Ebenezer's fingers shook as he lifted the cup. "You must take your holiday," he said. "You're very tired."

Ebenezer's pale eyes lifted to the predikant's face. For a moment his expression was veiled, and then it grew sharp and intent, as if he were listening. "I'm afraid . . ." he began, and then stopped. "I feel very disturbed. For some time . . ."

"You're tired. You work too hard, and none of us are young any more."

Ebenezer shook his head. "Often, nowadays, I think of the time we were children. I suppose that is old age. The orchard is very sweet, when the plow has gone over it." He set down the cup in its saucer. "You could talk to Julius."

Mr. Bond made a slight movement, and again Ebenezer's eyes sharpened. "Or do you agree with him?" The words were spoken so softly that they seemed hardly able to survive the brazen weight of the heat.

"I don't agree with Julius. Not in the sense you mean."

"Then I ask you to say what you do mean. The time has come when each of us should speak his mind. You've been a strength to this community as long as I can remember. Before ever you were called to the Church. And yet, I am being honest, forgive me . . . since Cottesloe, you've said nothing to guide us. Some of our people have questions, doubts, but you have remained silent. Old friend, I know that this is a time when we need your strength as never before. We need your reassurance that our faith in temporal policy springs from our acceptance of the will of God. You know that people must be reminded constantly of their duty to man and to God. They need the rock of faith. In Peace Drift, you are that rock. I ask you now to comfort your flock. Tell them, tell me, that you won't lead us into the wilderness, that you remain faithful to the old things. Believe me, it is necessary."

"What if I myself have doubts and questions? What if I have no comfort in me to give others?"

Bond leaned forward in his chair. "If I have kept silent, Karl, it was by design, not accident. For fifty years, I have believed it to be God's will that black and white should not mingle. Then came the discussions at the time of the Church Clause. The publishing of the book *Delayed Action*. The statements of our Synods after Cottesloe. The quitting of the World Council of Churches. All these things have forced me to question myself. There is a time when one is face to face with oneself, if that is not a contradiction of terms, and then one must withdraw, particularly if one is a churchman. Go into the wilderness, keep silent, and wait for the Word of God. That is why I have said nothing. I've been listening for the truth."

"The devil also walks in the wilderness."

"Undoubtedly."

Ebenezer leaned forward and tapped his fingers on the table. "It is our right to call on you! We have been faithful to the Church, now let the Church be faithful to us."

The predikant's heavy head sank deeper into his shoulders. "You talk as if the Church belonged to the Volk. Let me say clearly that on this point I have no doubts whatever. The Church belongs not to the Afrikaner, nor to the State, nor to South Africa, but to God. It is His, to do with as He will. If we forget that, then nothing can save us from His judgment."

Ebenezer relaxed. "I'm sorry, Cornelius. I don't mean to be impertinent, but I am in great distress of mind."

"There's another thing, Karl. You feel a sense of crisis, and you think my voice can provide a . . . panacea. But don't you understand that if I speak it will very likely have the reverse effect? The thing will be beyond recall? No one will be able to take refuge in silence, any longer? Are you sure that you want that, now?" He put his hand on his friend's arm. "Don't you think you're taking this quarrel with Julius too seriously? You aren't well, you need a rest. Why not just take things at their face value? Sometimes silence is wiser than speech. Men must sometimes wonder, and question, and be divided on important problems.

"True harmony does not lie in everyone thinking alike. It comes when those who disagree can still respect each other, love each other, and work together for the highest good."

Ebenezer said wearily, "Cornelius, you are avoiding the issue. There are ultimate, fundamental principles. The Church isn't a Parliament, to reach a compromise, give a little, take a little. There is a right and a wrong. Tell us which is which." He got stiffly to his feet. "Let us know where we stand."

He went slowly down the steps, putting on his Panama hat; disappeared through the gate and along the path.

The predikant sat on, looking at his raised hands, moving them slowly, palm upward, as if they were the opposing scales of justice.

38

LATER THE SAME AFTERNOON, Julius Kruger called on Mr. Bond. He found him working in the wood-and-iron office behind the Church. The building was unbearably hot. Flies banged at the wire screens over the window, and the bare boards smelled of carbolic soap. In the center of the room the predikant sat writing. At the entry of Kruger, he cleared some papers off a chair, and waited for an explanation of the interruption.

Julius plunged straight into an account of his quarrels with Ebenezer. He seemed less concerned with the cause of these

disagreements than with the personal sense of hurt they had
produced. He sat facing Bond, his heavy legs sprawled out,
his great fist pounding the table. "Why should Karl doubt my
good faith? I was born here, I'll die here. I helped to build this
town. Must I now be challenged, must I be asked for refer-
ences, like a stranger? Is it impossible to disagree with the
smallest point Karl raises? He wants this bunting, I want that,
is it a cause for rudeness?"

"One would not think so," said Bond. "There has been an
element of the ridiculous in all that has happened here, recently."

Kruger suddenly subsided. He stopped his table thumping
and stared at the predikant with his eyes puckered. "No. It
isn't ridiculous any longer. It is serious, Cornelius, and sad.
There can be danger even in the ridiculous. It sounds ridiculous when a man is bitten by a mad sheep. There is something
funny in the sound of it, but if the sheep is rabid, no one laughs,
least of all the man who is bitten." His fingers fidgeted with
a pen, and he shook his head. "A civil meeting is no place to
discuss politics or religion."

"These were discussed?"

"In a sense. It was a question of who was to conduct the
Service. Somehow, Mr. Prentiss and Karl became involved in
an argument, and we had a hard time to smooth things down.
Molteno pointed out that we were not gathered to discuss fine
points of religious doctrine, and there were apologies. But the
good spirit was ruined. It was unfortunate and unnecessary.
After the meeting a number of people stayed in the hall, arguing, and had to be turned out by the caretaker."

"Was my name mentioned?"

"Well . . . only as a good example, so to speak."

"Because I have not . . . given tongue?"

"Because you have taken time to consider, before giving
tongue."

Mr. Bond looked at Kruger steadily. The conference at Cottesloe, which had examined, among other things, the attitude

of world churches toward the question of apartheid, had provided an urgent subject of discussion in every parish in the country. Certain of the Church members maintained that the doctrine was morally indefensible; others, while rejecting unjust domination of the white group over the black, believed that a policy of racial differentiation was not only realistic, but could be made to accord with the teachings of the Scriptures. A third group felt itself unqualified to decide a matter which was more properly the concern of the Synods, but insisted that the Church must retain its right to discuss, and if necessary criticize, every aspect of national life.

At last the predikant said, "And you, Julius, what do you want me to do?" His face was turned away, toward the window.

Julius shrugged, absorbed in his own grievance. "I'm a layman, I leave it to you." He frowned. "I would once have said that nothing could cause a breach between Karl and me."

"Would you?" Bond's voice was dry. "Then you have deceived yourself. You must remember that what we have to deal with is no small matter, but something basic and final. Up till now, we have concerned ourselves with twigs and pebbles. We have fought over flags and anthems, about the shape of thoughts which we call language, rather than about the thoughts themselves. Now comes the real labor. We have to build a nation. The question is whether that nation shall be white or multi-racial. It is significant that only to mention this self-evident fact causes a stir among us. Yet it can no longer be avoided. We are to be honest with ourselves. Karl accepts this. He has the courage of his convictions, and he sees that if you deviate ever so slightly in your views, Julius, you move a little away from him, and each small step will take your further, from him and from what have been your own beliefs up till now. Ultimately you threaten all he is and does. That is the breach between you. These other irritations are only signs of this deeper disturbance."

"But . . ." began Kruger, and the predikant shook his head.

"Karl has just been here, and he rightly said that at this

time moderation is a word politicians use to deceive themselves. We are talking not of policies, but of principles. You can alter your approach to the principle, but in the end you cannot alter the principle itself. Karl has chosen his principle. Differentiation, separate development. He sees everything, law, economics, religion, as motes of dust floating in that single shaft of light. Either it is entirely right, or entirely wrong."

He folded his hands on his chest and fixed his gaze on Kruger's face. "No, Julius. Be honest. Karl is warning you to consider your position. Think well, of the honors you have won, the offices you hold, the friends you cherish. If you call yourself a reformer today, you will call Karl an extremist tomorrow. The division will widen. I know you. You aren't a man to stand idle and let the world go by. Karl has warned you and now I warn you. You can't shuffle off your decision by telling me you are a layman. It concerns the layman. It concerns you. So think, before you take another little step, of what you are doing. Think that you must pay the price of your actions, whichever way you walk."

Kruger met his eyes. "What advice are you giving me?"

"The advice that you can't avoid the decision any longer. Between Karl and something else. You must decide what is right, and not pretend there is no decision."

But Kruger was shaking his head, pushing himself back from the table and getting up. "I don't see it as you do. I see that even if a thing is right, there is a right way and a wrong way to go about it. Karl and I disagree about method, not principle."

The Dominee looked at him gravely, without speaking. Kruger paced over to the window, fiddled with the catch and threw it open. A bumble bee that had been dashing itself against the wire zoomed into the room and out again. Kruger came back to the table. "The whole situation is false. It has all been precipitated by the robbery at the store. It's built up from there. Once catch the thief . . . the agitator . . . and we'll have peace and quiet again. That must be our effort. To restore things to normal. Then everything will solve itself."

39

EVERY SECOND Saturday afternoon, Abel was free of duties at the Garage. These hours of leisure were particularly enjoyable, better than the routine freedom of Sunday. When he left the workshop at noon on Saturday, it was with a legacy of hours that must be spent with care and forethought. A poor man must extract from leisure the last squeezings of enjoyment, the same pleasure he extracted from buying. As for example: one stood before the shop window, considering imagining . . . how would I look in that hat? Would I feel happy in it? Proud? Would it be proof against rain, against dust? Would it attract the right sort of attention, respectful and admiring? And then, the feel of the hat, the trying on, the bargaining, the going away to reconsider, and the final possession, the walk through town, wearing this hat. When a man was poor, he must spend his money and his time with care.

This Saturday, he accumulated happiness from various small circumstances. From the heat, which he liked, because on a hot day there was no pain in his leg; from the brassy smoothness of the sky; the smell of his meal of beans, stewing with a good slice of bacon over his paraffin stove; from the knowledge that he had sugar and tea in the cupboard, and half a packet of cigarettes in his pocket; from the whole, round, complete freedom of the afternoon ahead.

He took his good shirt from the drawer, put it on, knotted his tie with exactness, before carrying a chair out into the sun. He sat eating with the warm enamel bowl balanced on his knees, chewing with gusto, swilling down the food with drafts of strong sweet tea.

There was one small round cloud in the sky, as there was one cloud in his thoughts. Sizwa. He decided that this afternoon he would go over to the housing area where the factory workers lived. Someone might have news of Sizwa.

148

Anyway, it was nice over there. Clean houses, with vegetable plots. People to talk to; perhaps he would listen to Absolem playing his guitar, and someone would be sure to invite him to take a little food in the evening. Later, he would go with the rest of them to the meeting up at the Mission. There would be singing, and a chance, after the service, of meeting friends from up the valley. He'd be home well before the curfew.

So he laid his plans, and so it happened, at least until the evening, but then things took a twist of their own. An elderly woman delayed him with discussion of her son's debts, the furnishing company were threatening to take away his furniture, he was out of work and couldn't pay. By the time Abel had listened to the full history, the others had gone up the hill past the Hospital. He set out after them, taking his time. His short leg made haste impossible, and it was a pleasant path, cushioned with pine needles that smelled as good as washing dried on the grass. Once he stopped and bent to stir the mast with a finger. He shook his head. Very, very dry. The wind has dropped, there wasn't a sign of rain.

The sun was down. He skirted the clear ground behind the Elizabeth Hospital, and reflected that there was too little of it. The scrub land should be plowed, or burned off within the safety of brakes. Although he had never owned so much as a vegetable patch, and had spent most of his life in urban areas, Abel loved land. He sometimes thought that if he failed his examinations too often, he would like to live on a farm. Perhaps, one day, he might keep a small garden.

He left the afforested area, and emerged on the road alongside the railway track, at the Mission Halt. On his right the highway ran north and east toward the Reserve, and above him, nearly as high as the rising moon, were the Mission buildings. He crossed the tracks and took the path upward.

It was at a bend in the path that he came face to face with Sizwa. The big man was sitting on a bank, singing to himself. Abel stopped, astonished. He said, "What are you doing here?"

Sizwa rose and stretched his arms over his head. The twilight made him larger than life-size. He had been smoking a cigarette and now tossed it down. It rolled down the slope, scattering sparks. Abel quickly stamped on it.

"You fool, you'll start a fire," he said, and Sizwa laughed.

"I mean to." There was smooth satisfaction in his voice, that made Abel peer up at him in dismay.

Sizwa moved his outstretched arm in a slow arc, covering the valley below them. "I am the spark," he said, "in the dry grass. When my enemies are burned off, my people will spring up strongly." He dropped his oratorical pose and said conversationally, "I've been waiting for you. I can do with some cash."

"You've got money of your own."

"Not cash. I don't want to go into town."

"Why not?" Abel sat down on the bank. "I don't like that way of talking. You're up to no good."

Sizwa merely laughed, his eyes glinting in the half-light.

"You tell me what you're up to, Sizwa."

"Organizing a boycott," said Sizwa. He used the English word, giving it a staccato force. Abel's heart thudded.

"A boycott of what?"

"You'll see." Sizwa bent and picked up his stick from the grass, weighed it in his hand. "Are you going to lend me some money?"

"No I am not. It's against the law, what you're doing."

"Poor Abel, so good, so frightened! Don't you want to hear about my plans?"

Abel shook his head in panic, but his eyes could not tear themselves from Sizwa, who gave the stick a whirl and said nonchalantly, "I have enough support, without you."

Abel heaved himself to his feet. "Listen. Don't be a fool. You can get a good job. Good money. And save for your taxi. That's what you want to do, buy your taxi and settle down. Come back to town and act like a sensible man."

Sizwa put out a hand and thrust Abel lightly away from him. "Hurry, little boy, it's time for you to sing in church."

Abel said wildly, "How do you know I won't betray you? Do you want to be called agitator? I can get you arrested!"

"You won't." Sizwa was already moving away across the hillside. Some fifteen paces off he called back, "You're too frightened. Insects like you have no courage; if you fall on your backs you can't turn over, just lie there kicking your legs. Only fit to hide in a crack in the wall. Go and take shelter in Church, with other cockroaches!"

Abel shouted after him, "You'll end in jail. Sizwa, come back, Man, you don't know what you're doing. Come back here!"

But Sizwa was running now, springing like a buck over the tussocks of grass. His laughter came faintly back to Abel.

Abel watched him until he was out of sight around the curve of the hill. He felt angry, fearful, pitying; and under all, he felt the stirring of an illicit excitement. Violence, he knew, was pointless and wicked, it came back on those who had done nothing. Abel accepted the good laws, and endured the bad with patience, for he came of a law-abiding family. And yet, in Sizwa's presence, he was aware of a moving excitement, dark and warming as brandy. Sizwa seemed to be free of the burdens of other men. He acknowledged no laws but his own. His voice, rolling through the dark, was the expression of all the hopes and resentments that Abel had ever felt. It was not only that he had the power to express himself, it was something in him that made him seem taller than ordinary people. Dimly, with mixed pride and apprehension, Abel recognized in Sizwa the new Africa of which he so often spoke. Sizwa was indeed the spark in dry grass. The word slashed on a wall at night. Uhuru, Kwacha, Freedom.

So it seemed to Abel, here in the half-world between night and day. He started up the path once more. What should he do? He ought to talk to someone about Sizwa. But to whom? Old Gwevu? What could the old man do, except suffer pain? The police? The police? Abel winced away from the thought.

Up at the Mission they had started the first hymn. Sizwa's

words buzzed in Abel's ears. Hymn and words alike seemed far away. Abel felt he belonged to neither. He struggled on up the path. How hot it was, how empty the fields. His leg ached and his heart overflowed with loneliness.

What should he do? What could he do?

He began to hum the music of the hymn, softly and then louder, pressing down his doubts under a fervor of singing.

40

WHILE ABEL MADE his way up to the Mission, Ben and Nella watched an American gangster film in the Town Hall. The film, which was of great antiquity, jerked spasmodically, and at times broke down altogether. When this happened the patrons whistled, stamped their feet, and shouted at the projectionist. Nella, Ben saw, was an uncritical audience. She sat with her eyes glued to the screen. The fact that the hero wore his hat continuously, and never altered his expression even when pumped full of lead, seemed to daunt her not at all. When the exit doors clanged back, and they escaped into the at least smokeless heat of the main road, she took Ben's arm with a sigh of contentment. "My, that was exciting."

He smiled down at her flushed face. Her nose shone. Her naïveté, he was surprised to find, did not irritate him. Nella was naïve, inquisitive, and provincial, her build though good was smaller than he thought desirable, and her honesty at times was downright unnerving. She was evidently not the girl for him. Yet he had to admit that during the past week, he had found himself ticking off the days of his stay in Peace Drift, with a sort of anxious frustration. Moreover, she had tricked him into an honesty as defenseless as her own. He seemed to have forgotten how to duck. Nothing but a bloody punch ball. It was inexplicable. She was pretty, but nothing special. He took her hand and turned it over, looking at their linked fingers. Her nails were small and oval, with a natural shine. Nice, capable hands. But he'd never before wanted to go to bed with a woman because she had nice hands. Much less wanted to be close to her, talk to her, take her home to meet his father, find out what she looked like in decent clothes instead of the awful things she wore here. He was annoyed with himself, puzzled, a little amused. He also realized that he still had time to turn back and get free of her.

She glanced up at him with a frankly measuring look, and he thought, there she goes again, the woman has no guile. Ten days ago that look would have sent me running for cover. Now I'm a sitting duck. So is she. Someone ought to protect us. He sighed and said, "When are you going to ask me to supper?"

"I was thinking, Ben, perhaps it's a bad idea. We might be better to let this go."

He was startled at how much the words hurt, and said quickly, "No, I don't think so."

They were strolling past the Hotel, and the light fell on her face. Her lower lip was thrust out in concentration. She said nothing, and he persisted, "You mean, because of your father?"

She shook her head.

"He hasn't changed his mind about asking me?"

"No."

"You, then?"

"Perhaps."

"Listen," he walked more quickly, forcing her to hurry, "listen, you may as well take a chance on it. Ask me."

"All right. Wednesday?"

"Umh."

They reached the river and turned off along the path that led to Ebenezer's back gate. They passed houses, their backs turned like grumpy old men. Even by the water there was no respite from the heat. The moon struck lambent fire from the willow branches.

At the gate they stopped, and Ben lifted Nella's face between his hands and kissed her with great and tender care. At last she said, "No, stop."

"Listen, again," he said. He chose the right words of affection and said them to her, my dear, my heart, my little dove. She smiled, putting her hands on his shoulders, and listened as carefully as he spoke, storing up the words to think about later, but she gave him no words of her own.

Nevertheless, when she slipped off toward the house, he watched her out of sight with satisfaction. Walking home along the river, he began to rehearse in his mind what line he should take when he dined with her father.

41

BEN WAS AMONG the first to arrive in Church. He found a seat at the back, and watched for familiar faces. Julius Kruger, Mr. and Mrs. Loubscher from the Ridge, Mannie Reimer, and several others to whom he could not put a name. Karl Ebenezer took his place diagonally in front of Kruger. Ben could see the strong planes of Ebenezer's profile, the prominent cheekbone and hollow temple. Nella had something of her old man, after all.

The air was warm, still, and green, like water in a fish tank. The congregation sat motionless in an unsuccessful attempt to lower the rate of perspiration. Ben ran a finger around inside his collar. The things one did to impress a girl's father.

His gaze strayed to the pulpit. It was the one beautiful object in the Church. Must be pretty old. Perhaps came from Holland? Idly he imagined it surging and bobbing like driftwood on advancing tides of frontiersmen.

The service began, taking him by surprise. He jerked upright, looking round guiltily, as if he felt his mother's accusing eye. He found he was thinking in Afrikaans, a child again, over-taken by that stern discipline that was missing in the Anglican community.

Here, he reflected, was the backbone of Afrikanerdom, its re-ligious discipline. It was a strength and a weakness. The Afri-kaner tended to make religion of everything that most nearly concerned him, from politics to rugby. At best he was a cru-sader, dedicated, brave and idealistic. At worst, a bigot and a bully.

Prayer and praise continued. Ben thought, I am half taking part, and half an onlooker. I haven't yet found my identity . . .

Dominee Bond was mounting the pulpit. Ben was shocked by his appearance. He moved slowly, and his face was putty-colored except for the purple shadows under the eyes.

Now he stood with his hands clasped on the rail before him. His eyes moved over the assembly, and in that moment, some-thing in him communicated with those watching him, some-thing that rang in the silence like a startled cry. Then he said, in his deep, clear voice, "It is written in the tenth chapter of the Gospel of St. Matthew that Jesus said to his disciples, 'Do not imagine that I have come to bring peace on earth. I have not come to bring peace but a sword. Indeed I have come to sow discord between a man and his father, between a daughter and her mother, and between a daughter-in-law and her mother-in-law. A man's enemies will be the people of his own household. A man who loves his father or mother more than me is not worthy of me; he that loves son or daughter more than me is not worthy of me; he that does not take his cross and follow in my steps is not worthy of me. He that wins his life shall lose it, and he that loses his life for my sake shall win it.' "

He paused, put up a freckled hand and passed it slowly over his mouth. In a louder voice, he said, "Yesterday, two of my oldest friends came to see me, and each in turn asked my ad-vice. I gave certain answers, but when I was alone again, I found that I had not given guidance, but had received it."

His glance once more touched them, lightly, almost abstractedly, and he said, "I realized, last night, that it is possible I have come to the end of my work among you; that it may become obligatory for me to retire from my ministry."

In front of Ben, Kruger heaved his heavy shoulders forward. A woman in the front row of seats dropped her handbag and the contents rattled across the floor. Bond's hands ran apart along the pulpit rail, slid together again. He said, "Obviously, you deserve an explanation of such a statement. I will try to give one, although it isn't easy . . .

"Well, you know, really, what my life has been. Most of it has been spent in this valley. I was born in Peace Drift, when it was only a village. The rail tracks came only as far as the Halt, and there were fields where the shops are now. My parents had the house next door to our first Church Hall. I had three brothers and two sisters, so there was not much my father could bequeath in the way of property, but he did give us the legacy of his faith. He and my mother taught us that God appointed the world, each thing in its proper place. There was a place for work and play, for man and wife, adult and child, for the wise and the foolish, the black and the white. To try to unmake that law, my father said, was to offend against the fundament. And why should anyone try to alter a pattern that was orderly and peaceful, since a law that works for good is a good law?

"I grew up in a community that was simple and clear-cut. At school; at home; when I went away to University, when I traveled, when I returned to take up my ministry here, I lived in the discipline and security of our faith. I had no doubts myself, and when I addressed you, you accepted what I said without question. That was my life, and it was a happy one.

"However, God does not necessarily leave a man alone to enjoy peace of mind. Even in the Promised Land, time moves; so, here in Peace Drift, time moved and brought its changes. The village became the town, customs altered, and in the outside world, wars exploded. Theories arose to challenge my settled way of life. I think I can say I met the challenge with unchanged conviction. Remember now, I am not making an apology, nor am I claiming credit. I am giving certain facts as they occurred.

"To put it another way, in its particular and local context, the greater part of my life had been spent in the knowledge that the separation of the races, even within the Church, was in accordance with the Scriptures. Now my knowledge was called in question. I do not say this was good or bad, merely that it happened.

"My calling naturally took me among the nonwhite members of the community. I can say without offense to you that my work among them was my greatest reward, for among them I found the poor, the mourners, the hungry. It was the fruit of my labor to see them come to the Church we built for them, to see them receive the light and comfort of His word.

"I knew that certain of the laws of the land brought misery to certain of these people. Laws are not, as some people like to pretend, just pieces of paper. They are written into the lives of men, women, and children. Still, I felt these laws to be necessary. When our people at the Mission questioned me about them, I gave the answer I had always given, the same I gave to those of you who questioned me. I continued to give it, even when, in these later years, the congregation on the Ridge grew smaller, and when a new generation refused to come there at all. Once a woman said to me, 'If these things are the will of God, then He is a God for white people, and no God for one who is black.'

"You may guess how it distressed me to hear such a thing said. I knew, however, that one must not allow duty to be obscured by emotion, and that temptation often approaches in the pathetic guise. Such doubts as I had seemed to lie in the fringes of my life, connected with practical matters, and not, I thought, in the fundamental core. I was upheld for a time by faith, like a child whose head is kept above water by his father's hand, and who says, 'Look at me, swimming here, by myself.' Only when the hand is removed does the child learn the truth; that he cannot swim, that without support, he will drown.

"Don't be misled by people who tell that drowning is a pleasant end. There is a time when one beats the water and cries aloud for help.

"My drowning . . . you can say, the dimming of certainty . . . began some years ago. I don't want to detail for you the history of events, both within and without this community, that brought me to such an experience. Perhaps I was alone in it, but I think not. I think many of you were, and are, faced with a similar experience. Let us call it a trial of the spirit. It must be endured in the spirit, and solved in terms of the spirit. It is also a personal experience, in which each of us is alone.

"Events, as I say, led me to the point when I had to decide what I must do to save my life. Naturally, I prayed for help, and as often happens it was given in a way I had not foreseen.

"Yesterday these two friends came to see me. Again, I need not go into finer details of what was said. It is enough to tell you that one of them exhorted me as if I were a layman. Both suggested, at this time of crises in all our lives, that we were not merely Christians. As if we could be more than Christians, as if, for certain reasons and at certain time, we could voluntarily abstain from our mere Christianity, and our faith be suspended.

"One said it was my duty to strengthen and unite the Volk in time of trouble. The other said that though this was recognizably a time of trouble, that trouble was something external to the valley, due to the presence of an agitator in our vicinity.

"Well, I sat a long time, thinking over what these two friends had said. It occurred to me that no agitator causes more unrest, more distress, more disruption in quiet places than the human conscience. Here indeed is an element quick to seize on weakness; argumentative, intransigent, not easily silenced. It occurred to me that my own personal trouble in the town did not lie in a political dilemma, nor in its practical solution. My trouble lay in the attempt to conceal that I have doubts. It lay in the effort to pretend that there was no agitator in my mind. It lay in my own wish for peace, my desire to preserve the unity and strength of my people. It lay in silence.

"So let me now express what has remained unsaid. Let me now say that it is my own belief that in refusing to relax the color bar within the Church, we are failing in our Christian duty. That this in turn is not strengthening, but weakening, our whole people in their Christian life, and particularly the Afrikaner section of that people. That we have here shaped for ourselves the threat of destruction, not from without but from within, because we have set our loyalty to the Volk above our loyalty to the Cross.

"That is true for me, at any rate. I have come to what seems to be a division in my loyalties. Since I am a Christian I must seek the spiritual unity of my people. In the spirit, my neighbors cannot be divided into black and white, for in the spirit we are all equal and one in the sight of God. But in practice, I help to create division. That is the situation which I have put out of sight for so long, and which, if I am to save my life, I must now face.

"As I have already said, I am not seeking to advise you, but am telling you of something that has taken place in my own life.

"For some time, last night, I sat in my office. When it was dark, I left the town and walked up to the Mission. There was a service in the Church, and I stood at the back and watched the congregation. They gave me a sense of loss, of unreasonable anger, and of failure. Failure not as a layman, not in terms of safety, or social security, but failure as a Christian in terms of Christianity. I saw myself at last; an old man, deserted by the conviction of a lifetime, a failure, in danger of spiritual death. It was a bitter, bitter realization."

The predikant paused. Sweat was running down his face, and he seemed to struggle for breath. "I tell you honestly . . . I would give much . . . almost anything . . . to take refuge now in silence. But yesterday it was made plain to me that I should not take such refuge, any longer.

"My fault has lain, over the years, in counting the cost, in ignoring the plain injunctions of our Lord that we should cast our bread upon the waters, give rather than receive, and take no thought to the morrow.

"It's a hard moment, in the life of a Christian, when he is asked to consider his allegiance to God above his allegiance to family, friend, or group. But the teaching of the Gospel, in one of the hardest lessons we are given, is clear. He who saves his life, shall lose it. He who loses his life for the sake of the Lord, shall win it.

"I have spoken of my own, personal experience. If I have done wrong in saying what I have said, then my error will be questioned and corrected in the proper place and at the proper time. I am ready to leave the ministry, if that is felt to be desirable. I am not ready, however, to remain silent.

"To everything there is a season, and a time to every purpose under the heaven. For me, whatever the consequences may be, this is a time to speak."

42

BEN LEFT THE CHURCH before the end of the service. He stood alone on the wan summer turf, wondering what to do. He knew that the predikant had just made a declaration that might not only end his ministry, but might well split the community to the bone.

Would it be wiser to go home at once, before anyone else came out of Church? Bond's words would make the local people close their ranks. Ben himself would rate as an outsider, unwelcome witness of a scene that should have remained private.

Yet he felt he had a right to stay. He felt that now, everything in town was his concern, that he belonged to Peace Drift. He stood grimly waiting for the people to leave the building.

As he had expected, they wasted no time on him, but hastened past, some worried, some puzzled, some vehemently angry. Even Kruger gave him no more than a cursory glance and a curt nod.

Ben waited for Nella to appear. She stepped out through the door at last, blinked against the sun, caught sight of him, and came across.

"Well," she said, "it's done."

"You expected it?"

"I expected something. He's been worried for some time, I knew. Then my father told me they had a discussion, yesterday." She swallowed and he saw that her eyes brimmed with tears. "Why do these things happen to old men?"

Unsure whom she was thinking of, Ben said, "He believes it to be his duty, I suppose. . . ."

She rounded on him. "Oh, you don't know what you're talking about. You don't know us, you're only a visitor to the town."

"The hell I am. I was born here."

"But it isn't your home. You aren't involved, like the predikant, or my father, or me."

Ben said furiously. "The predikant may go into his own wilderness, that's his affair. Your father has problems which are his affair. And I'll play the fool with a foot in both camps, which is my affair. But I'm damned if I stand here drowning in waves of self-pity!"

Before she could answer him, a brisk step sounded behind them and Ebenezer appeared. His shoulders were stiffly erect. He held his Panama hat so firmly that the brim was crushed. As he drew near, Ben saw that the old man's mouth trembled uncontrollably. He put out a hand. "Are you all right, sir?"

"Certainly I am all right." Ebenezer's eyes gave him a sharp warning. He said to Nella, "Your hat is crooked, girl." And turning back to Ben, "I believe we are to have the pleasure of your company on Wednesday evening?"

"I'm looking forward to it."

"Good, good. Come, Nella."

Ebenezer drew his daughter away. He spoke to none of the

people lingering in the yard, but marched resolutely through the gate and up the road toward the river.

Ben watched him go.

Retreat in good order, colors flying, blast of martial music!

He decided the time had come to go back to Strasser's house. And, my boy, he told himself, if you had any sense you'd leave the area now, before this God-awful town minces you smaller than a cat's dinner.

43

As LONG AS HE was in sight of the Church, Ebenezer kept up his brisk pace, but on the river path, by the lackaday willows, he slowed and leaned on Nella's arm. She could feel how his muscles were tensed.

Only when they were back in their own garden did she ask him whether he thought the predikant would resign. Her father moved his head vaguely, as if he hardly heard her. The contours of his face were set. She wanted to put her arms around him, but she saw that his mind was already driving on beyond the personal implications of the predikant's statement. He was not considering the possibility of affront to himself. He was estimating effects not on his own emotions, but on his little kingdom of Peace Drift. His eyes roved about the garden as they walked up the path, but he did not see the magenta pride of India, nor the dusty pink and white geraniums. He saw problems, the town, people moving to this camp or that. Officials, the press, a thousand things to be weighed and dealt with. Already he was putting himself beyond the reach of Cornelius Bond. Pain was isolated by aseptic thought. Soon that whole section of his life would be neatly and finally excised.

As they climbed the steps to the porch, he said suddenly, "This polio campaign. You work in units, not so?"

"Yes, Pa."

"And the young man Nevis works with you?"

"No. On a different unit." How well Kruger had guessed her father's reaction to Ben. His friends know him better than I do, she thought. I'm the one who has the lion by the tail, and if I want to let go? If I love Ben?

Her father stood tapping his hat on the palm of his hand, studying her. He said, "One must entertain the stranger within one's gates, but one should remember that he is a stranger. Not one of us."

Although she had said the same thing a few minutes back, she burst out, "Don't, Pa."

"Don't what?" His tone was bland. She turned on him with the same anger that had roused her against Ben.

"Don't put me in a category. I'm not part of a military plan, I'm a woman, I'm . . ." she hesitated, "I'm your daughter, Pa. Isn't that enough?"

He looked at her a moment, his eyes baffled and watchful. Then he went off into the house.

She pulled the rocking chair from its corner, sank down in it, and shut her eyes. She thought, I am myself. Ben and my father must learn that. I shall go the way I want to.

A voice inquired of her, but which way is that? Where do you want to go, and with whom?

44

THE POLIO CAMPAIGN in the outer areas started the following morning. Strasser and Ben were up and dressed by five o'clock, loading equipment into the three ambulances that Strasser was using as mobile units.

Once again, Ben was impressed by Strasser's efficiency. He carried in his head every detail of a complicated and exact schedule. Nothing had been left to fate. He had even arranged for cars to follow the vans, carrying interpreters, an African policeman, record players with loud-speakers, and, in one case, a team of dancers to entertain the waiting crowds. This team sat gravely in the second car, wearing their scant traditional dress with an air of calm resignation. Contemplating the whole cavalcade, Ben was prompted to say, "What, no elephants?"

Strasser said tartly, "I would have them if I could afford them." He left Ben chuckling and went off to supervise the departure of the first ambulance, which was to cover the area west of the town.

After breakfast, they collected two African nurses from the Elizabeth Hospital, and headed north across the Ridge to Kruger's farm. Strasser seemed completely happy. He made little jokes, laughed at them heartily. Once he pointed over at the Reserve territory. "That's where the real work lies. That's the real crusade."

Ben glanced at him with some dismay. Strasser had an almost obsessional belief in the importance of his plans, he really thought the world was to be reformed by the prick of the hypodermic, hygiene, and the scientific approach. Strasser said, "Once Kruger's lot has accepted inoculation, our work will be much easier. That's the heart of old Gwevu's clan, over there, and he pulls a lot of weight."

Ben said nothing, feeling out of his depth. The response to immunization of Africans in the city had been good, but here . . . he tilted back his head, looking at the brow of the escarpment and the lower hills. Even a mile from the town, one was in a rural area. Here, earth was the reality, cement and brick the mirage. A stone leaped and clanged against the undercarriage of the ambulance. A bird flapped overhead. Its long cry streamed back . . . Africaaaaa . . . Africaaaaa . . . an omen good or bad?

At Kruger's house they found the answer. The old farmer came rapidly down to them, and said to Strasser, "Here's trouble. I tried to telephone you, but you'd already left."

Strasser's smile faded. "What trouble?"

"The children are not here. The adults are, because I told them to be, but they've left the children at home."

Strasser's hands flew up. "Utter incompetence. I've publicized for weeks that the children are what we want most."

Kruger shrugged. "You can talk to them if you like."

They started toward the stable yard. Strasser said, "But, I cannot understand it. Last week, when I checked with the area assistants, they reported that people were well-disposed. What can have gone wrong?"

"It seems someone has spread the story that inoculation will make the children sterile."

"Impossible nonsense! Who can have told them such a thing?"

"Anyone. A witch doctor, perhaps. There's professional jealousy everywhere, you know."

Strasser eyed Kruger. "You don't think that is the answer!"

Again Kruger shrugged, but Strasser insisted, "You know who started this tale?"

"I can guess. You shouldn't have sacked your cook, doctor, he has a lot of friends around here."

"But I had no personal quarrel with him. I paid him a month's wages. He must have known I have to consider my work, my official position?"

"Meneer, Sizwa is not a philosopher. He sees things to suit him, not to suit you."

"We must agree to differ. I still think I was justified. However, the important thing is the polio campaign. You must admit that it is designed only to help these people?"

In the stable yard, close to the shade thrown by an ancient fig-tree, were gathered some hundred and fifty people. In their midst, seated on an upturned paraffin tin, and discoursing in a leisurely voice, was old Gwevu. He rose at Kruger's approach, and came to where the ambulance and cars were parked, waiting.

Kruger returned his greeting, and said, "Have you spoken to them again?"

"Yes. They say they don't want the medicine."

"But why?" Strasser burst out, and Gwevu's eye scanned him calmly. "They say it will make them sterile. They ask, why is it you want the young people and the children."

"I have taken the medicine myself," remarked Kruger. "Do I look like an ox, now?"

Gwevu chuckled, but waved a deprecating hand. It was plain that he had no confidence in new-fangled medicines, but was too courteous to say so. Deadlock seemed to have been reached.

Ben listened while Kruger pointed out that several of the young men showed the scars of vaccination. That this had not prevented their marrying and producing sons. Gwevu sighed, and said, "Inkosi, I've told them, but I will tell them again."

He turned to the gathering and addressed it in a clear, carrying voice, one hand moving in emphasis. The people listened in passive silence. Strasser muttered under his breath, "If we can't persuade them, we'll never get the children."

Most of the young men stood together, near the fringe of the crowd. In the broken shade their bodies were dappled, like leopards. It was clear that their minds were made up. One of them muttered something, and the remark raised a laugh from his fellows. Kruger glanced quickly toward the ambulance and the cars. His face became sharp with annoyance.

When Gwevu stopped talking, a token discussion followed. Shoulders shrugged, hands flicked in negation. Kruger stepped up to Gwevu and spoke to him rapidly. Gwevu said, with an air of delicate amusement, "I will take one of your pills, yes, but it is of no use. They have no wish to take the medicine."

Strasser said, "You are being ridiculous. Where's your authority? Order them to."

Gwevu looked at him. "Can you order them to? Is there a law that says they must take it?"

"No but . . ."

"If there is no law, how can I order?" Gwevu's voice was silky. "I will swallow a pill, out of courtesy."

He did so. One or two of the elders in the crowd followed

suit, but neither exhortation nor example could induce the bulk of the company to accept the dose. Presently they returned to their duties, some to the nearer fields, others up the paths that fanned across the valley.

The yard was empty except for the members of the campaign team. Old Gwevu, with two seniors of his family, also lingered, but withdrew to the shade of the fig tree.

Ben said, "At least the dancers haven't deserted."

Kruger turned on him. "No, my good young fool, because they all belong to the Pembe faction. That was the last straw, coming up here with your tame sheep, into the heart of the Vuli clan. One of those young men pointed out that if ever there was a sterile lot, it was your pretty boys there."

He crossed toward Gwevu, and Ben followed. Kruger, glancing at him, grunted, but made no comment. In the shade, the three Africans stood together. Kruger said something to Gwevu, who shook his head. "I'm sorry, Inkosi." There was such regret in his voice that Ben realized that the situation seemed grave to him as well as to Strasser. Kruger and Gwevu faced each other as men who have talked their way past inessentials to the heart of the matter.

Kruger said, "Where is Sizwa?"

"I don't know."

"Do you think he persuaded the young men to refuse?"

"Perhaps. Not in person, but news travels." Gwevu's tone was sad. "I'm sorry, but there it is. You and I have outlived our time, as I said."

"Not a kind saying."

"Dying men speak the truth." Gwevu put his hand on his chest. "Find Sizwa, if you can, but I think it is too late. You cannot stop the rumors, any more than you can be a young man again."

Kruger and Ben watched him move away with his clansmen. Kruger said, "Now that bloody little doctor of ours will run to the police."

This seemed to Ben an extraordinary remark. Certainly police intervention seemed desirable. Old Kruger was no doubt a law unto himself and resented any sort of authority beyond his own.

They rejoined Strasser. For the first time in their acquaintance, Ben pitied him. He said, "I see I have deceived myself. They've lost faith in me."

Kruger said grimly, "They would not have done so unless someone got at them. Make no mistake, this can blow up into a regrettable incident, as the papers have it."

Strasser snapped, "I'm not interested in that aspect. My duty is to push through immunization, and I shall do so. This is a nation-wide thing, and we are using a live vaccine. Any large community that remains without immunization is a danger to itself and to others. The campaign must proceed. I shall go to the police. They must get to the root of the matter."

His cold intensity gave evidence of why so gifted a man had won so few friends. Ben said, "You don't feel that may do more harm than good, making a martyr of Sizwa, I mean? Why not fight fire with fire? Isn't there anyone in the town, some African with influence? I was thinking of that chap at the Garage. He's an educated man, and you say he's got some sort of following. What's more, I'm pretty sure he's had polio himself. Couldn't we get him to do a spot of propaganda for us, a sort of counter-campaign? It's only an idea. . . ."

. . . "and not a very good one," said Strasser. He glanced at his watch. "I shall go straight to the police."

He climbed into the ambulance. "I shall withdraw from any conspicuous part in the plan. That will relieve the personal ill-will between myself and Sizwa."

Kruger shook his head. "Not a chance. You can't hope to dis-associate yourself from it now."

"My mind is made up." Strasser started the engine. Ben was forced to climb into his seat. The ambulance jerked forward, the other vehicles following.

They spoke little on the return journey. In town, Strasser went straight to the Police Station. Ben, after a moment's thought, walked down to the Garage in search of Abel.

45

DRIVING UP the Ridge to the Mission, early on Monday morning, Nella realized that in a short time she might encounter Dominee Bond. She had no idea what she would say to him if she did meet him. His resignation seemed impossible. Peace Drift without him could not exist.

Sure enough, as she turned into the Mission yard, the predikant's round figure emerged from the school building and approached the car. Close behind came Mr. Kumalo, a young teacher who had the polished plumpness of an aubergine, and Sister Matadi from the Hospital. The predikant rumpled his hair with one hand, and as Nella climbed out, said, "Good morning, we're in an uproar. It seems no one wants our medicine. Now what do you make of that?"

He looked tired, but quite cheerful, not at all like a man who has staged a revolt, in fact he seemed oblivious of all but the lack of patients in the yard. The schoolmaster cried, "The vaccine is mixed, everything here. We were working since five A.M. But nothing, nobody." His hands indicated an utter vacuum.

Nella said, "It's early yet."

The young man shook his head. "Only a fraction of the children are in school."

Nella said to the African nurse, "Can you explain it? Have they mistaken the day?"

"I don't think so. In the outer districts, they may make a mistake. But there have been notices in the schoolroom, and the children were told several times to take the message home to the father and mother. I was here myself on Friday and I spoke to them. It must be the parents are keeping them at home."

"Why?"

The other woman shook her head. "I don't know. But I have noticed that the children here are all from the south side of the town. That is the Pembe faction. Now why is that?" She herself was a Xhosa from far down the coast, and not involved in local squabbles.

The predikant said, "Yes, that's so. Well, perhaps there is some reason unknown to us. We must do what we can, here. The tables are ready at the far end of the hall, Sister Ebenezer."

They found a few parents and children in the hall, and completed their immunization dosage. Then they waited for over an hour, but no new arrivals appeared. At nine-fifteen, Nella decided they must move on to the next assembly point. The Africans, with their two clerical workers, packed the equipment into the ambulance. Nella moved toward her own car. Before she reached it, the predikant caught up with her. "Nella, how is your father?"

She had almost forgotten the events of the previous day. She said, "Angry."

Bond contemplated her, with a half-smile. Nella was crystal-clear, and absolute. Her laughter, tears and anger all broke like a spring from the rock of her character, limpid. He said, "Let me give you some advice. Stick to your guns. Don't take sides."

He saw that he had hit the mark. He went on, "It isn't necessary to agree with people you love, although it is, of course, what they want."

She heaved a sigh, and he said firmly, "No doubt you wish you were many miles away in another town. But let me tell you, you are lucky. Only a few people catch so much as a glimpse of the life they pass through. They come, they go, smoke on the veld. They face no issues, have no chance of reaching understanding. They are the people in the parable, blind that see not. But you have a spark of recognition in you. Give thanks for it. It lights the way."

She said rather crossly, "I only want to be ordinary. I hate change. And I'm afraid."

His face returned to cheerfulness. "Oh, as to that, love is eternal, but fear only lasts a lifetime."

When the team left the Mission, it moved to Sullivan's farm,

and from there to van Tonder's, Maxwell's, Loubscher's and
McLeod's, moving south and east round the perimeter of the
town. At each place they found the same story. A small attendance of members of the Pembe clan.

Sullivan, when asked, said he had heard his employees discussing the vaccine, saying it made people sterile. They de-
clined to tell him where they had heard the rumor. He gave it
as his opinion that it had been started as a malicious joke, and
added that it should not be hard to find the culprit. "No one
really likes agitators, because no one likes being frightened. Not
one likes them, except I suppose other agitators. Like war
hogs."

Offered a polio pill, he accepted it happily. "Take more than
that to fix me," he observed, and would have embroidered on
this theme had Nella given him the chance.

46

IT WAS TEN O'CLOCK by the time Ben reached the Garage. The
owner told him that Abel, being on late shift, would not arrive
until noon. He suggested Ben call back then, but Ben, thinking
of Strasser pleaded urgency. Turnbull then said that Abel might
be in his room at the back, or up on Railway Hill. "He spends a
lot of time watching the station yards. Likes engines, I suppose."

Ben left, conscious of the man's inquisitive stare. He called at
Abel's room, but the door was locked. He found his quarry, at
last, on Railway Hill, sitting on a slope of grass in the thin
shade of a belt of scrub. Abel held a paperbacked book in one
hand, and in the other a slab of bread and dripping. Hearing
Ben's somewhat stertorous ascent, he half rose, apparently considering escape. Ben shouted and he sank back and waited till
Ben stood on the slope just below him.

Ben said, "Can I talk to you for a moment, please?"

Abel's thin face assumed a patient resignation. He held his slice of bread apologetically, as if it might be rude to chew and swallow, but at last took a delicate bite that seemed to say, "What can I do, the hill is free?" His eyes watched politely as Ben pulled himself up into the shade.

"God, it's hot." Ben sat down, pulled off his jacket, and loosened his tie. "I'm sorry to interrupt your meal."

"It doesn't matter." Abel smiled. "I was reading. It's quieter up here." An engine whistled, and he added, "Most of the time."

Ben proffered a cigarette, which was refused. He lit one himself, leaned back on his elbow. The blue curl of smoke vanished at once against the arch of air. "You know," he began, "that I'm working with Dr. Strasser on the polio campaign?"

"Yes."

"We started on the outlying farms, today. We went to Mr. Kruger's place, first, and collected ourselves a boycott. Almost total."

He glanced at Abel. The African sat motionless, staring at the grass between his feet.

Ben said, "Have you any idea what may be behind it?"

No answer, except a flicker of the eyelids.

"I came to ask your advice. Your help. Apparently there's a rumor going round that the vaccine causes sterility. I thought you might help us to end that nonsense. Perhaps go around to the tannery and the sawmill, explain how important the vaccine is, say it can do nothing but good."

Abel said, "Why should I do that?" His voice was cool.

"You had polio when you were a child, didn't you?"

Abel smiled. "Sir, if I had two strong legs, I'd be working on a road gang, or cutting cane on the coast, or cooking someone's dinner. My leg taught me to read and write."

"And work in a Garage."

"Where I can learn about machinery, and have good hours, so that I can study." Abel looked up. His eyes were neither hostile nor friendly; merely, they waited.

"You're an educated man. You must see that this boycott can do your people no good. Tell them so."

"They might not believe me. They might only say I'm flirting with the whites, which is an insult . . . like calling a white man a liberal." He smiled faintly.

"But these situations are explosive. Sooner or later, if the boycott continues, it will stop being a joke. A man will get excited, throw a stone, burn down a hut, and we'll have bloodshed."

"It will come, fast or slow, if there is an agitator at work."

"But you can't just sit back and do nothing. You can't just . . . wait for the thing to hit you?"

Abel shook his head. He pulled a long blade of grass and wound it around his finger. "I know what I can do and what is impossible."

"Are you afraid of Sizwa?"

Abel looked up sharply. "I am either afraid of everyone, or no one. I am not sure which."

To that, Ben could find no answer. After a moment, Abel went on slowly, "In a time of unrest, a man relies on his own people. Why don't you go to your own people? Call in Saracens and guns? They can come, along that road over there. But I think it's already too late."

"You're ready to let violence take over."

"No. I hate violence. But it's a weed, doctor, it grows; it doesn't come from nowhere, from nothing. You should have cut out the root, years ago. That's why I say it's too late."

Ben rose to his feet. Below them in the yards, an engine burst into a stutter of acceleration. He said urgently, "I know it's difficult for you. I still think you should throw in your weight, however small, with what's good for your people and mine. It's a human problem, nothing else."

The dark face lifted toward him, was turned away.

"Please," said Ben, "will you speak to them?"

There was no answer. Ben's hands dropped. He said in a flat voice, "I shouldn't have wasted my breath."

He moved off down the hill. Abel watched him go. The paperback he had been reading lay forgotten on the grass. The fingers of one hand moved to caress the calf of his shortened leg.

47

As VENTER WALKED into the charge office at ten-thirty, he passed Dr. Strasser on his way out. Venter, noticing the grim set of his face, asked Mannie Reimer what was up.

Mannie said, "There's a whispering campaign being worked, against the polio teams." He repeated what Strasser had said about the events at Witteboom, and added, "We checked with Sister Ebenezer, at Sullivan's place. Same thing there, and at the Mission. Our orders are to pull in Sizwa as quick as we can."

"They think it's him?"

Mannie shrugged. "Seems the answer. Well, don't just stand there, son, we've got work to do."

48

On WEDNESDAY AFTERNOON, Abel came off shift at three o'clock. He hung up his overalls, collected a brown paper parcel from his locker, and walked down to the Railway Station, where he joined the queue waiting for the bus to the Reserve.

He had been there only a short while when he heard his name called. Glancing around, he saw Reimer, leaning from the window of a police car. Reimer beckoned and Abel went over to him. The Sergeant, he thought, was exactly like a buffalo. The same broad muzzle, blue-green eyes, and, when he was angry, the same vindictive tenacity. Now the buffalo-eyes watched him intently. "You going over to the Reserve?"

Abel affirmed that this was so.

"Why?" said Reimer.

"My maternal uncle has been ill. I'm taking him some food and medicine." Abel hoped that Reimer would not ask to examine the parcel. He was suddenly, and frighteningly, aware of the force of Mannie's anger. The fact that it might not be directed against him personally was no comfort. He stood nervously shuffling his feet.

"Where's your friend Sizwa?" The words gave Abel a sensation of being backed against the wall. He hesitated.

"Sir?"

"You heard me."

Abel gave an embarrassed laugh. "Oh—Sizwa—I don't know where he is at the moment."

Reimer's eyes studied him. His face was carved in stone, the thick fists resting on the wheel of the car were stone, he was the stone man of the Law. His silence was more threatening than any formal warning could be. Dismissed by a curt nod, Abel walked back to rejoin the queue. He watched Reimer drive away. Panic urged him to leave the railway yard, escape to his room, and take no further risks. He waited, hesitating. The bus drew up at the curb, and the conductor and driver climbed out. The woman behind Abel jabbed him sharply. "Aren't you going to move?" He entered the bus and sat down near the back.

When the conductor and driver returned, and the bus started up the hill, he thought, I can get off at the Halt. I needn't go on. But when he was asked for his fare, he paid for the full journey to the Reserve.

All the passengers except an old, deaf woman with a hen in a wicker cage, and a young boy accompanying her, alighted at the Mission Halt. The conductor, a skinny, talkative man sat down facing Abel and launched into conversation. He was in a very bad temper. Early that morning, it seemed, there had been unpleasantness. Two wide boys, town tsotsis, had tried to get away with paying half-fare. The driver had had to come around and flex his muscles before they'd pay. "Scum," said the conductor. "They come up from the Coast and try to treat us like a lot of peasants. I know that sort. Full of talk about liberation and free drink. You don't travel on this bus free, I said. I may have been born in the country, but I can tell a cent from a penny, I said. You pay the same as anyone else, or you'll get bashed." He spat expertly from the window.

The old woman took an orange from her pocket and handed it to the boy. He peeled it and broke it in two, handing the old woman half. The smell of the fruit filled the bus.

They had left the plantations behind, and now climbed through rough pastureland; and then, about three miles on, they began to lurch downhill toward the Reserve. There opened up a vista of flat, brown, shining dams, scattered over a pattern of small-holdings, patches of corn and pumpkin and wispy scrub trees. All were very brown with drought.

"What liberation?" asked Abel. The conductor, who had been cleaning his nails on the edge of a ticket, took up the thread of talk without difficulty.

"Oh, they talked some nonsense. They say there's someone up there who'll help them. A bird? I said." The conductor rubbed his nose, gazing back at Mission Hill.

"That's dangerous talk," said Abel.

"Well, I didn't talk, they did the talking. I'm not a fool and I don't want to go to jail. But the valley's full of talk. I hear it, being on the bus all day. They say this boycott is just the beginning. It's all planned by this bird in the hills, the one who broke into the store. Me, I simply tell them to shut up, when they talk like that. I'm a peaceable man. There was a fight yesterday, right here in my bus, now what do you think of that? Someone shouting, 'One man, one vote,' and someone else trying to punch his head because he was putting his foot in a basket of vegetables. The noise! That's enough, I told them,

you can all get off and vote in the road." He sucked his teeth.
"I hope they catch this bird. He's bad for business."

They reached level ground, and Abel stood up. "Can you
put me off at the next bend?" He was in fact short of his stop,
but, remembering the Sergeant's baleful curiosity, he decided
to give the conductor no clue to his destination. A talkative man
wasn't to be trusted.

As Abel swung down to the ground, the conductor leaned
out. "There's a bus back to town at ha'-pas'-five." And as he
drew away, he added with a grin, pointing skyward, "Look out
for the bird-up-there."

Abel watched the bus out of sight, and then took a narrow
path that led away from the road, up a neck of valley running
into the foothills.

49

MANNIE REIMER, on his way to Sullivan's farm, thought over
his talk with Abel. Abel, he felt, could stand watching. He was
a friend of Sizwa, and Sizwa was certainly at the bottom of the
boycott. But was Abel mixed up in it? Mannie thought not.
Abel was a type to keep out of trouble. Keen on his books and
trying to pass exams. Not much guts.

But here Mannie checked himself. Sure, Abel was scared,
but you could never be certain that sort wouldn't pull a fast
one. Abel must be kept an eye on.

This whole thing had to be done right, and done quickly.
The boycott was already in its third day. Strasser was nearly
rupturing himself, because expensive vaccine was being wasted.
You couldn't use the stuff more than twenty-four hours after
it came out of deepfreeze. Larkill was carrying on nastier than
a polecat, and the boycott was turning people sour, everywhere.

At Redcliff, Mannie obtained Sullivan's permission to question some of his workmen. He wanted to find out how the whispering campaign had started. He got no change, however. Everyone knew it was there, no one knew where it came from. Or if they knew, they weren't going to say. Afraid. That was it. Fear. Mannie's nostrils wrinkled as if the smell of fear were a positive thing, for Mannie, as a policeman, was afraid of fear. It was fear that made violence. Fear made a mob, and a mob increased fear.

Up at the farmhouse, he found time to accept a cup of tea from Sullivan. He asked Sullivan jokingly if he'd lost any more ducks. It amused him to show that he'd heard of that little incident.

Sullivan was unabashed. He shook his head. "You know something? I think your agitator stole my ducks."

"My agitator, sir? Haven't got one. Larkill's agitator, maybe."

Sullivan's round eyes brightened at this sign of a sore point. He said, "Everyone says there's an agitator."

Mannie shook his head sourly. He drained the dregs of his tea and looked up at the fold of hills above the farmhouse. "If you're right about those ducks, he's got a damn cheek."

He left soon after.

He would have been surprised to know that his remarks had piqued the indolent Mr. Sullivan to a quite unprecedented activity. He was, in fact, already busy in his photographic darkroom.

50

ABEL NEARED the end of the path. It ran now through a cleft between slabs of dank gray rock, with a sluggish stream at their base. Abel picked his way up until the gorge widened into a small amphitheater. On the left of the stream, the rock rose almost sheer, on the right was a stretch of flat ground. In the center of this was a ramshackle hut with decaying thatch.

The place had once housed a herbalist, who was convicted of poisoning several of his acquaintances. This history, and the natural threat of shadow and isolation, invested the hut with malignity. No one came here willingly.

Abel stared about him. Nothing moved. He forced himself to shout, and the sound leaped along the rock walls. Returning silence laid a gentle finger on the back of his neck.

He ducked his head through the low round doorway of the hut, stepped inside, and struck a match. The ashes of a fire lay at his feet. He bent to touch them and found them faintly warm.

There came to his ears the faint "clonk" of stones striking together under water. Someone was fording the stream. He stooped to the doorway, his hands braced against the lintel arch.

In the middle of the clearing, shaking water from a raised foot, stood Sizwa. He glanced at Abel, bent, and rolled down the legs of his trousers. Abel stepped forward, dusting smears of ash from his fingers. "So this is your home, now?"

Sizwa straightened and shrugged. His stance conveyed boredom. He was power dismissing the negligible. "I only sleep here."

Abel shivered. "It's not a very nice place."

Sizwa smiled. "That's why I chose it."

"And that," said Abel tartly, "is why I guessed I'd find you here. I worked it out, and so will the police."

Indifferently, Sizwa said, "You aren't very clever. I followed you all the way up the valley and you never noticed me. That limp gives you away."

"Well, I didn't limp all the way here to have a chat." Abel moved over to a rock and sat down, laying aside the parcel he carried. "I brought you some meat, and tobacco."

Sizwa tilted his head. "But you did come to talk."

In the enclosed space, their voices fell hollow. Abel felt he was talking in a dream. He raised his voice a little. "Now, listen, Sizwa. The police are after you. They say you started the boycott of the polio medicine. The town's like a wasp's nest."

"What's it to do with you? I told you to mind your own business."

"Did you start the boycott?" There was a patient acidity in Abel's tone, and Sizwa looked at him under his lids.

"Perhaps."

"It's not perhaps. It's yes or no. You know what you've done, surely?"

"I know what I'll discuss with you, mealie grub."

"You can talk or keep quiet. It doesn't matter to me. But you're right, I have something to say. First, you can be sure that the police will look for you here. Stories won't frighten them away. I worked it out. . . ."

"If you know how the police think," said Sizwa, shifting his weight to the other foot, "why don't you trot back to town and tell them where I am?"

"Because I came as your friend. I don't want to see you in any more trouble. And I won't let you make fools of my people."

Sizwa burst out laughing. "Your people? Who are they?"

For a moment the two watched each other, then Abel said, "Sizwa, I understand you. I know the thing that works in your heart. You can give it new names, but it's an old, old thing. What you want is power. You want a country of fighting and burning, where you think you can rule like a king. You will send men out to die for you. For you and your sort, there are always deaths."

"And for you?" Sizwa bent forward. "What must there be for you and your sort? A safe place, a hole in which to hide? You aren't a man. Go back, clean motorcars for white men and leave the way open for people with guts."

Abel rose. "You ask, who are my people? Why, surely, people like me, who want to live a proper life. We have waited so long that we have learned what it is we are waiting for. It is to stand tall among tall men. I won't allow you to set us back, to teach that Africans are only able to plow fields and mend roads. I know as well as you that life has been hard for us. But I haven't waited so long, patiently waited, so that fools like you can break me down again.

"You said, once, that the white men don't see us. Well, nor do you. You don't see me, you don't see my people. Some time there will be leaders who do see us, and see what we want. Then we won't be used and thrown away. But you aren't that leader. So I can't follow you.

"Let me tell you now, you can have until Friday to end this boycott. I give you that time because I was your friend. Until Friday. After that, if you are still making trouble, I will tell the police everything. That you are here, that you are working the boycott, that you saw the man who broke into Oakes's store. I shall help the police to prove everything against you, and I will persuade the factorymen and the men at the mill to oppose you. I can do it. I know that. I can do it because I understand you."

Sizwa laughed again, and swung his arm. "Run home, little lame man, you frighten me to death! Run home to the police."

Abel bent down, picked up the parcel from the ground and placed it on the rock. "I'll leave these. Remember what I say, Sizwa. You have two days."

Sizwa was still laughing, his dark red mouth turned up to the sky. The sound echoed round the rock walls, fell back from them, trembled in the earth, as if Africa itself mocked the lame man.

Abel made his way back down the valley to the point where the bus would collect him.

The sun had gone down. The Reserve was a place of shadows, blue, green, ocher. Somewhere out of sight, a young boy was singing.

Abel was very tired. He sat down by the roadside to wait for the bus.

IN THE FIRST DAYS of the boycott, Ben remained something of an onlooker. He had come to work, and it seemed there was to be no work for him to do.

But he knew that he had moved a long way from the half-deliberate nostalgia of his first day in the town. More and more, he identified himself with Peace Drift and its inhabitants.

He listened to their talk in the Hotel Bar, in the streets, and on the farms at which he and Strasser made their abortive visits. There was no doubt of the tension they felt. One or two, like the man Oakes, took refuge in wild words. The bigots, black and white, blamed the boycott on the objects of their bigotry. Puritan blamed Catholic, worker blamed boss, each political party blamed the next.

Part of Ben's mind protested against the absurdity of the situation. For there was much that seemed to him absurd. Absurd that old Dominee Bond, so kindly, tending his roses and his flock with the same air of childish happiness, might become the victim of a witch hunt. Absurd that civic bodies should wrangle. Absurd that the dismissal of a wayward cook should disrupt an entire community.

He thought of what Abel had said. In time of trouble, people took refuge with their own kind. He remembered Abraham's warnings about fragmentation. With growing anxiety, he watched the town crack along the lines of old controversies, and then disintegrate into sullen, sour, and potentially dangerous factions.

It was this that made him realize that Peace Drift, absurd or not, was a microcosm. Here, in this sleepy dorp, was the cell of the national body. Malignity might begin here as well as anywhere else.

He knew, too, that each day made a personal escape more

difficult. He must decide soon whether to leave the town and return to the crowded isolation of Johannesburg, or remain in Peace Drift, which now took on the aspect of a gladiatorial arena.

It was Nella who decided him. He saw her only for a short time each day, and then their conversation was mostly of the hamstrung polio campaign. She referred only once to her own problems. They centered around what Dominee Bond had said on Sunday. Her little society was suffering the repercussions of his words. Nella was unhappy, she had withdrawn from Ben her endearing candor, and her smile was a rarity.

To leave Peace Drift became, simply, to leave Nella uncomforted.

In this light, Ben considered his undertaking to dine with the Ebenezers on Wednesday. He half thought of calling it off, but decided that that would solve nothing.

Walking along the river path to fulfil the engagement, he thought he would play things safe. Avoid implication. Avoid all controversy. No religion, no politics. A nice, polite, safe line, that was it.

But as soon as he was through the front door, he saw that it would not be left to him to direct the path of conversation. Ebenezer had other ideas, and Ebenezer was undoubtedly master in his own house. His taste was everywhere supreme. Stern daguerreotypes of bearded patriarchs; dusty chenille curtains; rows of leather-bound philosophy in the book shelves, and in the center of the mahogany dinner board, a vase of faded everlastings. None of this, Ben felt, could be of Nella's choosing.

Ebenezer, standing to carve a roast duck, ended his polite preliminary sparring and moved straight into the danger zone. What, he wanted to know, was the truth about the boycott? Was it true that the Vuli refused immunization, while the Pembe accepted it? Was the boycott politically inspired? What, in Ben's view, were the proper countermeasures to adopt?

The old man spoke suavely, but under his sharp eye Ben

discarded the last of his illusions. In this town Ebenezer was certainly omnipresent, if not omnipotent. He was on to Ben. Knew how he felt about Nella, knew his political leanings, knew or guessed at his relations with Strasser. There was no hope of avoiding issues. Ebenezer had foreseen such an attempt, and blocked it firmly. Nella, perhaps, might be allowed to choose her loyalty, but her father would make sure it was a deliberate, conscious choice.

Swallowing a mouthful of duck, Ben said, "Strasser has handed the matter over to the police. I don't think that's the complete answer, though. Not in the long run. It does nothing to end the unrest which allows such a boycott to develop."

Ebenezer bent a considering look on the young man. He thought he looked uncomfortable, but also obstinate. Was that what appealed to Nella? More than a clear eye and a quick smile, this underlying determination? A phrase of Kruger's came to his mind. "Some day you'll meet an opponent worthy of your steel. Respect him." Was this that opponent, across the table?

Ebenezer smiled faintly. "I agree with you, one should fight fire with fire. The best way to counter a whispering campaign is to silence it with the truth, declaimed loudly through accepted media. Don't you think so?"

Ben seemed dubious. "You mean, publish and broadcast denials that the vaccine is harmful?"

"Nothing so negative. That might really strengthen the rumors. No, I mean that our accredited representatives among the Bantu must explain, quietly and reasonably, that the campaign is positively beneficial, and the boycott pointless and destructive. These things are best done through the proper authorities, don't you think?"

Ben smiled at him. This mention of the proper authorities . . . Did the old devil know, or was he guessing, that Ben had made his own approach to the African, Abel? He tried to think who might have carried the tale. Who had been present when first he suggested the idea to Strasser? Kruger? Not by nature a talebearer, one would have thought. Strasser himself? Too much of a fence-sitter. Possibly one of the members of the team, a Pembe dancer for instance. Well, so Ebenezer was well informed. And if he wanted a scrap, he could have it. He said, "Medically speaking, I feel the immunization is so important that I would use any means of ending the boycott, official or unofficial."

Ebenezer nodded. "Indeed? But I doubt whether indiscriminate, individual attempts are ever much good. In fact, I'm sure they are useless in the Africa of today. One must regularize, regularize. It's unwise to allow . . . ah . . . enthusiastic amateurs . . . to take matters into their own hands."

"Even when the proper authorities are distrusted by the people?" said Ben. "Surely, in an emergency, there's room for discretion?"

"In an emergency, there is more than ever need for recognized authority." A velvet gleam appeared in Ebenezer's eye. "Nominated Bantu authorities are, of course, a newish concept. They are bound to meet with a certain die-hard opposition. Once firmly established, they will be accepted by everyone."

Ben saw the abyss open. He glanced at Nella. She sat with her eyes on her plate. Fine thing, he thought, if I throw down the glove to her old man the first time I cross the threshold. With something of an effort he turned the conversation to safer ground.

During the rest of the meal, Ebenezer followed this lead, but afterward, when they moved out on the stoep to drink coffee, he returned to the attack. He forced Ben to express opinions on the subjects he had thought to avoid. He was an excellent debater, tenacious as the Old Man of the Sea, his convictions supported by specialized information, his arguments developed with close logic. Although Ben strove to retain his calm, he felt himself grow hot and intense. The only comfort was that Ebenezer too lost his aloofness. They were long past shadowboxing, now, and argued about basic principles. It was clear to all three on the verandah that the point being established was that, on all matters of importance, Ben and his host stood diametrically opposed to each other.

Nella sat a little apart, her face in shadow. She seemed to be watching the river that burned a flat silver beyond the garden boundary.

Did she realize, or admit, that the two men were engaged in an undeclared battle for her loyalty? As Ben turned back to Ebenezer, the old man stabbed the air with a finger. "Dr. Nevis, you are a Liberal."

"I am not. I don't, for example, support one-man-one-vote."

"Of course . . . you, er . . . qualify your principles."

"I qualify the vote. Qualification is my principle."

"And you follow that to its logical conclusion? That in time Africans must be allowed to dominate the politics of this country?"

"Domination implies injustice. I believe in constitutional safeguards, as you very well know, sir. Moreover, I think that the white man is too important to this continent to become redundant."

"In spite of the fact that he has become so in other parts of Africa?"

"I don't believe he has. He's frivoled away his prestige, lost out to Communism, just as Britain and France and America did in the Far East, because he failed to understand what it was his compatriots needed. Although I'm sure white skills and techniques are important to Africa, they will be supplied by the people most acceptable to Africans. That is where we must pit ourselves against Communism. I mean to be among those whites who are acceptable. I believe that we have been caught up in a process of history. This is a shrinking world. If we wanted to avoid the present crisis, we should have begun several centuries ago. The *Golden Hind* and the *Dromedaris* should never have been allowed to sail, there should have been no Columbus, no Stephenson, no Wilbur Wright and no Yuri Gargarin. Now we can't go back to a golden age when east was east, etcetera. China is next door to Paris, and the world is conditioned by ties of trade, and by an international flow of ideas. It's no longer practical to be an isolationist, even if it's possible . . . which I don't believe it is."

Ebenezer took a silver case from his breast pocket, extracted a cheroot, and lit it. As the match flared, Ben could see in his face not only antagonism, but a strange, secret appreciation.

The old man said, "Doctor, at least you're an honest man. You are wrong, of course, but at least you realize that there is a crisis in Africa. That is more than can be said for most people, who think we can drift along without making any alterations or sacrifices whatever. Luckily for this country, however, you are in a minority. You will not be given the chance to implement views that would undoubtedly destroy us. The people of South Africa have rejected multi-racialism, as they reject Communism."

"The electorate has. What about those without a vote? Have they rejected it? It seems to me that whatever you or I think, their views will provide the ultimate answer."

"The nonwhite races," said Ebenezer firmly, "are not citizens of the Republic. When they are established as citizens in their own territories, governing themselves . . . independent states within the larger boundary of southern Africa . . . then there will be a proper acknowledgment of the way we have met this huge challenge of our day. Then there will be a proper gratitude."

He rose to his feet. "Well, if you will forgive me, I'm rather tired. Come again and see us. I've enjoyed this talk. Nella, don't forget the lights when you go to bed."

He disappeared into the house. Ben went over and sat on the bench beside Nella. "I'm sorry. I didn't mean to spend the evening arguing."

"He wanted it." Her voice sounded sad, and he put his arm around her shoulders. "Perhaps he doesn't think I'm worth bothering about."

"He thinks he's right. He's convinced he's right, and that right will always triumph. It's simple for him."

He took her hands. "I'm just as convinced as he is. Just as serious. He feels now he can beat me at his own game, but what if I show signs of success?"

Her hands twitched in his and he tightened his grasp. "You understand, Nella, what you may be letting yourself in for?"

"I don't want to think about it." She moved her shoulders restlessly. "I hate quarreling . . . I won't take sides, Ben."

He sighed, wondering how long she could continue to think that way.

Drawing her to him, feeling her respond to his kiss, he was conscious of a small, treacherous satisfaction. Here was one argument that Ebenezer could not counter. In the pull of the flesh lay his greatest advantage.

52

ON THURSDAY MORNING, Strasser decided to abandon the campaign in the areas north of the town, and concentrate on the southern farms, where Pembe labor was in the majority.

Ben felt this to be a vain hope. The boycott seemed to have set firm over the whole valley. Strasser, with his sharp tongue and aloof manner, did not have the popular appeal to defeat it. But one could hardly tell him so, and accordingly the teams set out early in the morning. This time, each was accompanied by a native policeman.

The first stand reached by Ben's unit was a wind-blown hill top in one of the poorest parts of the territory. A small group of people were assembled, and Ben saw that they were a dirty, slovenly lot, and their huts, further down the hillside, neglected and tumble-down. He told his helpers to set up their equipment, and sent the interpreter to invite custom. After a few moments this man returned at a trot. "They're bad people, sir," he said. "Very poor, rude people. They don't want us. I think we must try the next place." He looked frightened, and Ben, knowing him to be a cautious soul, said, "I'll go up myself and talk to them. You'd better come with me."

They advanced up the slope. The people at the top neither moved nor spoke. The wind plucked at their scant clothing. Ben understood why the interpreter was nervous, and why the Pembe were not generally liked. An unattractive lot, slack-mouthed and sly. They smelled powerfully unwashed. When Ben offered a greeting, they preserved their ungracious silence.

The interpreter did his best, proving quite eloquent, but the spokesman of the group repeated his refusal. They had been told by their employer to be at the assembly point, and they were here, but they knew their rights. They did not have to swallow the medicine, and they would not. They would like to get back to their work at the earliest possible moment.

While this altercation went on, Ben fell to watching a child on the edge of the crowd. It was painfully thin, its belly distended, its eyes those of an old man. Wanting to talk to it, he crouched down and extended a hand. The child stared, and when Ben spoke, backed away. He put his hand into his coat pocket and found a tube of fruit drops, which he proffered to the child. Its eyes brightened, it darted forward, both hands cupped together to receive the gift.

Ben dropped the sweets into the child's palm, but before the child could unwrap them, a man darted forward and snatched them and threw them down the hillside. He then turned, shouting at Ben and the interpreter, his arm raised.

Ben was unable to follow what he said, but it was evidently hostile. The interpreter shouted back, waving both arms. The crowd began to press forward. The rancid smell of their bodies was overpowering. Ben said, above the clamor, "What's wrong?"

The interpreter made no answer, continuing to argue with the aggressive man. Several voices joined in. Out of the corner of his eye Ben saw the native policeman and the two African clerks coming up the hill at a run. He took a step or two away, and signaled the policeman and his companions to stay where they were. Then he returned to the throng and waited for the shouting to die down.

This happened quite suddenly. Yells became mumbles, the crowd thinned, and the aggressive man marched away towards his hut, with the child.

Ben said to the interpreter, "What was that about?"

"They thought you were giving the child one of our pills. They say you would like to put a spell on them."

"So I would," said Ben. "However, there's nothing to do but move on. You were quite right, I should have taken your advice."

They returned to their vehicles and climbed in. As they drove past the end of the settlement, however, a shower of small pebbles banged against the ambulance, one shattering Ben's window. The policeman demanded they should stop and find the culprits, but Ben refused. He had conceived a dislike of the place and its unpleasant inhabitants, and he had no wish to provide fuel for their fires.

He told the rest of the team to say nothing, but this was lost counsel. The story got around in no time, with embellishment, and whereas the people of Peace Drift accepted it as the characteristic nastiness of one small family group, the people outside took it for stone-throwing, which, as everyone knows, is important, significant, and of universal interest.

53

EARLY ON FRIDAY morning, a reporter on the Hopetoun newspaper told his editor that he had had a telephone call from a contact of his, saying there was a big story building up in Peace Drift.

The editor, Cochrane, who was a cautious man and already overworked, asked why the hell Ballinger wanted a contact in a place like Peace Drift. Ballinger replied that Oakes had given him some stories in the past, and added that, in his opinion, Oakes was currently unhinged. "Told me his shop's besieged by hostile natives, and they're all due to be murdered in their beds. He says there's a boycott of the polio campaign. He says the police are being stoned, and it's all caused by an agitator in the hills."

"Oh, go away," said Cochrane.

"To Peace Drift? I could do with a break. And it might be straws in the wind, mightn't it?"

"Might be wind," retorted Cochrane. "Here I try to keep my nose clean, and you come with Zulu Rebellions. You can check up with the authorities there, but don't go making alarm and despond, for Christ's sake."

Ballinger drifted off. He was a conscientious young man, despite his air of indolence, and exercised discretion. But it is difficult to obtain information without giving it, and by that evening, the residents of Peace Drift knew that their private affairs were of public interest.

"They're all right, they won't publish any nonsense," said Larkill to Ebenezer, who called in to see him early on Saturday.

"At the moment," retorted Ebenezer, "I am concerned with deeds, not words. I suggest you take strong action. Why have we no police reinforcements? I want this man Sizwa arrested, and I want this other creature who burgled the store arrested too, and in record time, please note. We can't have this town turned into a circus any longer. We must have law and order, and that is your job, Captain Larkill."

Larkill, who had, after all, urged strong action some while back, was left with the inference that he was slack and inefficient. He vented his spleen on his subordinates, engaging them in an exhausting and fruitless search of a number of dead-end valleys.

On Saturday night, however, it was known that reinforcements were being sent, and later they arrived, five riot trucks,
snub-nosed, the back portions enclosed with wire.

Their advent, and the efforts of the local men, proved finally
to the townsfolk that they were threatened by dangerous and
desperate criminals. The timid became nerve-ridden, the aggressive openly belligerent. Archie Oakes's hysteria threatened
to start an epidemic.

54

PROBABLY IT IS TRUE that, in any village drama, the cast remains constant. A crisis calls on the same few virtues and vices,
and it's seldom that a guest star appears to take a leading role.

So now, as might have been foreseen, Larkill bullied, Oakes
flustered, Strasser alienated affections; while Ebenezer regu-
lated, Mannie Reimer calmed, and Abrahams increased good
will.

Mannie had always exemplified the law at its best, unbiased,
humane, and effective. People were prepared to put their trust
in him, and this went for the odd informers who make no small
contribution to police work. Mannie knew from them that
Sizwa was constantly on the move through the area. He had
left the Reserve on Wednesday night. He was now south of
the town, now north. Always just out of reach. There was no
doubt he was being helped by certain of his clansmen, but
not, it seemed, by old Gwevu. That disciplinarian had expressed quite clearly his aversion to Sizwa's actions, calling
them pointless, foolish, and malevolent. Gwevu in his own way
represented law and order, and greatly disliked having his authority challenged by his grandson.

It was, Mannie knew, only a matter of time before Sizwa

was arrested. But as he said to Julius Kruger, who called in to see him at his office, "My real worry isn't with that bastard. It's the people here that frighten me. Bad-tempered and scared. And I'm frightened something'll spark off faction fighting between the Vuli and the Pembe. I'm scared someone'll set fire to huts or something. With the fire hazard so high, that could mean big trouble. I can't make out what's got into this town."

Kruger shook his pendulous cheeks. "Where the carcass lies, there will the vultures gather."

"We're not dead yet, though, Oom."

"Sick, the predikant says." Kruger's small blue eyes were thoughtful. "You ever seen vultures, Mannie, waiting for something to die? Hopping closer all the time?"

Mannie shrugged off this flight of fancy. "Well, I'm a policeman, not a predikant." He pulled out a handkerchief and mopped his forehead. "Man, this heat! I sweat like a pig. Rots the strap of my watch."

"Paper says we can expect hot winds. Keep the fire-spotters busy. Nice, eh?"

Mannie sighed. "All we need, Uncle. All we need."

55

ABEL TOO HEARD news of Sizwa's movements, and it filled him with apprehension. Never had he known such confusion of mind as he knew now. He slept badly, dreaming of Sizwa. Faces not his own seemed to watch him from the shining metal of the cars he worked on. Voices chirruped like crickets in the machinery. People like you, they said, only want a safe place.

Oh, how true it was. Never had he loved his room so much, his own place with his books, and the nice quiet little yard where no one came to bother him. Now even the yard was full of shadows, urging him this way or that, the young doctor, Sizwa, the man in the hills. All right there in his yard, talking and pushing him around.

There was no quiet.

He had given Sizwa until Friday. Two long days wore thin and died, Friday was here, undeniably, and there was a new rumor that Sizwa was south of town, making a nuisance of himself.

During his lunch break, Abel took a grip on his courage and went across to the tannery.

56

IN HIS OFFICE, Abrahams studied Abel thoughtfully. Funny little figure, he thought, almost as funny as me. Should be we were wearing little velvet coats, like the animals in children's books.

The two knew each other from the days when Abrahams first arrived in town to take over the tannery—with the effects of malaria on him, and all his possessions in one tin trunk. They had quite a lot in common. Ambition. And, thought Abrahams, fear. He's as scared as I am.

He said, "Why do you want to talk to them?"

"About the boycott."

Abrahams blew out his cheeks. "The strength of the crocodile is water. Why do you want to dive in? Could be we'll be in trouble, holding meetings. . . ." He drummed his short fingers. "O.K. You go down in the yard and speak to my foreman. They'll be in the canteen, having lunch. If they'll listen, you can talk."

Abel started for the door. Abrahams called after him, "Don't keep them too long, now."

When Abel had gone, he sat up for some time. Foolishness.

So he was a fool. That wasn't news. He got up and walked to
the window in time to see Abel talking to the foreman, Albert.
Albert glanced up at the window. Abrahams raised his hand
and nodded. The two Africans moved over to the canteen
building and disappeared through the door.

57

THE CANTEEN was a large, square room, with several tables,
and chairs, and a counter at the far end. Abel looked about
him, while Albert called the men together. There were about
thirty of them present, some Vuli, some Pembe, all men who
thought of themselves as town dwellers.

They stared at Abel, as they shuffled forward to the longest
of the tables. They wore the careful expressions of people ready
to listen but on their guard. Abel moved to the head of the
table, and they took their places, cleared their throats, and
looked grave.

Abel had had two days to think out what he'd say. Now all
thoughts flew away. He stood for a moment or two, tongue-
tied. Then, abandoning all hopes of oratory, he launched
straight into his plea, telling them of his meeting with Nevis
on Railway Hill.

They listened attentively, which encouraged him. He quoted
old Gwevu, and declared that the boycott was wicked, dangerous, and against the interests of the community. "It is not true
that this medicine causes impotence. We have seen it given to
the white children at the Clinic. It was the same medicine,
from the same bottle, we know that. We know it in the town,
but do the people on the farms know it? It is for us to tell them
the truth. We must take the lead, persuade everyone to accept
these pills."

"What is it to do with us?" said a sharp voice at the far end of the table. Abel knew the speaker, a thin man whose right cheek was disfigured by a cicatrice. The man went on. "We have had nothing to do with the boycott, on the farms or in the town. Why get mixed up in it? We're all right here, good jobs, good pay, we don't want to get mixed up in anything."

Abel said coldly, "I know you have good conditions. If you remember, Moses, I explained them to you, when at first you could not understand them."

The thin man scowled. "Well, I still think it's better to have the cash, and no meals provided here. But we are not speaking of that now."

"I agree. We are speaking of medicine. Now, have you sent your son to the Clinic? You call me the lame one behind my back, but have you done anything to protect your boy against lameness?"

Someone further down the table chuckled. Moses was known to have a son on whom he doted.

"You sent him?" repeated Abel.

Moses gave a sheepish nod. Abel said, "Then you surely agree that others should do the same for their children?"

"That's all very well," a fat man with a high voice leaned forward. "But Moses doesn't belong here. He's not a Vuli and he's not a Pembe. Now I'm a Pembe. And this is Sizwa's boycott and Sizwa's a Vuli. Where I live, on the north side of the town, a lot of people sympathize with Sizwa. If my wife takes the children up to the Mission, perhaps on the way home they'll be frightened, or even stoned. Perhaps my house will be burned down. Perhaps, in the nature of things, I'll fight back. Then it's off to jail for me, and how does that help my children? I agree, the thing is to keep out of this whole business. Keep out of trouble."

Abel spread his hands. "Friend, do others respect you? Have you a voice in the town? Are you the first to be praised? No, no, nothing of the sort. And I will tell you why. It's because you always keep out of trouble. You have no authority in your own tribe, because you live in town, and know very little about cattle. And in town, where you live, you hold your tongue. Now there are many of us like you. Thoughtful people, who know right from wrong, and know quite well what should be done. We have waited a long time for good pay and good housing, and now that it's come, we have to see we don't lose it by sitting on the backside and doing nothing.

"In the past you have complained because you have no chance to settle your own affairs. Now a chance comes to us, to stop a thing that is evil and foolish, and you tell me we must do nothing. Keep out of trouble.

"Shall I tell you again who will suffer if the boycott continues? Not the tsotsis, but people like you and me. We'll be caught by the grindstone. There'll be raids in the middle of the night. We'll be afraid to see our children go off to school. We are against that, all of us. Then we should show it. We must show ourselves to be worthy of respect and of responsibility."

He looked along the table, at faces stubborn, thoughtful, indifferent. He brushed his hands over the surface of the table, thinking that he did not care about these people, did not want their friendship. He wanted to go back to his own place, and eat his meal alone, and be at peace.

Moses suddenly thrust his face forward. "You were Sizwa's friend. Why have you chosen to speak against him now?"

The faces lifted toward him. He must answer quickly, but no words came. Moses was smiling, pleased with the point he'd made. But Albert, who up till now had listened in silence, rapped the table. "Just a moment."

He blew a cloud of smoke in the air, balancing the moment while the men turned towards him. Then he said, "When I was a child they used to tell us a story of two men, great companions, in the same regiment together. In the singing of praises there was little to choose between them, so great was their repute as fighting men. But at last, in a certain battle, one lost his courage. The other saw it, and rather than let his friend be disgraced, and slaughtered by others who had no feeling for him, he himself stabbed his friend. Now you must know that Sizwa has disgraced himself. He will be arrested, and I say, the sooner the better, because I have no feeling for Sizwa. Abel here has perhaps chosen the way of a friend. We do not know, of course, but that is how it seems to me."

Abel said, "I spoke to Sizwa. I warned him that if he continued to agitate, and to involve us, I would come to you and I would also speak to the police." He saw astonishment in their faces, but he no longer cared whether they thought him treacherous. He said, "You are men who have some influence. If you also have good sense, you will do as I suggest, and help to end this trouble."

Before they could answer, he turned and walked out of the room. He heard murmuring break out behind him, and started to close the door, but it was tugged from his hand and Albert slipped through and joined him.

"Well," said Albert, "I think they'll do as you ask."

Abel shrugged. "I don't care what they do. I'm going home."

"But not, I suppose, to the police?"

"No. I can't do it."

"You should, for your own sake. And for everyone's good."

Abel shook his head. He left Albert and hurried away across the yard. He felt sick, and it was nothing to do with the rank stench of hides.

Why had he acted against Sizwa? Why was a peaceable man expected to act in such a way? Resentment surged in him, over Sizwa, the authorities, the young doctor. So absorbed was he in his own thoughts that he ran full into the doctor himself, on the pavement outside Strasser's gate. Ben started to say something, but Abel pretended not to hear, and hurried on to the yard behind the Garage.

Home at last. He stood trying to regain his composure. A hot wind was blowing from Railway Hill, it dried the sweat on his forehead and the breath in his lungs.

He said aloud, "Sizwa, go away now, while there's time."

In the immense and impersonal arch of the sky, his words vanished without trace.

58

DURING THE NEXT few days the boycott waned. Whether this was due to the efforts of the police, to the reassurances of Ebenezer, to Abel's action, or a combination of all these things, is a matter for conjecture; but certainly, Strasser was able to report that an increasing number of Africans were attending for immunization. He told Ebenezer, whom he met one morning in the Bank, that the boycott was dying a natural death, a description which Ebenezer found singularly naive.

Throughout this time, the heat wave banked up, a hot wind blowing steadily from the east. It seemed that the heat became absolute, a pure flame licking the crucible of the town. In the dryest part of the valley, to the south, grass fires broke out constantly. Northward the spotter-plane was persistent as a bumblebee. The air was painful to breathe. The townsfolk sealed doors and windows against the dust-sharpened gusts, pavements threw up a quivering mirage, and tarred surfaces became mucous. Even under the trees the light assumed an acid green brilliance.

Only the early morning was bearable. On Saturday, Ben, tired of tossing on a sweaty sheet, rose at five and walked around to Ebenezer's house. The servant who answered his knock told him that Nella was awake, and in a short while she appeared, in a cotton wrap, her hair in two plaits on her shoulders.

She ran down the steps to the lawn where he waited. "Is something wrong?"

He smiled. "I'm hot, and I have no car. Take me for a swim before breakfast?"

She gave a gasp of exasperation. "You! I though someone was dying!"

"I shall very likely die if I don't lower my body temperature. Come on, get your things and we'll go up to the Cascades."

Her frown vanished. "All right. Go down to the Garage. I won't be long."

He waited, leaning against the Garage wall. Presently Nella joined him. She wore a green swim suit under a white toweling wrap. Her hair was coiled on top of her head.

"We'll go fetch your shorts," she said.

"Must we?"

"Certainly. The Cascades are on Sullivan's farm."

"Very well, if Sullivan's so prudish. Your father will be annoyed, however. . . ."

"Why?"

". . . if we go all the way to Johannesburg, just to fetch my shorts."

She said uncertainly, "You're teasing me? You've got them on underneath?"

He smiled down at her. Even when she blushed her skin was smooth and cool. "Whatever you say," he agreed amiably. A feeling of great contentment spread over him.

They drove up the Ridge, past Sullivan's farmstead, to the foot of the red kloof. The stream, falling in a series of water chutes and pools, was a favorite bathing place, and Sullivan allowed the townspeople free access to it.

They climbed the steep path beside the water to the largest of the pools. Some fifty feet across, its fast-flowing volume was ice cold, even in summer.

They swam for about ten minutes. They were in the lee of the kloof, sheltered from the wind. The water swirled past them, streaked with foam, and in the surrounding bush birds flashed and chattered. When cold brought an ache to their bones, they pulled themselves on to a flat boulder in midstream.

Nella rubbed herself with her wrap, stamping her feet and gasping. Ben sat down, watching the water run from his limbs, to dry almost at once on the hot rock.

A patch of pale blue silky sky was visible. Nella stared at it, sighing. She said, "Oh how happy I am." She turned and laughed at Ben, and slid down beside him.

He took her hand, kissed the fingers and the palm. "We're in love, you know."

She nodded. He put his arm around her shoulders. Her flesh, still cool, was deeply sunburned. "You're like a chestnut," he said, "brown and shiny." She leaned against him, and he added, "But softer, I'm glad to say."

They stayed an hour at the pool, diving into the water, drying again in the sun. At half-past six Nella twisted her hair up and secured it, and put on her wrap. "Come, we must hurry. It's nearly breakfast time."

They took the path down. Nella hurried along in front, turning her head to peer about her. Once she tripped and giggled at herself.

When they emerged into the open, the heat struck them with full force. The ground burned, and Nella broke into a trot, heading for the car. Ben grumbled, "It's too hot to run."

Near the bottom of the path, she checked, staring toward the face of the krantz that towered above them. She put up her hands to shield her eyes. Following her gaze, Ben said, "What is it?"

"I thought I saw something flash. Just out of the corner of my eye. It was like metal."

"Gold in my teeth."

"No, you fool."

"Probably water, higher up."

"But it moved. I saw it move over to the left." She shook her head. "Oh, well." She began to run again, and Ben followed at leisure.

On the way back, they saw Sullivan at his boundary fence. He invited them home to breakfast, fed them ham and eggs, and listened to Nella's chat with an indulgent smile. When she mentioned the flash on the cliff face, he said, "You often get that, when the rock's wet."

But after they'd gone, he sat thoughtfully over his coffee. Drought and the hot wind had made the rock-face exceptionally dry. He went to his room and took up the photographs he had recently developed, the ones he had taken the day he and Kruger went to look for a dam site. In one of them, it was possible to discern small black spots. Blurred. Baboons, making for the east side of the krantz, which, barren of feeding grounds, was steep and impregnable as a fortress.

Sullivan stood, chewing a finger. Should he say something? A wild guess, after all, he didn't want to be laughed at. It was too hot to trail into town on a fool's errand. Later, perhaps.

He dropped the pictures back in a drawer.

59

"DAMN THIS BLOODY CLIMATE," said Sullivan. "I can't bear the thought of a brunette, let alone a blonde. Present company excepted, of course."

The lounge of the Hotel was nearly empty. Two electric fans whirred, and their draft spun the flypapers dangling from the central lights. The only people who had braved the dust storm outside were Ben, Sullivan, Abrahams, Strasser and Nella. They sprawled in easy chairs close to the barroom door, chatting desultorily. They had been there about an hour when the main door swung back, letting in the whine of the wind, and the thickset shape of Julius Kruger. They called him over. He collected a brandy and came, coughing, hitting his chest with a clenched fist.

"Man, I'm full of dust. The plantations are red with it." He sat down and took a mouthful of brandy. "Ach, now it's turned to mud!"

Strasser, who alone looked moderately wide awake, leaned over the arm of the chair and said to Abrahams, "I've said again and again that for most people, politics are unimportant. What matters is income, health, jobs. These interests will always dominate the situation. You say yourself, your workers opposed the boycott for these same reasons of personal security. I've seen it happen, over and over. Ordinary people aren't interested in political philosophies."

Abrahams swung his hand at an insect. "And yet, in state after state to the north, the Africans, offered a choice between social security and this strange new dynamic which they talk of as freedom, or the search for the African Personality, or whatever, have refused the safer way. Don't delude yourself, Strasser. The drive to end colonialism won't be turned aside by talk of better amenities."

Kruger studied the brandy in his glass. "Man is a political animal," he said. "You should both know that, coming from Europe."

They looked at him carefully, and Abrahams said in a dry voice, "Coming from Europe, we both know that politics is not the whole animal, not perhaps even the most important part. Am I making heresies?"

Kruger smiled sideways at him. "Maybe. Go on. I can always listen."

Easing himself a little lower in his chair, Abrahams laced his hands in front of his chest. "Now take this town, for instance. We've had great trouble here. Now, where did it start? One moment we're a nice town, a quiet town, the next we're upside-down."

Strasser said impatiently, "As Kruger has said before, it stems from the arrival of the agitator. The burglary of Oakes's store, the dismissal of my miserable cook, the rumors, everything started from that one point."

"But why, from such a small source, do we have such big results? No, doctor. Sometimes a village, a town even, will come through war and revolution with small moral damage. Another time, a political campaign or perhaps only one crazy poison-pen writer will create real havoc. It's a question of fundamental human relations. If these are good, then we are safe. If they are bad, we are in danger. This thief was simply a detonator. And why was it possible for this to be so? Because we have grown accustomed in this country to turn to politics for the settlement of problems. In many ways, commercially for instance, we are quite an efficient nation. In human relations, we are hopeless muddlers." He pointed a stubby finger at Kruger. "Isn't that why you call for unity, for good will? Let me tell you, you cannot achieve that politically. Politicians, you see, tend to stress our differences rather than our similarities. They play oranges and lemons with our emotions, stand this side or that, compete, divide. It's easy to make people combine against something. Very hard to make them combine for something."

Kruger grunted, and Ben said, "Why don't they call a multi-racial meeting for this area, to discuss the boycott?"

"All races?" said Strasser.

"Yes, of course."

Kruger finished his brandy. "There are existing means of interracial consultation."

"Not for ordinary people. As Abrahams said, it's ordinary human knowledge and personal relations that are weak. I don't see how one co-operates with people if one's ignorant of them, if one never meets them."

"No, no." Kruger shook his head. "There you have the way to racial integration, and the end of the white race in Africa. I'm a realist, my friend."

Ben said, "That's your official answer. But unofficially, sir, in your own sphere, you consult with other races all the time. You know what goes on on your farm, and in the town. You make it your business to meet Africans, Coloreds, Indians, and you know how your nonwhite associates feel and think. But there are hundreds of thousands of people, particularly in the towns, who live in boxes. The only members of other races they consult are their cooks, and then only to discuss the menus for the day. We have a servant-employer relationship, but that only brushes the surface. I would like to meet people, particularly professional men, in open congress. Now why are you against this?"

"Because," said Kruger, "it's no use appointing bodies for discussion, and then sidetracking them with unofficial talks." He rose to his feet. "You will find that in any country, young man. There is always an element that refuses to acknowledge the proper channels for complaint and negotiation. Your suggestion would merely play into the hands of extremists who want to overthrow the recognized Government." He nodded affably all around, said goodnight, and went off, edging between the empty tables.

Ben sighed. "I lose every damn argument." He rubbed his neck. "Where did I go wrong?"

Abrahams smiled. "No doubt your definition of an extremist and his differ. Kruger argues a priori from his fears to his principles."

Ben nodded. "I'll be ready for him, next time."

Sullivan suddenly heaved himself upright and waved a hand above his head, groping for the bell that would summon the bar waiter.

Nella said, "Have you been asleep?"

"Thinkin'." He pressed the bell stop. "It's compulsive. Sweeps over me like a wave. Leaves me weak for days."

"What were you thinking about?"

"Oh, cabbages and kings. Ducks, baboons, and the light in your eyes. If that waiter doesn't hurry, I'll scream and scream. Run, Moodly, man! Same all around?" He ordered drinks and then sank back, apparently exhausted.

Nella saw that he was very well pleased with himself. His round eyes were sparkling. He banged his heel on the floor and sang to himself under his breath.

60

WHEN KRUGER RETURNED from church on Sunday morning, his house servant told him that Baas Reimer had telephoned and wanted Kruger. The number he had left, however, was Sullivan's.

Julius went to his antiquated wall telephone, and rang Sullivan, who proved mysterious, but repeated Mannie's request. Would Kruger please come across to Redcliff at once, and bring his rifle? No more could be said, in case others were listening on the party line.

Kruger hung up, changed rapidly from his Sunday clothes into ancient flannels, lifted his rifle from the cupboard, dropped cartridges into his coat pockets, and drove over to Redcliff.

Turning past Mission Halt, he saw two riot trucks drawn up in the shadow of the gum trees. One of them moved away at his approach and headed up the hill to the Mission.

Down at Sullivan's he found a Landrover in the driveway. Mannie, Venter and Sullivan waited beside it. Kruger swung his legs out of his car and Mannie came over.

"Oom, you know this country. Would there be any good place for a chap to hide on the kloof?"

Kruger eyed him sourly. "Not more than two or three hundred. Did you get me over here . . ."

"Wait for it!" Mannie held up a hand. "Sullivan has a hunch. Someone's been foraging off the land around here for some time. Took his ducks, and the Mission's reported losing vegetables at intervals. Then yesterday, Nella Ebenezer told him she saw something like metal moving on the cliff. Sullivan took a look at the pictures he made that time you and him were looking for a place to put the dam. Remember? He says that in the one photo, you can see the baboons moving away from their feeding grounds, and in another, there's something looks like smoke, high up the face."

206

Kruger's eyes were sharp. "You think it's the man who broke into the store?"

"You think he could hide there?"

Kruger frowned, trying to recall the long-past days when he and René van Zyl had been kings of this high country. At last he said, "Yes, far up near the top there's a shelf, that's wide enough. Us kids used to use it as a hideout. You can reach it from the plateau, if you climb down beside the first waterfall."

Mannie nodded. "We have to back the hunch. Larkill's away in Hopetoun, can't wait for him. My idea is, we let the trucks go up to the Mission. Let anyone think that's what we're after. You can't see the kloof face from the Mission. Us four will go on in the Landrover and try to catch this chap from behind."

They climbed into the Landrover and drove to the Mission, where Mannie stopped to talk to the rest of his men. Then Sullivan took the rough cart track that zigzagged toward the plateau. The vehicle lurched and bumped, and the wind buffeted it so strongly that at times it seemed likely to overturn. Once on the high flats, there was no cover. Sullivan's eyes began to stream.

From the back, Venter said, "He's got that gun he took from Oakes's store."

"We won't give him time to use it," said Julius, patting the rifle on his knees.

Mannie looked around. "Don't kill the bastard, Oom. I want to ask him a question."

"Where did you come from, Baby Dear?" sang Sullivan, and swore as a swirl of dust half-choked him.

Now the track was running level. They stopped the Landrover and climbed out. About them stretched a treeless grassland, tossing, shining, bisected by a shallow rivulet.

"We follow the stream," said Kruger. "It leads to the kloof."

They walked along the water's edge. Only the wind broke the silence. Once a rock rabbit sprang up and scrambled for the shelter of some boulders. They neared the point where the grassland ended in empty space. Mannie and Kruger crossed the stream and moved right. Sullivan and Venter deployed to the left. Mannie signaled them to keep down, and they crawled slowly toward the lip.

"Big laugh," thought Mannie, "if there's nobody there."

But near the edge he lay flat, rolled on his elbow, and waved Kruger to his side.

"There," he whispered.

Below them, about fifty feet down on a flat shelf of rock, a man lay asleep. His head was in shadow. They could see his outflung arms and the dusty soles of his boots.

Mannie said grimly, "Give 'im a fright, Uncle."

Kruger loaded his rifle. Further along, Sullivan lifted his gun to his shoulder, watching Mannie.

Kruger steadied himself and sighted. His finger closed. The crack of the shot echoed and sprang around the curve of the krantz, dust spurted near the sleeping man, he leaped up, gazing wildly about him.

Seeing Kruger, he dived toward his pack. Sullivan's rifle barked, the pack jerked beneath the man's outstretched hand. He stood upright, flung his arms above his head.

"Cover him," said Mannie, and Kruger and Sullivan did so, while Mannie and Venter ran to the strip of bush bordering the waterfall. They lowered themselves down the face, clinging to branches.

The man below stood motionless, his eyes on the leveled rifles. He offered no resistance when Venter handcuffed him. Mannie was unwrapping a long oilcloth bundle. It contained the rifle stolen from the store. Mannie wrapped it again, picked up the pack, made a rapid search of the rest of the shelf. He and Venter hauled the man and his belongings up the face.

The party made its way back to the Landrover. The captive said not one word. He stumbled somewhat, and his breathing was stertorous, sometimes breaking into a painful cough. His dark eyes looked vacant, almost disinterested. Mannie watched him curiously. Not hard to see him as the thug that beat up an old lady. That would pound a dog's head to pulp. But an agitator? That was something else, again.

At the Mission, Mannie, Venter, and the prisoner rejoined the police squad. Kruger and Sullivan went back to the farmstead, Sullivan very annoyed because he had not been allowed to accompany the police back to town. He took the credit for the arrest, and refused to admit that Mannie had showed generosity in allowing him and Kruger to be of the party that cornered the man.

He was still complaining when Kruger left him.

Kruger himself was glad to be free of further responsibility. He found himself very tired. Not as young as he had been. Anyhow, that was that. They'd got him, and now things would go back to normal. He heaved a sigh of relief, turning homeward.

It did not occur to him that the removal of the cause of evil does not immediately arrest its effects.

61

BEN, WHO HAD WAITED for an hour for Strasser to appear, at last sat down to luncheon without him. At two o'clock Strasser appeared, exuberant. "They've caught the man that burgled Oakes's store. Oakes is going about puffed up like a toad. They caught him with the gun on him, too. A white man."

"Good God! Did Oakes tell you?"

"I've been at the Station. Oakes was there, to identify his goods. I was called over to see the prisoner. He's got a threatened pneumonia. Coughing and half-drowned. Exposure, no doubt. Larkill wanted me to check him over. I made the most of it, I was interested. In my opinion, the man is a psychopath. Very low mental age, about twelve years, I should think. He gave his actual age as twenty-five. Says he lived here once, as

a child. He has the absolute, characteristic record. Only child
of a mother of low intelligence. Reform school. Early delin-
quency. He will end in a mental home or on the gallows. Violent, vain, stupid, all . . ."

"But not a political agitator?"

"Oh I think one can say certainly not that. One could not
train such a being to anything. Probably ineducable, and quite
unable to profit by experience." Strasser took a draft of beer.
"Ironic, is it not, that the town has been thrown into a panic
by this creature with the mind of a vicious child? A whole town
. . ." he spread his hands eloquently. "Ah well. Now he is under
lock and key, we shall have a little peace."

62

THE RING of the telephone, three times repeated, woke Ebenezer. He got slowly to his feet, dropping his book on the
floor. It was just three o'clock. In the rocking chair at the end
of the stoep, Nella slept, her head dropped sideways against
the backrest, her wrists hanging limp. Ebenezer went into the
house and answered the telephone.

When he returned, his daughter was awake, leaning forward
and rubbing her neck. She looked up and said, "Is it for me?"

"They've rung off," he said, still standing.

Her brows snapped together, in an expression that always
sent a pang through him, her mother's look when angered.

"Who was it?" she said.

He spread his hands. "I wasn't sure. I said you were asleep."

"But who did it sound like, Pa?"

He said unwillingly, "Perhaps Dr. Nevis."

She got up and walked past him into the house. He heard

her enter the study and use the telephone. A few minutes later she reappeared, in a clean cotton dress, with a sun hat in her hand. She did not look at him.

"You're not being reasonable," he began. It was so rare for her to be angry, to challenge him, that he was shaken, and only when she was down the steps did he lean over the verandah rail and call "Nella!"

She turned and looked up at him. He said sharply, "I don't want you to let your feelings for that young man go any further. I don't want you hurt. Do you understand?"

She frowned as the wind pulled a strand of hair across her eyes. She was thinking, nobody knows me like Pa, nobody else can see right through me. She said, "I'm a grown woman, Pa."

As she walked away down the path he leaned forward and shouted, "He's not interested in you, in us . . . he'll go away, back where he came from. . . ."

She neither turned nor slackened pace. He watched her go, the wind cracking the crisp cotton skirt against her legs. He groped behind him, found the edge of a chair, and sank down. He sat there quietly for a long time. When the fat old servant came out of the house with the tray of tea, she said to him in surprise, "The young mistress gone, baas?"

"She will be back presently. Put the tray there."

His voice was calm, but as he poured tea into his cup, his right hand shook so badly that he had to steady the wrist against the edge of the table. Parting, he thought, never comes over a major issue. When the time comes, a flapping slipper, an irritating sniff, a quarrel about the right way to make toast . . . that is enough. The steel is eroded, and a slight pressure breaks the link.

He sipped his tea. No politics, no arguments. I must think of something nice for her, to show how much she means to me, my Nella.

But a bird among the willows mocked him, "Too-late, too-late, too-late."

63

THE SUN had already begun to move toward the rim of the escarpment when the mongrel dogs of Gwevu's kraal set up a high barking. Gwevu himself, who had been asleep, came out of his hut and scanned the valley below. The kraal was almost deserted, the young people being busy with their own affairs.

There was no one on the footpaths lower down, but the dogs kept up their clamor. Gwevu picked up a knobkerrie, and walked up toward the fringe of the plantations above the kraal. He moved slowly, his eyes on the ground. The wind stabbed like a blade. When he reached the shade of a thorn tree, a little below the tree line, he stood waiting, his thin flanks braced against the tilt of the land, his face impassive. He guessed who was approaching. He could hear the steps now, quick but clumsy.

Stones rattled down the slope. The man appeared, sliding down the bank between the pine. His chest heaved and shone with sweat. He raised a hand in greeting.

Gwevu looked at him without sign.

The man called, "I need food."

After a pause, Gwevu said, "Sizwa, come down here."

"I can't be seen."

"Come down!"

Sulkily, Sizwa advanced, to tower over the old man. Fixed by a stern eye, he at first glowered, then sank unwillingly to his haunches. Gwevu took his time about moving to a small boulder, where he sat down. Then he said in a mild, almost conversational tone, "You've come a long way."

"Not too far." Sizwa jerked his head. "Grandfather, I haven't time for gossip.

"Nor for courtesy, it seems." Gwevu considered the young

212

man. His opaque eyes were unwinking, his flat, wrinkled nose and hollow cheeks might have been modeled in terra cotta. He said, "Now you come running to me for food."

Sizwa glanced up quickly as if he would speak, but Gwevu gestured him to be silent. "You run to me for food. You say to yourself, go home to the old man, because he loves you, you are his pride, since as a child you rode on his shoulder. Go to the soft old fool and he will protect you."

Sizwa's eyes narrowed, his heavy lips parted.

"Perhaps," continued Gwevu, planting the stem of his stick and resting his chin on the knob, "perhaps you told yourself that if this old man will not help you because he loves you, then he will help you because of his shame. He will not want his grandson to be taken by the police."

"I will not . . ."

"Wait! Be silent!"

Gwevu seemed to take thought. Then he said, "Close to us is the place where our ancestors are buried. When you came to manhood, I prayed them, 'Look at this one, enfold him, make him worthy of his line.' It is a good line. We have been leaders, have not disgraced ourselves in war. On important occasions, our praise-singers took pride of place, because such was our due. We know who we are.

"Certainly, I would give a good deal to keep our reputation high. Also I owe something to my own kin. On the other hand, one could say that I owe something to myself. I have a position to keep up, after all. I should consider the law, which you have broken, and the respect owed to me, which you have neglected to observe."

He looked at Sizwa, and the wrinkles around his mouth deepened as if he tasted something sour. "Is that true? That I should think of you, the grandson, or of myself, the grandfather? That it is a matter of reputation?"

He shook his head. His eyes wandered along the valley. "Reputation means a good deal, particularly when one is very young, or even in the middle years. But an old man begins to see that reputation is a stone that must be carried everywhere. It grows heavy. . . ."

Sizwa started to rise, but the thin hand wagged at him, as if returning him to dust.

"Do you know what we are for? We who have a position and a reputation? We are appointed to carry this stone, this weight, for our people. To give bowels of courage to the weak, to give wisdom to fools, to see that there is enough food for the hungry. Are you one of us, my grandson?

"When you were a child, you were well taught. I and others gave you enough to allow you to stand tall among the tallest.

"All these things, I have considered during these past days. I have heard what you have done, and I have thought about it carefully. I myself do not give much credit to this new medicine. But then, no doubt, I am old, and perhaps a time has come when a younger man, with fresh ideas, should take my place. When the bull is old, he is replaced, that is the course of nature. But he is not replaced by the rogue animal, for him the herd rejects and drives away. Are you the leader, or are you the rogue?

"I have thought it over, and I think the answer is clear. You are a man who thinks only of himself. The time has not come when I can die happy, knowing that everything is in good hands."

He rose to his feet. "You must go now. You have no place here. I will give you nothing more, because what I have given in the past you have abused. You are not worth further gifts."

Sizwa shot upright, and took a step forward. His great height emphasized the frailty of Gwevu, who stood quietly watching him. Sizwa half-lifted his arm, and Gwevu said, "What good will it do if you strike me?"

Sizwa dropped his hand. He thrust past the old man, lunged away up the slope, scrambled up the bank, and disappeared among the trees.

Gwevu waited some time before he returned to the kraal.

There he summoned a boy of ten. "Go quickly down to the farm," he said. "Say that they must tell the white lord, Sizwa has been here."

He did not wait to see the child run down the hillside. He went back to his hut, and sat there in darkness of eye and spirit.

64

THE AFTERNOON wore on without the wind's abating. The whole sky now was in ferment, cloud, dust, leaf, sun itself seemed bowled together in a sort of burning torrent. Old Mr. Palmer was blown off his feet and broke an elbow, and during tea, a corrugated iron sheet was torn from the sawmill roof and tossed over the road into the railway yards.

Mannie, coming off duty at five-thirty, paused in the shadow of the Town Hall to glance up at the clock. He was one of those people on whom watches keep poor time. He declared it was due to surplus electricity, but his wife said it was sweat getting into the watch case.

He adjusted the minute hand, his eyes screwed up. Bloody wind; a man couldn't think with the whole street blowing up his nose. He was in a restless mood. Sunday was a depressing day, anyway, without the wind, whine, whine, like a spoiled child.

It was Sunday, he was off duty, and the sensible thing to do was go home and have a cold shower and get the weight off his feet. At the back of his mind, though, something niggled him. Something someone said? What? Couldn't remember. He sucked his teeth, staring across the road, and then walked over to the Garage. It was closed. He put a palm flat on the hot wood of the door, and leaned there, thinking. Then he walked briskly around to the yard at the back.

Abel's door was shut and locked. Mannie tried the handle and banged, but the silence rolled up softly as the dust. He walked home across the town, then.

He took a shower, put on clean clothes, and went into the living room, where Marie had tea waiting for him. Afterward he tried to settle down with a book. His sons, running in from the garden, distracted him, and he shouted at them to be quiet. Marie appeared in the doorway.

"What's the matter with you?"

He smiled at her apologetically. "I don't know. I feel restless."

She said kindly, "It's because you've caught that man. Now it's over, you feel restless. It's natural." She went away to the kitchen, and he heard her singing there. He read a little more.

The garden outside grew dark, the church bells started their sad tune. Mannie moved to the window. There was a single star over the Town Hall, a pale green star, coming and going between the clouds like a little goldfish. Up over the plantations, the spotter-plane was making its last trip, with lights winking.

He turned away from the window and hurried to his bedroom, pulled off his slippers and put on outdoor shoes, rummaged in a drawer and found a torch. He slipped a loaded Smith and Wesson into the pocket of his coat. Putting his head around the kitchen door he said, "Don't wait supper for me."

Marie's face came around, a startled moon, but he was already out of the door, and running up the path.

He moved by back ways through thickening darkness, up the hill to the native shanties. His feet carried him by guess over the unpaved tracks, between rubbish dumps and across open ditches. He reached a house near the edge of the settlement. In the space before the door, over a wood fire, a woman was stirring an iron pot that gave off a bitter smell of herbs. She was old, her skin withered. As he approached, she called out in Afrikaans, "Yes, my master, what do you want now?" and burst into laughter.

Mannie said, "Has Abel from the Garage been here this afternoon?"

She shook her head. "No, no," and laughed again.

Mannie said patiently, "I'm not making trouble for him."

"That's what you always say, you policemen." She mocked him with the licence of the old, stirring the pot as she spoke. "No trouble, with a gun in your pocket?"

"Come on, Mother, I haven't got all night."

She banged the stick on the top of the pot. "Well, he was here. Some time. I can't be expected to remember everyone."

"Where did he go?"

"Up, down, how do I know?"

He pulled out a coin and tossed it and caught it, so that it flashed in the firelight. She said, "Perhaps to the Church. . . ."

"Not perhaps, old woman."

"Well, then, to the Hospital, to see a friend. Then he'll go to church."

Mannie tossed the coin. It fell in the dust at her feet, and she bent for it without haste. When she straightened, he was gone.

65

ABEL REACHED the Elizabeth Hospital at six o'clock. It was the visiting hour, and the entrance hall was fairly full. Several Africans and Indians sat on the wooden benches along the wall. The woman at the inquiries desk was busy on the telephone. As she talked, she poked a pencil through her hair, which had a white, unearthly shine because she tried to straighten it with cosmetics. Abel knew her, she was well off, and even owned a motor scooter which Abel had fixed for her once. Normally she treated him politely enough, but tonight she looked away as he came through the door. She was a very cautious woman, always trying to be on the winning side. She thought everyone was anxious to bring her to disfavor with the hospital authorities, in order to steal her job from her.

There was a queue in front of her desk, and Abel joined it. He knew the man in front of him, a fat, excitable fellow from the Hotel kitchen.

Abel smiled at him. "What are you doing here?"

"My wife had a daughter last night, a nice, fat child."

"That's good news."

"And you? Have you a sick friend here?"

"I wanted news of young Sibisi, the one who had the trouble with his chest."

"Oh yes." As if he had remembered something, the fat man licked his lips and said, "Aren't you a friend of Sizwa? I often saw you together, when he worked for the doctor."

Abel saw the alarm in the fat man's eye. Now, he thought, I should play safe, say I was a friend, but not any longer. Say, I'm the man who helped to end the boycott, and quite respectable.

He felt his face stiffening in dislike, and he could not bring himself to speak. The fat man said hastily, "All right, I understand. A man has to be prudent. I know there's nothing in being friendly with a person, but when that person becomes dangerous, I chuck him away like an old shoe."

Abel said explosively, "Sizwa is worth more than the whole of your family put together."

"All right, all right. There's no need to be rude. I was only saying I don't accuse you, like some, of betraying a friend." The fat man turned a shoulder. "Some people don't deserve sympathy."

Abel looked at the floor. A few days ago, this fat fool had been Sizwa's crony, laughing at his songs, hanging on his words. Suddenly, Abel hated them all, the fat man, the clerk at the desk, the indolent watchers by the wall, and the aloof, alien Indians. He thrust away from the counter, pushed past his neighbors, and made for the doors. Young Dr. Nevis was standing just inside them, talking to Dr. Mdunge. Nevis called

Abel's name, but Abel ran out into the courtyard and up the drive.

He took the road through the plantations, toward Mission Halt. He could not keep up his pace for long, and slowed to a walk. The dust road wound before him like a road in a dream, without end.

I am alone, he thought. My own people distrust me, and the white men have no place for me. He thought of the desk clerk, an educated woman. Am I like her, trying to pretend I'm better than my own people?

He felt a longing to go back, to forget the skills that he had acquired at such cost and effort, to be again at home with his people. He stopped and unlaced his shoes, pulled them off and tied the laces together, slung them around his neck. Now I'm a country boy, he thought, with a faint smile.

Puffs of warm silken dust spread as he walked. The trees about him sobbed and tossed like mourning women. His leg ached, and when he reached the railway line, he sat down on the bank to rest.

There was a ring around the moon. He remembered how, as a child, he had seen such a halo, one winter's night, as he came from the hills with a bunch of herd boys. The slow-moving cattle had glittered, moving through the frosty veld, radiant as if they had been blessed by the Princess of Heaven, she who appeared in mists. . . .

. . . He should pray, but to whom? To the ancestors, to the gods, or to the one God. Who would answer him? In whose charge was he?

He felt the fear of vastness close on him. The huge sky and the massive hills crushed down on him. They were like a voice repeating a question, who are you, who are you?

Up there, perhaps, lay the answer. The hills waited, the sky waited. He got to his feet and took the path to the Mission, drawn upward like a moth toward the moon.

66

MANNIE PUSHED without ceremony through the crowd at the reception desk. He said abruptly, "Has Abel from the Garage been here?"

The girl's eyes grew sharp with curiosity. "Yes, sir, he was here, about quarter of an hour ago, but he never wait to speak to me. Just went."

"Where to, you know?"

"Oah, he didn't say to anyone, sir."

Mannie went outside again, and stood hesitating on the front steps. A man ran through the doors and nearly cannoned into him, said, "Sorry, Sergeant, I didn't see you."

Mannie said, "Hullo, Dr. Nevis."

"What are you doing here?"

"Wasting my time, doctor."

Ben grinned and started down the steps. Mannie called after him. "Can you gimme a lift as far as the Halt?"

"Sure. Run you up to the Mission if you want?"

"No, just to the Halt."

Mannie sat silently in the passenger seat, and Ben, though he wondered why the policeman had no transport of his own, did not like to question him. He sensed in Mannie an unusual tension. The large body had the alert stillness of a listening animal.

That's it, thought Ben, he's like a dog on the scent, coursing about half-blindly, and all you can do is stand back and make no sound or sign, because he runs by instinct, and thought distracts him.

He dropped Mannie at the Halt. Mannie gave hasty thanks and set off up the hill path without a backward glance.

Ben, feeling uneasy, drove slowly back to town.

67

As ABEL LEFT the shelter of the railway cutting, the height of the gale struck him, pouring down the defiles of the escarpment, flailing the exposed hillside with dust and flying pebbles. His bare feet slipped on the baked path, and he leaned forward and clutched at tufts of grass razor-stropped by drought. Twice he was forced to rest. At last he was nearly at the level ground about the Mission. He halted, trying to peer through the skirts of the wind.

One part of his mind said, run for the bright lights over there beyond the trees. But another part said, wait. When at last he discerned the shadow among shadows, the darkness on darkness, he was not surprised. He called, "Sizwa!"

The shadow moved closer. Sizwa stood a little above him, on the curve of the hill. He carried no weapon save his heavy stick. Abel scrambled toward him. He saw, close up, that Sizwa's eyes were red with fatigue, and his stomach concave below his ribs.

Abel sank down on the grass, panting. "You're mad to show yourself here, don't you know that?"

"I know." Sizwa's voice sounded dusty. "I know the police are after me, and who set them on. I've been waiting for you. It's you who were foolish to come."

Abel peered up into the darkness. "And I knew you would be waiting. But I didn't talk to the police."

"No? The boycott just broke by itself?"

"I talked to the men at the factory. But not to the police." Abel tried to collect his thoughts. "You must go away, there's nothing here for you any more."

"So my grandfather tells me."

"You've seen him?"

"Yes." Sizwa's voice was indifferent. "Gwevu is an old man. I am young. I shall stay."

Abel got wearily to his feet. "Listen to me, Sizwa. You're finished here. No respectable people will accept you, now that Gwevu has denied you. No one will give you work or food because you are wanted by the police. And the hotheads will have nothing to do with you, because you've failed once, and that means you're finished. All you'll get here is arrest and prison." He fumbled in his pocket. "Look, here's a pound. It's all I have now, but I'll get you more. Go away, to Johannesburg. Let me know where you are, and I'll send you money until you're settled. Take it, go on. You can pay me back some time."

Sizwa spat into the grass. "Are you trying to buy your life, now?"

"I'm trying to help you."

It seemed to be the last thing left to say. Abel took a step forward, holding out the pound note. Sizwa's hand shot out, knocked the money aside, and caught Abel by the throat.

"I can see what you're doing." The hand forced Abel's head around. "There's your help . . . friend."

A man was running up the slope, doubled against the thrust of the gale. He shouted, waving his arm. Metal glinted.

Sizwa laughed. "You have too many friends, friend."

Abel caught at Sizwa's wrist. "I didn't bring him . . . I know nothing. . . ."

He saw Sizwa's arm swing back, the stick whirl around. Desperately, he threw himself sideways. The blow glanced past his head, tore at his ear and thudded into his shoulder. The wind was needles of agony, there was banging in the sky. Abel sagged backward and rolled downhill into darkness.

When he opened his eyes he saw Sergeant Reimer running on the sky. Not on the sky. On the hill above him. The Sergeant put his foot in a hole and fell, swearing. Abel was lying head-down on the slope. He levered himself around cautiously, then lay still.

Later he managed to sit up. His ear was torn and blood ran down his neck. He searched for a handkerchief and held it to the side of his head.

Footsteps sounded and Reimer slid down to him. His hands moved the handkerchief, moved quickly over Abel's head and shoulder.

"You're all right, not dead yet. Can you stand?"

Abel said thickly, "There was nobody. I fell."

Mannie said, "Don't gimme that. Come on, get up." He added, "Where were you going?"

"To church, sir."

Mannie grunted. He got an arm around Abel and began to half-lift him up the hill. He seemed in a frenzy of impatience. The two men staggered toward the lights of the Mission.

68

IN HIS FARMHOUSE, Julius Kruger kept vigil. Usually he went to bed at eight-thirty, but tonight he was too restless. The heat, the excitement that morning, and now old Gwevu's report that Sizwa was in the vicinity made sleep seem as far away as the sea.

Kruger sat smoking his pipe and thinking.

He thought of Sullivan, irresponsible and clever. Did he have any strong opinions, at all? Perhaps he disliked the United Nations, but that was a safe hate, since what could a man do about the United Nations, after all? Sullivan was the common man, with his beer, his women, his refusal to commit himself. Theories, thought Kruger, ebb and flow, the centuries go by, and only Sullivan remains, intact, immune, in a queer way incorruptible.

He thought of old Gwevu, and of Sizwa. He wondered whether they'd got hold of Mannie yet, to tell him about Sizwa's latest move?

He remembered Sizwa's birth, how pleased old Gwevu had been. Man, that was growing old, when one could remember the grandson as a child. Now a revolutionary. What made a revolutionary? Or were all men revolutionaries, always in revolt against their own fathers, their own past?

Smiling, Kruger thought again of what Sullivan had said once, when they argued about the State. Kruger had told him that the State was of supreme importance, but Sullivan had shaken his head, with that sudden obstinacy of his.

"The individual is just as important. . . ."

"What would you be," asked Kruger, "without the State, without trade, economic treaties, scientific projects?"

"I don't know." Sullivan smiled, and added in a dreamy voice, "Sullivan for President. Sullivan the Movie Mogul. Pope Sullivan the First. . . ."

The common man.

Thirsty, Kruger went to the back of the house to find a glass of iced water. Sipping it, he opened the back door. The wind was blowing toward him, and he was about to retreat when he heard the clang of the Mission Bell. Almost simultaneously, the telephone started to ring. He slammed the door shut and lumbered back to answer the phone.

69

DOMINEE BOND had elected to spend that night up at the Mission. A room was always kept ready for him, and there he found sanctuary when he felt himself in particular need of rest and seclusion. From this small space, with its battered iron bedstead and its cupboard that would not quite shut, he could see the cataracts of stone that soothed his spirit, for like many of the psalmists, Bond was a hillman of the hills.

Tonight he sat by the window, his Bible on his knee, but he did not read. He watched the dark surge of the pines below, and the moon that leaped like a dolphin ringed with light through cloudy surf.

He thought the gale had abated a little, but it was still strong.

A sound caught his attention, and he glanced down into the courtyard, where the church hall made an angle with the schoolhouse. A door banging? He listened, but could distinguish only the hymn-singing and the roar of the wind. Finally he rose and went out into the hall and leaned over the banisters.

"Jeremiah?"

A young servant boy came from the kitchen and looked up at him. Bond said, "I think someone is knocking at the side door, Jeremiah. Will you please see who it is?"

He went back to his room, having no wish to make his presence known unless he were needed. He heard the side door open, and footsteps hurrying through the house. The step seemed familiar. No doubt he would be called if it were important.

Mr. Scheepers, the caretaker, would attend to it. There was his voice now, so like that of an anxious budgerigar, dear old Scheepers. Bond smiled faintly, leaning his fists on the windowsill, feeling the house tremble in the mountainous sweep of the gale.

A point of light was moving on the edge of the plantations, southeast of the Halt. He watched it bob down the brake between two sectors. It pursued an uneven course, obscured sometimes by the thickness of the trees. The predikant cupped his hands against the glass and stared out, then threw up the window and ducked his shoulders through. There was an incandescence between the tree trunks, widening now, soaring with a terrible beauty. He slammed down the sash and lumbered toward the stairs. As he started down them, he saw Mannie Reimer, Scheepers, and an African standing in the lower hall. Reimer stepped forward and began, "Sir, I borrowed your telephone. . . ."

"Never mind that now. Someone has fired the eastern sector. Mannie, phone the emergency number, and you Scheepers, run and ring the alarm at once."

The men in the hall scattered. Mr. Bond went to his study,

and working with urgent calm collected the rucksack of first-aid kit, checked it, added a flask of fresh water and one of brandy, then fetched his car from the shed.

The church bell was clanging, six times, pause, six again. Lights snapped on in the workmen's quarters, the headman Duma appeared, running along the length of the compound, shouting. People streamed from the church hall, and Reimer mustered them and gave them instructions.

Men began to trot down the footpath to the Halt, carrying sticks and cane knives. Duma and Reimer crossed the courtyard together and jumped into the car. Through his anxiety, the pastor felt a sense of pride that the emergency drill worked so smoothly.

As he edged the car through the arch of the courtyard, he said, "Whose land is it?"

Mannie said, "Bill Maxwell's, sir. About two miles east of the Halt."

"It was deliberately fired. I saw."

"Yes, I think so."

"But who would do such a thing?"

"I can guess."

Mr. Bond sighed. As the car lurched down the Hill, they saw a fresh tract explode into flames that roared a hundred feet high, leaning, groping blindly toward the central plantations. Dense smoke rolled across the tree tops, brilliant with burning matter. The roar of fire and wind thickened.

Duma said, "Baas, the first brake is too narrow."

Birds rose from the threatened sector, screaming. In the valley the church bells took up the clamor, and the sirens of the three fire engines whined up from the town. Two of them passed the Halt as they arrived. The third turned right, heading for the dam behind the Hospital. The buildings were on main water from the town, but the pressure was bound to be low.

At the Halt, the predikant lined up his team of helpers, to await orders from the trained fire-fighters. The police had set up a roadblock at the Halt, and volunteer cars were confined to the town side, but a few were allowed through, among them Bill Maxwell's. They caught a glimpse of his white face, as he shot past, racing for his homestead.

The crowd was thickest around the railway line. Sullivan and Kruger arrived with work parties and were directed on. Riot trucks nosed forward, spilled out policemen, four with walkie-talkies strapped to their chests. A bulldozer chugged along brake two, widening it.

His own team set to work. Mr. Bond sought out Larkill. He found him standing on the back of a truck, shouting orders. His face was already streaked with sweat and smuts.

The predikant caught his attention. "Can I go to the Hospital? Are they getting the patients away?"

"The doctors are seeing to it, sir. You can go there, if you want."

"Can they save it?"

Larkill wiped his sleeve over his eyes. "They're sending soldiers from Hopetoun. That may take an hour. Dynamite may stop it. Nothing else will, in this wind." His face cracked in a skull's grin. "They forecast rain for tonight. You better pray...."

The predikant glanced at the escarpment. It seemed to him that the clouds were a little lower, the wind not as fierce?

He set off along the road to the Hospital. On his left, the sky was smoky, but not yet red. He hurried, coughing. A little way on he came up with the African who had been with Mannie Reimer. He walked uncertainly, a bloody rag pressed to his head. After one sharp glance, Bond took his arm and helped him forward.

The shouts at the Halt grew fainter. In the Hospital grounds, people were hurrying, but with a quiet deliberateness. Even the noise of the fire was muted. It sounded like a dog chewing a matchbox in the next room.

Close at hand, pumps hammered. They had got the hoses going, and their spray blew a velvet softness into the stench of burning vegetation.

70

HALF AN HOUR LATER Ben, who was ushering a group of patients from the center block, caught sight of Ebenezer and nearly laughed. In this crowd of scarecrow workers, some stripped to the waist, some in raincoats over pajamas, Ebenezer moved correct and dapper. His light suit was spotless, his tie exactly aligned, and he wore his Panama hat. He was talking to Mannie Reimer, and as Ben approached, said briskly, "Good evening, doctor. You'll be glad to know that everything is going well down in the town. They are putting the patients into the Town Hall. The women are in charge, and there'll be soup and coffee, very shortly." He moved off with a brisk step. Mannie said, "How many still to go, doc?"

"Only the serious cases. Strasser won't move them unless it's unavoidable. How's the fire?"

"It's jumped the first brake. But the second's much wider, and the wind's dropped quite a bit. They're fighting south and east, now." The walkie-talkie on his chest kept up an incessant small chatter, like a mad old woman.

"What started it, lightning?"

"Anything could have started it. The wood's tinder, and the ground's as dry as newspaper." Strasser and Ebenezer joined them, and Strasser said, "There are cases that can't lie about on the floor of the Town Hall. Two may need oxygen. They must go to the White Clinic."

All three men looked at Ebenezer. After a moment's thought, he said, "Yes, this is a special circumstance. They can be accommodated in the old office at the end."

Ben watched the little man as he talked. His neat beard wagged, he made precise gestures with his thin hands. In the path of an inferno, he did not appear even to feel warm.

For the first time, Ben feared him. This grasshopper figure,

228

ludicrous as it might seem, symbolized a larger tragedy. Here was hubris inviting disaster, the inexorable thrust of Fate, and the voices crying Woe! And I, thought Ben, am in the cast with him, must take my chance, like him, of good and evil fortune.

For a short space he understood the loneliness of Karl Ebenezer. He acknowledged the obduracy, the quality of noble despair in him. He knew that seldom, among friends and allies, would he encounter a force to equal this of his principal adversary.

Ebenezer moved away, and Strasser said, "I have six I won't move until I must."

Mannie said, "She's rolling fast, sir."

Behind the main buildings they could see across the cleared ground to the marching phalanx of trees. Behind these the smoke now had the granulated glow of brown sugar.

"If she jumps Brake Two before the dynamiters get here, the grass'll catch, and the trees on both sides of the Hospital. They can't bring enough water by hoses or the dam. And the men up close can't hardly breathe that air. Two of them's collapsed already."

Mannie spoke gently, his eyes on Strasser, who said hopelessly, "If we all went up there and helped? . . ."

"They got plenty of men. It's not men that can do it. Only explosives, and rain. Perhaps the Army types will get here in time."

Strasser nodded. "Well, the patients are ready to leave. Let me know the latest they can be shifted with safety. All three ambulances can go down, and I'll have personnel with each. You'll find me in the entrance hall if you want me."

DOWN IN THE TOWN, order began to impose its patterns. In
the Town Hall, the Anglican minister and his wife, with the
workers of the Women's Guild, settled the patients from the
Hospital in something like comfort. Venter, with two African
policemen, kept an eye on the shops and saw that the main road
was not blocked by sightseers. The manager of the Hotel, Mr.
Malcolm, combined business and public duty by serving as a
supplier of coffee, buns, and official information.

Abrahams, who had come down with a consignment of drugs
and dressings from the Hospital, stopped on his way back to
snatch a hot drink. While he was drinking it, a battered sports
car drew up at the curb, and two young men scrambled out.
One carried a press camera. The other, seeing Abrahams, came
quickly across to him.

"Mr. Abrahams? I'm from the Hopetoun paper, sir. My
name's Ballinger. Can I have your story?"

Abrahams said, "I've no time, sonny." He put the cup down
on the hotel steps and made for his car. The youngster trotted
beside him. "You going up? Give us a lift? The police are being
sticky about extra cars going there."

Abrahams hesitated. He felt a sharp distaste for the idea of
publicizing disaster, and at the same time admitted he was
being unfair. As he stood looking at the reporter, and the photographer, who now joined them, he was tempted to say, "This
is a private burning. Go away and leave us to it."

But before he could speak, a hand reached past him and
grabbed the reporter's arm. "Mr. Ballinger, I've been looking
for you. I can give you all you want."

Archie Oakes was gazing avidly at the pressman. His pale
face shone with sweat. He said, "I should be the one you talk
to. I telephoned you first."

Ballinger shrugged. "You know what started the fire?"

"Sure I know, I know it all, the whole story. Come back into the Hotel, we'll have a little drink and I'll give you the whole thing."

Abrahams said suddenly, "I shouldn't listen to this man if I were you, gentlemen. He's not in a position to give information, since he's been down here in town all night. If you want a lift up, come with me."

Oakes began to bluster. Abrahams opened the back door of his car, and the two young men slid in.

Abrahams started the engine. Oakes was leaning through the window, expostulating. Abrahams put his hand on Oakes chest, thrust him back and edged the car forward.

But Venter appeared in his path, his hand raised. He bent and shouted, "Wait until the troops are through, please."

They saw the snout of a troop carrier drawing level with them. An officer called to Venter, "Which way?"

Venter started to go over to him, but Abrahams slid along the seat and signaled to him. "I'll lead the way."

Venter nodded. "O.K., Mr. Abrahams."

They pulled away from the curb, edging through the crowd, which broke into a cheer at the sight of the army vehicle. The reporter said, "Three troop-carriers behind now." He leaned back in his seat. "Why did you change your mind about us?"

"If you want the truth, don't try and get it from Archie Oakes."

"Why not?"

"He's not one of us," said Abrahams. After a pause, he added, "For us, this is personal, you know." They climbed the hill fast. The car was filled with a flickering, smoky light. At the top they turned right, and before them lay the fearful magnificence of the fire.

"Jesus," said the photographer. "This'll cost you plenty of Rand."

"It'll cost us plenty." Abrahams wondered if the amount would ever be fully assessed. Not only the financial disaster.

Remembering Oakes's avid face, he shook his head. To Oakes and his kind, the fire meant headlines. Yes, tomorrow the nation would read about Peace Drift, and so, perhaps, they should; read, learn, bend the power of interest and pity on this valley. But the truth did not lie with Oakes, for truth was dispassionate, after all.

He dropped his passengers, and parked his car on the grass verge. The army vehicles lumbered on toward the police roadblock.

Abrahams climbed down from the car. He saw Dominee Bond ahead and walked to meet him.

The predikant said, "They sent me back from the Hospital. No more civilians. Now it's up to the Army."

"You mean, to God."

"Yes. If only it would rain."

Abrahams stared at the sky. "The wind's dropping, and the clouds are lower."

The two men sat down on the grass verge, to wait.

72

FOR THE LAST HOUR, Strasser and Mannie had worked together. The elemental threat of fire had burned away their antipathy, they seemed on this night curiously alike. The patients, all but six, were already down in the town, and now they turned to more material goods. They directed the moving of dangerous drugs, under lock and key, to the safety of the Mission, and then helped gangs to shift as much of the movable equipment as possible onto trucks, to be carried to safety.

They hardly noticed the thud and tremor of the blasting operations that were now in process. Their brief glances at the sky showed only that the fire advanced, retreated, moved south, and advanced again.

But at eleven o'clock a runner came to Mannie with a message. Mannie turned to Strasser and said, "Sorry, doc, you'll have to get the last patients out. They have to blast very close. It's going to bust windows and so on. And if it doesn't work, the roads may be blocked."

They walked along the corridor to where the half-dozen seriously ill patients were lying. Together they saw to their transfer to ambulances. One old woman wept continuously, and clung to Strasser's hand, refusing to release him. He told Mannie that he would see her safely bestowed in the town, and return.

Mannie nodded, and set about checking the Hospital to warn any remaining workers they must leave. He sent a man to fetch Nella Ebenezer from the theater where she was packing instruments for transportation.

As he crossed toward the main block, Larkill appeared with a shortish, sharp-faced army officer. Larkill said, "Anyone still working in the buildings?"

"Sister Ebenezer, sir, and Dr. Nevis."

"Tell them they must leave at once."

The Army man laughed. "Unless they want their eardrums broken." He turned away suddenly to shout at a group of soldiers who were moving toward the southern plantations. His language was obscene, his voice high and brusque. The soldiers altered course and trotted past, grinning. Larkill chuckled. Mannie saw that they were all enjoying themselves, and remembered how Larkill always spoke of his army days with pleasure. Well, if that was what they wanted. . . .

He said, "If you don't need me, sir, I'll get back to the Halt with the rest."

Larkill nodded dismissal. He set off down the slope at a run, followed by the officer. A small group of men was there, on the edge of the southern plantations. Must be the demolition squad.

Mannie rubbed a hand over his eyes. They smarted all the time, the smoke seemed to have got down to his guts. "Kippered," he said. Funny how one wanted a cigarette, with all this smoke.

He measured the distance between the Hospital and the fire.
It was closer, much closer. The flames had grown as tall as
Heaven, it looked like the sky had caught on fire, itself.

Mannie wished no one had had a chance to see this thing.
How simple it was, how terrible, and kind of . . . beautiful? A
man could see the temptation. Just put a match, and watch
it go.

The shouts of the soldiers became fainter. There was another
explosion. The shock of it beat on his ears. He heard the tearing
of falling trees.

It was Sizwa who started it, that was for sure. So they'd get
Sizwa, provided he hadn't got himself fried in his own oven. No
matter how long it took.

But it was dangerous, people seeing a fire like this, knowing
how easy it could be to set a valley on fire.

He shook himself and made his way to the out-patients de-
partment. Through the open door, he could see Nella showing
a soldier the fuse boxes that controlled all the Hospital current.
Other soldiers tramped from room to room, making a quick but
thorough search for stray loiterers.

73

In the records room, Ben checked the drawers of the last filing cabinet. All were empty, the case histories and important
documents safely cleared. The African staff had done a good
job. Ben slammed the drawer and kicked it to lock the cabinet.

As he did so, a movement at the door startled him. He jerked
round, to see Abel leaning against the door frame.

"What in God's name are you doing here? I sent you back to
town."

Abel put a hand to the bandage on his head. "I jumped off

the lorry." His reddened eyes gazed around the room. "How do they know he isn't here?" He looked at Ben. "He'd have to hide somewhere. . . ."

"Who?" Ben moved out into the corridor and tried to draw Abel after him. Abel's fingers closed on the jamb of the door.

"I mean Sizwa . . . my friend, Sizwa."

"He isn't here," Ben said gently. "We have to go now." He put a hand on Abel's shoulder. "We've been ordered to leave. The soldiers are in control, and we'll only be in their way." From the corner of his eye he saw Nella walking toward them along the corridor. As she joined them, he said under his breath, "He's a bit woozy. He got a crack on the head tonight. Take the other side."

They edged along the corridor. Mannie appeared in the outer doorway. "Come, come on. Get cracking."

The forecourt of the Hospital was empty of all save uniformed men, soldiers, policemen, and firemen. Nella said, "I'd like to stay."

"No, miss, you can't." Mannie's blackened face smiled faintly. "You're not captain of this ship. Even Strasser can't help here. There's plenty to do in the town, and your Pa's worried stiff about you. All this is no good for an old man like him."

Behind them, the lights of the Hospital snapped off. The soldiers tramped down the steps. A loud-speaker van in the courtyard started to blare, "All civilians must please leave the vicinity at once, and withdraw to Mission Halt. Fire groups Seven and Four are directed to sector Charlie, sector Charlie." The impersonal voice droned on, in English, Afrikaans, and Zulu. The patterns of men to the south scattered and reformed, against the bulk of the trees.

They climbed into Nella's car, Ben beside Nella, Mannie and Abel in the back seat. They were bumping along the road to the Halt. Nella saw that beyond the clearing, behind the Hospital, there was a blessed darkness. She said, "They're getting it under."

Mannie said, "And they'll get the chap who started it." He was watching Abel, but the African's head lolled against the seat, and his eyes were closed.

They dropped Mannie at the Halt, and drove on down the hill. A dull tremor shook the car, followed by the thud of an explosion. Above the plantations, the sky trembled, went black, was laced with scarlet and gold parabolas. The flames to the south diminished in extent.

Ben said, "The thing's a hydra."

They crossed the drift. Almost at once they had to slow and stop because of the crowd that filled the main street. Black and white jostled for a view of the bridge. Ben said to Nella, "Want to go home?"

"No. Drop me here, and I'll go to the Town Hall and make Pa come home with me. You can take the car on."

She climbed out. Ben slid under the wheel, pulled the car over to the wrong side of the road, and edged it through the press of people. One man, annoyed at being displaced, brought his hand down sharply on the bonnet and then yelped. The crowd laughed.

Ben swung the car in behind the petrol pumps of the Garage. Here, in the shadow of the building, was a small island of quiet. He said over his shoulder, "You mustn't blame yourself, Abel. . . ."

Abel said with soft bitterness, "Who must I blame? Sizwa?"

"Why not?"

"I saw him, last night, you know, doctor? I went up the hill to the Mission and he was waiting for me. He tried to kill me. He blames me." Abel gave a faint chuckle.

"You had to do what you did."

"The policeman followed me," said Abel, as if he had not heard. "Sizwa thought I'd brought him."

"They'd have caught up with him some time."

Abel leaned forward. "That policeman was looking for an agitator. You know, doctor, it's easy to make an agitator. You can do it by leaving things too long. By wanting peace and quiet, as

I did. There was a time when I could speak to Sizwa. A time I could have stopped him. But I just wanted to be quiet. . . ."

Ben rested his arm along the back of the seat. "It's no good, I tell you, blaming yourself. Sizwa's old enough to carry his own guilt. You acted in a perfectly responsible way."

Abel shook his head. "Doctor, I'm sorry, I don't know the way your mind works. I only know how I feel." He fumbled with the handle of the door. His face in the darkness looked blurred and swollen, as if the night had bruised its tissues. He said vehemently, "I have to find my place, that's all. I must find my place. That was what Sizwa tried to do. I could have helped him, but I didn't. Now who will help me? Who will be my friend? Listen, I have worked to learn, and to make myself better. I have a job, and money put aside. But what is that? You say I did this affair in a responsible way. But that does not give me my place. A white policeman used me to make a trap for Sizwa. I spoke to the men at the factory, because you asked me to, but that does not give me a place. They may think I'm a clever fellow, but that won't make them trust me, after what has happened. I've put myself too high, with learning, and with helping you. You understand what I'm telling you? I have to know what I am. Or perhaps people will say, he's an educated kaffir, and it's bad luck because for him, in these times, there's nowhere he can fit. I tell you, I hold out my hand and there's no one to take it. Where can I be at home? Where will they say to me, 'Abel, this is your own good place, be happy here?' Nowhere. I know. I had a friend, and now I have no friend. I understand that the blame for that must be on me. So I will try and think what I can do about this, but you cannot help me to do it. No one else can do it for me. No one else can see into my heart."

"Abel . . . wait a moment."

But Abel had opened the door and closed it behind him. He walked away along the alley beside the Garage. Ben sat for a moment, before edging the car out into the road.

The crowd was thinning. The wind had dropped. How quiet

it was. He saw that the fire was confined to a small area well south of the Hospital. The walls of the buildings stood up like white bones in a black flesh of devastated acres.

He stopped at the Hotel, where he found Strasser, almost hysterically jubilant. "Well, we beat it! Eh? A wonderful battle, wonderful! There's a reporter here. I'm going to have a word with him. Give him a few facts. No advertising, of course, but it won't do harm mention the Hospital." He smiled, clapping Ben on the shoulder. "I'm too excited to rest. You go and catch some sleep, and take over from me at six." He went off happily along the verandah, where a group of farmers were gathered, eating hamburgers and talking.

Ben left the car outside the Hotel, and walked along the river path.

74

BESIDE THE WATER the smell of burning was spiced with the sweetness of rose geranium; and the shouts of the crowd dimmed in the river's song. Ben felt that he approached an invisible point of stillness. Here, where the light burned in Karl Ebenezer's study, was the center of the whirlpool, the heart of the matter.

As he walked toward the house, the idea came to him that he was expected. The front door stood open. The hall was dark, but on his left, light showed under a door. He turned the handle and walked into Ebenezer's study.

The old man occupied a wing chair near the window. He sat upright, his legs stiffly crossed at the ankles. The single lamp at his elbow left the corners of the room in shadow. He seemed not to have moved for some time, for at Ben's entry, he moved awkwardly, rubbing his neck to ease the muscles.

Ben came over to him. Ebenezer watched him almost absently, a faint smile on his lips. His clear gray eyes were thoughtful. "Sit down, doctor." He indicated the chair opposite him, and Ben took it, turning it so that the lamp did not shine in his face. He said, "Is Nella asleep?"

Ebenezer seemed to wonder whether it was worth his while to answer. He said at last, "I expect so . . . but you didn't come here at two in the morning . . .?"

. . . "to exchange pleasantries. No." Ben settled in his chair. "Did you see the pressmen at the Hotel?"

"I spoke to them up at Mission Halt, briefly."

"What about?"

Again Ebenezer seemed to debate whether he would answer, and then said, "I did not make any statement to him. I asked the young man . . . Ballinger . . . to wait until tomorrow . . . today, that is . . . until I had had time to consider the whole position. To make some rough estimate of the damage."

"Do you think you can?"

"I can take an informed guess at it, in Rand and cents." Ebenezer tapped a knuckle against his nose. "You weren't thinking of the monetary side? I can assure you, I must. Tonight has been a disaster. The losses and expenses incurred by individuals are considerable. By the municipality, colossal. The productive power of the Ridge is axed. The telephone system is temporarily disrupted. Emergency measures must be taken for the hospital patients, the dam which normally supplies water up there is seriously depleted, so is the main water system. I wanted to plan a little, before leaping into print."

"Do you think that you'll be able to give the true story?"

"I appreciate that it is difficult at any time to present the whole truth. Perhaps impossible. I am not naive."

"Then what do you mean to say to Ballinger?"

"Really, young man, I find this cross-examination a piece of impertinence."

"I'm sorry. But I'm trying to tell you that I'm deeply concerned. This evening, for instance, Mannie Reimer said something to suggest that the fire was started by a saboteur. Is that going to be the official line?"

Ebenezer regarded him in silence, and Ben leaned forward. "You're thinking that it's none of my business, because I'm an outsider. That's true to a certain extent. But it gives me certain advantages. I could go away tomorrow and disclaim any interest in Peace Drift, you can take it I'm about as disinterested as anyone can ever be in a place they like. Yet I have to say that Teddy Abrahams is right. What you have to face here is a breakdown in human relations. The fear and mistrust that has arisen is quite out of proportion to the original causes. And that in turn has created fresh dangers and greater fears. The situation isn't trivial any longer. Yesterday you were a backwater. Today, you've got the Army here, and you'll be headline news by nightfall. The material damage you've suffered is, as you say, colossal. And yet, once again, Peace Drift is looking for an agitator."

"The inference being . . .?"

"That once more, we are trying to shift the blame, to find a scapegoat, to hunt down the enemy outside instead of the enemy within ourselves."

"Go on."

Ben took his time in answering. At last he said, "I was speaking to a man tonight. He said that he blamed himself for what has happened. It took me by surprise. I thought at first he was being hysterical. But he made me see that . . . that he was the only one, of all of us, who was willing to accept a personal responsibility for what's happened. And I thought . . . perhaps that's what is meant by the saying that a city may be spared for the sake of one just man."

"I'm afraid I don't see what you want me to do."

"I don't exactly know. But try and explain to that reporter that the fire wasn't a simple thing. Perhaps we can keep this thing where it belongs, as something to be solved from inside the town boundaries, by the people living here. Solved as a human problem, rather than as a political one."

"How?" Ebenezer's voice hovered between anger and amusement.

"Hold a local inquiry, to discuss the reasons for the fire. Release some of the pressures that have caused friction. Above all, end this talk of agitators. Don't you see, we have created the very thing we most fear? We must, we must treat the disease and not the symptom."

"A very proper sentiment for a doctor. What you're really after is a multi-racial meeting?"

"Yes, I think it should be so."

"And why come to me? Surely, I'm the last person?"

There was a short silence. Their eyes met and held, and Ben said, "I suppose because you're one of the few men who understands what I'm talking about, whether you agree or not."

"That may be true." Ebenezer sighed. "I appreciate your confidences, Dr. Nevis, but I can't share your views. To be honest, I feel you have a little lost your sense of proportion. When I say this, you must allow that I am sincere, as I allow you to be."

He put out his hand and rested it on the table beside him, the fingers tapping abstractedly. "You and I, as I think I said before, remember what many of our countrymen try to forget. That Africa is undergoing a period of change, that we are caught in a vice of history. We both know that the years ahead will demand of us a change equally profound. I'm an old man. I've seen these times coming, while you were still playing bok-bok in the schoolyard. We can call it the emergence of a new Africa. You agree?"

"Yes."

"Good. Now. There is the danger that this new order, under certain circumstances, may sweep away what is valuable of the old. Agreed?"

"Yes."

. . . "And this threat must be met, and overcome? No, wait until I have had my say. In like manner, I will agree with you that one cannot, whatever one may wish, ignore the dynamic of the force now abroad on the African continent. So we approach the crux of the thing. How are we to contain this dynamic, with justice both to ourselves and to the nonwhite races? What is the

realist's answer to this dire problem? I believe . . . and my belief
is the sincere result of many years of work and thought . . . that
if South Africa remains a single multi-racial unit, we . . . that is,
the whites . . . will be submerged by the black. This in turn will
mean the end of civilized rule here, with irreparable harm done
to all the races of southern Africa. It is not a conclusion I
enjoy, but it has been forced upon me, by long experience of
people and of this subcontinent. It is for these reasons that I uphold, as I have stated often and in public, the principle of separate development. I hope for the establishment of independent
nonwhite areas, autonomous in time, co-existing alongside the
white state of South Africa." He lifted his hand. "And I am
afraid that I look on attempts to sabotage this ideal as nothing
short of suicidal. To me, this man Sizwa, for we speak of him,
don't we, as an agitator, a threat to his people and to mine, al-
beit a small-time operator. It is because I feel only friendship
for the people of the subcontinent that I follow a course that is
difficult, and for me personally, very lonely. You must accept
that I act in good faith. I am prepared to make sacrifices in
order that what I value may survive. I act from love, not hate."

"You act from fear. How can you base friendship and love on
fear? Leaving aside all questions of practical application, it
seems to me that no party or principle can succeed in Africa
unless it tends to lessen rather than to increase fear." Ben rose
to his feet and crossed to the window. Beyond the porch a finger of bleached grass pointed to the jet polish of the river.
Above the water, a gray film hovered; smoke, mist, the end of
the night. He said, "The heart of the matter is one's opinion of
oneself. You underestimate yourself, and so you are already de-
feated."

"And you?"

"I have a good opinion of myself. I believe that my species,
Man, evolves toward full stature, and that mankind transcends
the obvious, or how is it we have survived so much? We've escaped the threat of a million years, we've escaped nonentity.
We have made history, explored our world, and haven't been

afraid to pay the high price of discovery. We've challenged space. We haven't allowed time and mortality to dismay us. Everything we have achieved has been rooted in faith, and in hope. I have faith in men, that they are fundamentally good, capable of learning, able to adapt and to succeed against odds. I have faith in God, not that I shall find life safe, but faith that I can be tossed into the universe and still return like a boomerang to His hand. And civilization . . . if I have one, it certainly doesn't belong to east or west alone, since I include such things as Arabic numerals and a religion born in Bethlehem. I don't look on civilization as the material fruits of experience . . . knowledge, skills, science, this or that Way of Life. It isn't a genie in a bottle, to fetch and carry a higher standard of living. If I think about civilization, it's as . . . something of the spirit . . . something that involves this continual act of faith. If there's no faith, there's no civilization, nothing but an attempt to hold about us the . . . the rags of a gown of glory.

"I think we must go among men, if we are to confirm civilization, because we as men are its bearers, and only we can transmit it to others of our kind. I don't say the method of approach need be crude and headlong, but I do say the approach must be made. The African nationalism which we both fear seems to me by definition to be an insistence on race. I don't think we can contain its dynamic by physical boundaries. One can't contain ideas in that way. Ideas have to meet in the minds of men. That is our problem in the modern world.

"The world shrinks, we grow closer all the time. The urgency lies in our need to find our points of accord with men of other races, our points of similarity. What is in danger in the atomic age is not our country, but our world, not our race but our whole species. This country is under fire because everyone, everywhere, who thinks at all, knows that our problem is ultimately his. This is a multi-racial world. We have to make it work, and the southern part of Africa is a testing run, that's all."

Ebenezer stirred gently in his chair. "My boy, you're an impractical theorist."

Ben gave a slight smile. "And I would say the same thing of you. . . ."

Ebenezer rose. "There doesn't seem to be much more we can say to each other, unless we are to fall to contumely. We must agree to differ. It's a pity. I respect you for saying to my face what most of my opponents prefer to say behind my back."

He led the way to the front porch and there halted and faced the younger man.

"Dr. Nevis, to come to less momentous subjects . . . our talks have been interesting. But since you have been frank with me, I will repay the compliment. Let us think of practical matters. You are, I believe, growing fond of my daughter. I know, we need not discuss why. I'm afraid that it's our bad luck that you and I are likely to remain opponents. Have you thought of the effect this will have on Nella?"

Before Ben could answer, Ebenezer raised a hand. "You do not know it, of course, but my own marriage was wrecked on just such a cleavage of sympathies. My wife's family had no sympathy with me, nor I with them. Everyone made the greatest efforts, but the marriage failed. There was no kindred spirit. The human relations . . . I believe you would say . . . broke down. It caused misery to the people I loved best." He put his thin yellow hand on Ben's arm. "I'm not in the habit of asking favors, but neither do I delude myself, even when I might like to. I don't want Nella to be forced to choose between us, later on, when her affections are perhaps deeply engaged. You've been here a very short while. You could go away now, and she would forget all about you."

Ben said harshly, "You expect me to make the choice for her? Are you sure it isn't that you're afraid of losing her to me?"

He regretted the words at once. Ebenezer dropped his hand. "Naturally, I'm afraid of that, but that is not my reason . . . it may seem inexplicable to you, but Nella loves me also. . . ."

"I'm sorry. I had no right to speak like that. But honestly, I don't think the decision lies with either of us."

"You've already spoken to her?"

"I didn't need to speak."

"I see. Yes, I see."

As they stood, a flash of lightning broke on the horizon, and both men glanced up at the hill. Seconds later, the thunder rolled. Ebenezer sighed. "We must let things take their course, then. Good night, Dr. Nevis."

Ben left him and walked back up the road, under the close arch of the trees. The main street was deserted. The stain of dawn spread upward from the east. As he drew level with the Hotel, he heard his name called and looking up, saw a group of men on the dark verandah.

Someone, Tim Sullivan it was, leaned over the rail. "Doc? Come and have breakfast."

Ben climbed the steps. Malcolm, Sullivan, Abrahams, and one or two others were slumped in a circle of chairs around a table that bore coffee jugs and a plate of sandwiches. The Hopetoun reporter sprawled nearby in a long chair, apparently asleep.

Sullivan handed Ben a mug of hot coffee. It smelled wonderful, but tasted metallic on his tongue. He sat down on the wooden steps, his back propped against a pillar. "Why don't you all go home?"

Sullivan groaned. "Too tired. I shall stay here for good, I think. National monument. Open Sundays, children half price. . . ." his voice was lost in a cavernous yawn. The reporter stirred and sat up. "That fire still out?"

Abrahams said from the shadows, "Now, he asks us. They're still patrolling. If the rain comes, that'll damp it down."

The reporter took a sandwich from the plate. "Can you use charred timber for anything?"

"For what? For firewood?" Abrahams snorted. "We have a national loss here, boy. You can be glad you got no shares in us. You and Ben can clear out and leave us to tidy the mess."

Ballinger's head rolled. "Who's Ben?"

Abrahams pointed. "Him. Dr. William Nevis, Stanley Ballinger from the Hopetoun paper."

Ballinger turned on his side and looked at Ben. "You leaving the dorp?"

"Perhaps."

"You don't belong here?"

And this was a fine time to know the answer, thought Ben. At his hesitation, Ballinger said, "Nothing personal, I mean. . . ."

Abrahams said, "He was born here, and with questions, my child, everything is personal." His eyes closed. "Personally, I like things personal. That's all I've saved from the hungry years. The first person. Me." He patted his chest. "So let the poor thing be happy, and work, and drink, and fight fires, and answer impertinent young men with questions." He sighed. "I'm talking nonsense. I better go home."

Lightning flickered over the Ridge, and a clap of thunder broke overhead. Large single drops banged on the tin roof, and Abraham heaved himself to his feet. "Now, really, I shall go." He ran down the steps, turning up his collar, and clambered into his car; Sullivan and the other farmers followed suit. Malcolm said good night and went off into the building.

Ben asked Ballinger if he had a bed for the night.

"Upstairs." Ballinger pointed at the ceiling. "I probably won't get to it. I want to talk to these army types when they come rolling down the mountain. Then I have to phone my paper again. The big boy'll be here soon, you know. And I've a couple of interviews lined up, side stories." He settled lower in his chair. "You know what caused the fire?"

Ben shrugged. "That would take all night."

"I've got all night. What's left of it."

Ben moved from the steps to the chair left empty by Sullivan. "Once upon a time," he said, "about three weeks ago. . . ." He closed his eyes. Ballinger leaned over and shook him.

"No sleeping."

Ben heaved a sigh, pulled himself erect, and while the storm thickened to a downpour overhead, went on with his story.

57

He went home for breakfast at seven.

Strasser was exultant, full of plans and instructions. The crisis of the previous night seemed to have stimulated him. He was twice called to the telephone in the course of the meal, once by an Army official, once by Ebenezer. When he came back the second time, he said to Ben, "I hope that now you'll stay on for a while? In view of the present situation, I'll be very busy. We would have to come to a business arrangement, of course. But you see what must be done, reorganizing the Hospital, alone. Ebenezer says they've learned their lesson and there'll have to be a far wider safety zone round the buildings. I've always wanted that Research wing, and now, if the land's available . . . You could find things here to interest you, and you have qualities to recommend you. You're young, up-to-date, but a local man."

Ben shook his head. "I'm sorry, sir, I have to leave."

"Some other commitment?"

"No."

"Well, then . . .?"

"I've decided to go back to Joburg."

"But why, when you're valuable here? This is an emergency. If it's a question of money. . . ." as Ben shook his head again, Strasser leaned his elbows on the table and said earnestly, "Nevis, I know I'm not easy to work with. . . ."

"It isn't anything of that sort."

"I know my failings. I'm not popular, not tactful. I haven't done well with people here. But you seem to make friends easily. You belong here as I can never hope to, and you would compensate for my shortcomings. I can promise I'll get you an appointment, and that there'll be work, interesting work. . . ."

Strasser's voice was almost pathetically anxious. "I will try to be not so difficult."

"I'm really sorry, sir. It's nothing to do with the work, or with you yourself. I just have to go. It's a private matter."

"I see. Well, if you must. When will you leave?"

"At the end of the week, as we originally planned."

Strasser made no further argument, but left the table, saying that he must go across to the Town Hall, and would pick Ben up in half an hour to take him up to the Hospital.

Ben smoked a cigarette over coffee, then went out into the garden at the back of the house. The smell of burned and sodden vegetation hung on the air. He studied the long curve of the Ridge. Nearly one third of it was black destruction. On the charred expanse, khaki figures crawled, and the blunt beetle-yellow shapes of bulldozers. A helicopter hovered over Mission Halt. The insect world was stubbornly repairing its damaged nest.

But the drought was broken. The sky was blue and moist as a child's eye. The ground was soft underfoot.

He walked around the house to the front gate. On the verandah of the Hotel he could see Ballinger, engaged in a lively altercation with a waiter. As Ben watched, Ballinger burst out laughing and ran down the steps to his car. He saw Ben and waved to him as he drove away up the Ridge.

The main road was already fairly crowded. Abel was on duty at the Garage, but the stoep of Oakes's store was empty. As the hand of the Town Hall clock moved to eight, the screech of saws began in the timberyard.

All we have to do, he thought, is achieve the impossible. Keep hoping, speak the truth, endure.

He saw Nella come down the steps of the Town Hall. She stared across at him for a moment and then walked quickly up the road, crossed over.

When she reached the gate where he stood, she was out of breath. She stood gazing anxiously up at him. "Dr. Strasser told me you're leaving. Is it true?"

"Nella . . ."

"Is it true?"

"Yes."

"Because of me?"

"I don't want you to be hurt."

"That's what Pa told me." She pushed against the gate. "Let me in."

He stood back and she thrust the gate open, ran around it, and faced him. "What right have you and Pa to arrange my life between you? Don't you think I'm sound in the head?" Her whole face was bright with anger. "You know nothing about me, nothing. You know nothing about love."

He started to protest, but she interrupted him with passion, "You have it all worked out, you and Pa, how much I am capable of. I must have one or the other. You will make a gentleman's agreement. Well, what if I don't agree? What if I say I will have you both?"

"Have your cake and eat it?"

She made an impatient movement, and he said, "Nella, you really must think this over."

"Think? I have thought. Long before you and Pa came down from the clouds, I was thinking. And I know I have nothing but love, Ben. I love my father, and I love you. I'm going to go on loving you both and having you both. This is my decision. This I will do."

Her fingers closed around his wrist. She said slowly and clearly, as if to a child, "You're to stay. You hear? You're to have faith in me, too."

He nodded, and she gave a slight sigh of satisfaction.

"Well, I must get back to my work. See you later."

But when she was halfway across the road, a doubt seemed to strike her. She turned and called back to him, "You won't mind living in a dorp?"

He leaned on the gate and laughed.

Watching her hurry back down the street, Nella, his woman, he knew that Peace Drift was only another name for the world.

ABOUT THE AUTHOR

June Drummond, a native of South Africa, makes her home in Durban. She received her degree from the University of Cape Town and has worked both in Durban and in London. Miss Drummond is the author of *The Black Unicorn* and *Thursday's Child*, which both received high critical praise.

This book was set in

Caledonia and Goudy Open types,

printed and bound

by The Haddon Craftsmen.

Design is by Larry Kamp.